BREAKAWAY

Kevin Lobster

Contents

Portland Storm captain Eric "Zee" Zellinger knows how to get the job done, but leading his once elite team to victory is fast becoming a losing battle. He can't lose focus now-not with his career on the line. But when his best friend's little sister makes him an offer he can't refuse, Eric could lose the drive the team relies on from their captain.

Still in a downward spiral after a life-altering event in college, Dana Campbell is desperate to try anything to break away from the horror of that fateful night-even enlisting the help of the only man she trusts completely.

No matter how irresistible she is or how tempting the offer, Eric might not be able to cross that line-especially with the team's chance at the playoffs on the line. Now, Eric has to take one last shot, but will he choose Dana's Breakaway chance at happiness or the move that could secure his career?

Chapter 1 - Breakaway

D AYANA

Amani's Family-Style Italian Restaurant was nearly empty. Not surprising, considering it was three o'clock on a Thursday afternoon in the middle of February. It wasn't the sort of place you'd expect someone to take a date for Valentine's Day—more the type of place you'd have a family reunion. But today wasn't Valentine's Day. That was tomorrow. And we weren't on a date. Far from it.

The only people in the restaurant other than the two of us and the staff were a retired couple seated near the windows. He had his nose buried in a newspaper, and she was knitting an incredibly ugly orange scarf. They were both ignoring the half full bowl of spaghetti and red sauce on the table between them, not to mention each other.

I looked at the door and made note of all the tables and chairs between it and me, mapping an exit path in my mind.

As soon as the waitress dropped off our drinks and walked away, Eric looked across at me. He cocked up a brow and gave me that always-ready half-smile I knew so well. "So what's this about, kid? I didn't think I'd see you any time soon. Not until the summer, at least." He left unspoken what we were both thinking: not here in Portland instead of in Providence.

He took a long draw from his water glass, and I tried to focus on all the familiarities: the loose-fitting, long-sleeved, navy-blue T-shirt that didn't quite mask all the muscle underneath; the stubble-lined jaw that proved he hadn't shaved in a day or so; the dark, almost-black hair that should have been cut over a month ago; the recent scar and corresponding bruise just below his left eye from taking a high stick in a game against Chicago last week; the way his left hand always looked ready to deliver an uppercut to a guy on the other team.

Focusing on those things helped me calm down, to slow my pulse and remember that this was Eric Zellinger, a man who had been my brother's best friend since they played peewee hockey together back home in Rhode Island. He'd been in my life nearly as long as I could remember.

Eric was safe. I could trust him. He was the only man in my life who I trusted implicitly, at least of the ones who weren't family. That's why I chose him.

"Does Soupy know you're here?" He set his glass down and unrolled the linen napkin from around his silverware, situating everything just so.

That was another bit of familiarity: Soupy. He'd called my brother, Brenden, that for forever, or at least it seemed that way. There's some unwritten rule in the hockey world that if your last name is Campbell, your teammates will inevitably call you Soupy. Girls weren't exempt from crazy hockey-nicknaming rules, either. I'd been called that by some of the girls' teams I played for, back before it all happened.

Even though I was trying to focus on the familiar, the comfortable, the safe, it was hard to the point of being nearly impossible. My tongue felt three times its normal size, and no matter how much I swallowed, I couldn't seem to stop the saliva from rapidly filling my mouth. I reached for my water glass to buy time and garner courage, but my hand was shaking like a 6.0 earthquake and I knocked over the glass.

Eric was on his feet before I could react. He righted it and used his napkin to dry the mess I'd made.

"Damn it. I'm sorry." That was all I could get out. I could feel that all-too-familiar heat creeping up my face—not a blush, nothing as simple and understandable as that, but the onset of a panic attack. My breaths came fast and shallow. I couldn't get enough air into my lungs. I had to get out of there. I had to leave. I couldn't—

"Dayana?"

Eric's hand came down over mine. Not forcefully. But firm. Secure. Safe.

I tried to focus on him, but my vision was blurred. I couldn't see well enough to be sure that it was him, but it was him. I knew it.

"Just keep talking for a minute," I somehow got out.

"Okay. I can do that." He didn't let go of my hand as he sat down across from me again. "You should have seen Burnzie in practice this morning. He got in against Ericsson on a breakaway, deked twice, and finished with this crazy spin-o-rama move just outside the crease. Tried to shoot it between his legs and go five-hole. It would have been brilliant if he'd scored. But instead, the puck shot off his skate and he tripped himself up. Crashed into the end boards face-first. Broke his nose in two places. He's going to be wearing a full cage for a few weeks. Somebody ought to remind him he's a defenseman, not a winger."

My breathing was starting to normalize, but I was still crazy hot, so hot I was sweating. But at least it was on its way to passing. "Shouldn't that be you? You're the captain."

"Nah. I'll leave that for Coach to deal with. Scotty's still trying to make an impression on the boys. Not all of them have bought into his system yet. We're over halfway through the season."

He didn't ever want anyone to see when he was frustrated, but I could always tell. There was a slight crease between his eyebrows when things weren't going well, just enough to reveal a well-masked tension. I could see it now.

The waitress came back with a basket of bread. She set it in the center of the table between us and smacked her gum loudly.

"Can we get another napkin and a refill on that water? We had a bit of an accident." Eric didn't even look at her when he spoke. His eyes never left me, and neither did his hand.

I wasn't antsy to pull my hand away, though. That was a surprising realization. It confirmed that I'd made the right choice, so I had to stick with it.

After she left, he said, "Is it better yet?"

I nodded. "Getting there."

"Better enough that you can tell me why you flew across the country without telling me you were coming? Providence to Portland isn't exactly a quick weekend getaway, and last-minute flights aren't cheap."

"I..." I pulled my hand away from his and fidgeted with my nails. I had to do something while I tried to tell him. To explain. I couldn't just sit still. "I need to ask you something, but you've got to let me get it all out without interrupting me or I won't be able to do it."

Clearing her throat beside us, the waitress refilled my water glass and handed Eric a stack of napkins. "Are you ready to order yet?" She gave a pointed look to the pair of untouched menus at the side of our table. She hadn't been gone long, but then again, she didn't really have much to do other than help us.

"Come back in fifteen minutes."

It was no wonder the Portland Storm had made him the team captain in only his second full season in the National Hockey League. Just the tone of his voice was enough to command respect and confidence. Somehow in the five years since his appointment, he'd only grown in his ability to make people sit up and take notice when he spoke.

She rolled her eyes and scowled, but she left.

"Sounds serious," he said to me. "Spill it."

This time when I reached for my glass, I was able to pick it up and sip without making a mess even though my hands were still shaking.

I set it back down and took a few soothing breaths.

"I meant spill your secrets, not the water."

My laugh was automatic. He'd always been able to make me laugh.

"Okay." I'd practiced my speech in my mind during every leg of my trip here. I knew exactly what I wanted to say, word for word, all laid out in a logical, reasonable order. I just had to get it to come out as I'd planned it. Should be easy enough, right? I couldn't look at him, though. Not for this. I looked down at my hands, watching almost subconsciously as I picked at the fingernail on my right index finger until I'd gotten it down to the quick, oblivious to the pain I was causing myself.

But I had to do this. I had to. Of course, as soon as I opened my mouth, nothing but a flood of babble came out.

"My counselor said she couldn't really help me anymore because after all these years, I still can't handle having a guy look at me a certain way or talk to me or flirt with me without having a freaking panic attack, and you know my anxiety meds only do so much to help, so she sent me to see a sex therapist. Which is all fine and good, except for the fact that the sex therapist says I have to actually practice letting guys flirt with me and hold my hand and...and more...and so she wants me to see a sex surrogate, which I don't know if you've ever heard of a sex surrogate or not, but I looked them up, and they're basically a cross between a prostitute and a counselor, and they cost a fortune which I can't afford even if my insurance would cover it, which they won't, and besides, A: oh my God, gross, and two: I wouldn't even know this sex surrogate guy, whoever he is, so how could I trust him enough to let him touch me, so there's no way in hell I can do that. So then the sex therapist said I need to find a man who I do trust if I'm ever going to get past all this, someone who can help me with it, and ask him for help. So I am. Asking. You."

Eric's silence was only magnified by how empty the restaurant was around us.

I wanted to leave. I wanted to get up, walk out of that restaurant, get a cab, and go straight back to the airport. To pretend I hadn't done this. I shouldn't have come. I should have just stayed at home, alone, and gone about my life as it had been for the last seven years. I may be twenty-six and pathetic and lonely, but at least I'm safe.

Tears stung my eyes when I finally got up the courage to look at him. I'd seen that same look on his face dozens of times through the TV, usually right before he pummeled a guy who'd gone in for a bad hit against one of his teammates. It was all anger, green fire, focused intensity. But I'd never seen him look at me that way.

I wanted to puke.

"You think—" his words were so soft I could barely hear him, clipped and icy "—I'm going to pay some quack therapist to fuck you? God damn it, Dayana, you're as good as my kid sister—"

"No! I—" I'd screwed it all up, just like always. I looked down at my hands again and realized my index finger was bleeding where I'd picked away too much of the nail. Methodically, I opened my napkin roll, dipped a corner of it in my water glass, then wrapped it around my finger, using the time that took to try to clear my thoughts again. "I don't want you to pay for anything, and I absolutely do not want to go to a sex surrogate, to let some man I don't know touch me and...stuff. But I do want to be able to have a relationship someday—to be able to let a man touch me without having another damn panic attack. So I..."

It took everything in me not to run out of the restaurant right that instant and not look back. The only reason I didn't is because I knew he could catch me—he was bigger, faster, stronger, always had been—and he'd convince me to tell him all of it.

"I want you to be my sex surrogate."

ERIC

Dayana had rendered me speechless.

I couldn't think of a time anything like that had happened in my twenty-nine years.

I'm not an overly loquacious guy, not normally. I tend to lead by example in the locker room, doing things the way they should be done and trusting that the younger guys will watch and take it all in, but I've never been shy about speaking my mind when it's called for.

Well, it sure as hell was called for now, but I couldn't come up with a single word to say. Nothing.

Shaking my head in disbelief, I reached for my wallet in my back pocket, pulled out a fifty—the smallest bill I had—and slapped it down on the table.

Dayana's head snapped up from the sound. Her eyes were huge—big and brown and so damn vulnerable. I hated seeing her like that, and I had witnessed that exact look way too many times for way too long. There wasn't a doubt in my mind that she needed help, but I knew that I couldn't be the one to help her.

Not like that.

I put my napkin on the table and pushed my chair back.

"Are we leaving already?"

"We're not talking about this here. Not in public." I moved behind her chair and pulled it back so she could stand. I held out her coat so she could put her arms in it. My fingers accidentally brushed against her collarbone when I released her coat. She jumped, but tried to act like she hadn't, like she was okay.

She wasn't okay.

Dayana Campbell hadn't been okay for even a single minute since the Boston College women's hockey team had played the University of Connecticut in her freshman year, when some crazy UConn fans, for lack of a better word, had thought it would be fun to gang-rape her afterward just because she was a better hockey player than any of their girls.

She was probably better than some of their men, too, for that matter. That might have played into why they did it. Who could know? What causes that switch to flip, where suddenly it becomes okay in your mind to do something like that, to hurt someone that way, to completely violate someone you don't even know? I hoped I would never find out.

The fact of the matter, though, was that she was a damn good hockey player. She'd scored a hat trick in the game, and she had an assist on top of it. It hadn't even been her best game that season.

There was little wonder that she'd been invited to play on the US women's Olympic team. If there was a women's professional hockey league, you can bet she would have been drafted into it. She was just that good.

Until that night. Everything changed that night.

They'd injured her body, which was bad enough, but they had destroyed her emotionally. She couldn't focus on the game anymore—all she could focus on were the catcalls coming down to the ice from the stands. She couldn't concentrate in her classes anymore—all her attention was zeroed in on how far away from her each man in the room was and how close she was to the exit.

Soupy and I had been finishing our senior year at Yale when it happened—we weren't with her. We couldn't protect her. When she was picking her college, we'd tried to get her to come to Yale where we could look after her at least for that one year before we turned pro, but she'd wanted to play for Coach Bassano. So, of course, we'd supported her decision. Coach Bassano was the best coach in all of women's hockey. We never could have imagined anything like that would happen to Dayana.

But it did.

The three men who'd raped her were expelled from school and put on trial. They each served a year in federal prison before being released.

One year. Where was the justice in that?

Dayana was still serving her sentence, and she hadn't done anything wrong.

And she wanted me to be her sex surrogate? How the hell did she think that was going to work? If she jumped just because my fingers accidentally brushed against her collarbone, how did she think we'd be able to do whatever it was she wanted me to do? It was like she was asking me to rape her, because that's what it would be for her. I couldn't—I wouldn't do that to her. Hell, she couldn't even handle letting Soupy and her dad touch her, hug her, all the things that families do. She wasn't ready. She might never be ready, and that pretty much killed me.

She pulled her blond hair up over the collar of her coat, letting it fall down her back however it wanted to, and she nodded at me, those brown eyes of hers always cautious. I was putting my own coat on as we walked toward the door, when the waitress stalked over and stopped in front of us, blocking the way. Blocking Dayana's escape route.

"You're leaving?" Her hands were on her hips, and she hadn't stopped smacking her gum once since we arrived. "You didn't order anything."

"Something came up. I left you a tip anyway."

I tried to brush past her and bring Dayana along with me, but the waitress moved to block the doorway.

"You're Zee, right? The captain of the Storm? Bobby, in the kitchen, that's what he said."

I'd brought Dayana here hoping I wouldn't be recognized. Amani's was always quiet this time of day, not too many people around. It was hard, in a town like this, to go unnoticed when you were a professional athlete. Everybody knew who you were, knew your business. I didn't mind too much. I'd gotten used to it. But Dayana didn't have to deal with that part of my life. She probably wasn't prepared for it. Soupy had spent more time in the minors than in the NHL, so no one really noticed him. Her dad had been in the NHL years ago, but only die-hard hockey fans recognized him unless he was at some hockey event. And back home in Providence, I was just a regular old guy to most people. Only the people involved in the hockey community knew me there. Not like here.

I looked over at her, and she gave me a tiny little nod.

"Yeah, that's me."

"Could you sign something for my kid? He's sick. Cancer. Leukemia."

At least that was all the waitress wanted. I nodded. "Yeah, sure. What do you have?" Even if I was in a hurry to get Dayana somewhere private where we could really talk about her ludicrous suggestion, I couldn't walk away without signing something for a sick kid. I fished in my coat pocket for a marker. Years ago, I learned it was best to always have one on hand, just for moments like this.

She went behind the cash register and jerked a Portland Storm window flag down from the wall. It must have been in that same spot for a decade or more—the logo was one that had been retired before I came into the league, and the empty space the flag had been covering was a stark white next to the rest of the dingy wall.

When she handed it over, I quickly scrawled my name on it and put my number—nine—inside the lower curl of my Z. I gave it back to her. "I hope your kid gets better soon."

"Yeah, thanks, Zee." She was already scurrying off to put it God only knew where. Then she nodded at where Dayana was inching closer to the door by degrees. "Your girlfriend's ready to go."

Dayana flinched at that. My girlfriend. She couldn't even handle hearing herself referred to that way. Her plan sounded crazier by the moment. Not that I'd say so to her. I didn't really think she was crazy—just her plan. But she'd take it to mean I was putting it all on her. Without thinking, I put my hand at the small of her back to guide her out of the restaurant. She immediately tensed even more than she already had, so I pulled it away and cursed under my breath.

"Come on. Let's get out of here."

We were barely on the sidewalk outside and heading toward the parking garage when I heard the waitress come back into the main dining room, cackling.

"Sucker! Got another one to bite. I'm putting this on eBay."

I should have known. She hadn't seemed all that torn up over her kid.

One look at Dayana was all I needed to remind me what torn up looked like.

I shoved my hands in my coat pockets so that I wouldn't inadvertently touch her again.

"Does that happen much?" She folded her arms across her chest and tucked her hands between her body and arms. "People lying to get you to give them stuff?"

"More often than I'd like. It's just part of the gig. But most people are good. Most are honest." I had always believed that. Sure, there were bastards in the world like the UConn students who raped Dayana. But there were also people like the Campbell family, the guys I'd played alongside my whole career.... There were more of the good than the bad.

Dayana seemed to only see the bad anymore, though, even when she was surrounded by the good. It was like she'd put blinders on.

Not that it was a choice. My mom had panic attacks if she had to fly. It had always been that way, and she couldn't control it. Dayana couldn't control her triggers, either. No one who has panic attacks can.

She just needed to learn to live with them. Mom lived with hers by going on road trips instead of flying. Dayana lived with hers by avoiding men.

Neither was ideal. But sometimes you just have to play with the hand you've been dealt.

Chapter 2 - Breakaway

DAYANA

Eric didn't say anything the whole way back to his house.

Normally, I didn't mind silence. I had a lot of it. It was comfortable to me lately. I lived alone and I didn't get out much, other than going to work.

Even at work I did most of the talking, not my clients. I was a personal trainer at Love Handles, a gym for women. It was safe for me there—no men. No one to ask me out for drinks after work. No one to smile at me in a way I could misinterpret. No one to trigger a panic attack.

Silence was usually my friend.

This time? Not so much.

This silence allowed my mind to wander too much. Even just thinking about a man touching me could sometimes trigger a panic attack, and the trip from near downtown where all the restaurants were to the older neighborhood where he and a bunch of rich people lived took a good fifteen minutes. That was way too long to think about the fact that I'd just asked Eric to touch me, and so much more. Hell, I hadn't even been able to really get the words out. Stuff? That's what I'd said. I couldn't even properly ask him for what I wanted—what I needed. I couldn't say the word sex to him. Not that I was ready for that—not yet. But I hoped I would be before I had to go back home to Providence, back to my job and my isolation and my life as I knew it.

He was bound to think I wasn't emotionally ready for this, that I wasn't mature enough. He still called me kid more often than not. That was how he thought of me, how he'd always thought of me. As a kid. A little girl. Not nearly ready to handle the emotional implications of even the smallest forms of physical intimacy or, God forbid, sex.

But that was just it. Emotionally, I wanted that connection. I wanted to be able to have a relationship, to have a boyfriend and go on dates and maybe someday get married. I'd been through enough counseling that I knew I was ready for that. I just didn't know if I could get to where my body could handle it.

Panic attacks are crazy beasts. They don't care what you think you're ready for. They don't care what you want. They just take control, and then you suffer.

I'd had enough. I was sick and tired of letting some wacko chemical response in my body determine where I worked or what friends I had or if I could ever allow myself to fall in love—or, maybe more precisely, to allow someone to love me.

This would only work if Eric would help me, though, and he didn't seem all that happy about my asking him, if his silence the whole way to his house was any indication.

By the time he pulled into his garage, I'd been trying to focus on my breathing for a good ten minutes so I wouldn't succumb to another panic attack. He turned off the ignition and got out. I'd barely undone my seatbelt before he had opened my door for me.

Instead of going inside, he opened the back of his SUV and reached in for my suitcases.

"You don't need to bring my bags in. I've got a reservation at—"

"Cancel it. I'll pay if they want to charge a cancellation fee." He moved past me and inside, one bag in each hand.

I had to follow him if I wanted to argue further—which I did. I wanted his help, but I needed it to go at my pace. Staying in his house? Not ready for that. Nowhere close to ready for that. "I don't want you to go—"

"I'm not going out of my way for you, so knock it off. You're Soupy's sister. You're not staying in a hotel when you come to visit me, not when I have five guest bedrooms that almost never get used."

I barely registered the rooms we were going through, the furniture, the things on the walls. It felt like it was all closing in around me, squeezing me through a too-narrow space. He started up a flight of stairs, and I followed because I didn't know what else to do. He had my stuff, my bags.

At the end of a long hall, he opened a door, set my luggage against the wall, and flipped the light switch. I stayed just outside the room.

"You've got your own bathroom in here and a closet. That door will take you out into the backyard if you need...if you need more air. There are stairs on the outside that'll take you down, and you've got a lock on that door and this one. I'm all the way at the end of the hall, and Babs is set up in his own apartment, pretty much. He won't have any reason to come up here. You'll just see him in the living room and kitchen mainly."

"Him?" That was the one word my mind latched onto of everything Eric had said.

"Yeah, Babs—Jamie Babcock. He's a nineteen-year-old rookie. Made the team out of camp and didn't have anywhere to live. I offered to let him stay here this season, get his feet under him some."

I swallowed hard, but it didn't help. The thought of someone else living here with Eric, another man, hadn't crossed my mind when I'd decided to do this.

"He's a good kid, Dayana. You'd like him, if you'd let yourself. He's got some sick mitts, too. A lot like yours, actually." Eric moved out into the hallway. Without thinking, I squeezed into a corner to allow him as much room as possible and then mentally berated myself as soon as I realized what I'd done. He lifted a hand as though he intended to touch my cheek but let it drop back to his side. "Take some time to get yourself together. I'll be in the kitchen when you're ready to talk."

I watched him walk back the same way we'd come before heading down the stairs. Once I couldn't see him anymore, I went into the bedroom and shut the door. Out of habit, I checked that the lock worked properly. It did.

Next I moved across the room to the door leading outside. It was locked, so I opened it and went out onto the landing. The stairwell looked newer than the outside of the house, sturdy and well constructed. As soon as I was inside again, I closed and locked the door, then examined the windows. All locked.

Everything seemed safe. Safe enough, at least.

My breathing still hadn't leveled out, so I cracked open a window to let in some cold air, took off my coat, and lay down on the bed for a few minutes. By the time the air was making me chilly, my pulse had returned to a more normal pace and I felt like more oxygen was making its way into my lungs.

I sat up on the edge of the bed and actually looked around the room for the first time, taking in everything that wasn't strictly a safety concern. It was done in a peaches-and-cream color scheme, soft and easy on the eyes. Soothing.

It didn't escape my notice that they were my colors. When I was six or seven years old, I told my parents I wanted a peaches and cream room, and they'd indulged me. Even now, the bedroom in my apartment looked much the same as this one.

The woods were all whitewashed, smooth and with a homey, beachy feel. I drew my hand over the top of the nightstand beside me and opened the drawer. It held two items: a flashlight and pepper spray—two things he knew I'd need to feel secure.

It didn't make sense. Eric didn't know I was coming, so how...?

The more important question might be, why?

Leaving the flashlight and pepper spray in the nightstand, I closed the drawer and crossed over to close the window, looking down at the stairwell one more time as I flipped the lock. It definitely wasn't part of the initial design. This was an older house. He'd told me it was part of a historical district here back when he bought it. He'd clearly had a lot of restoration and remodeling done to it. Houses like this didn't have outside stairs. They had steps leading up to porches and internal stairwells.

Eric had put the stairs in. He must have.

The scents of garlic and lemon met me when I opened the door to my room, and my stomach growled in response. I followed the hallway to the stairs and down. It opened up to a huge open area, living spaces coming together with the dining room and kitchen. This all looked so much more like what I would expect of his house than my room did, with sleek, modern lines, blacks and whites and grays with splashes of bright red tossed in here and there.

Eric was standing in front of the stove with pots and pans going over three different flames. He smiled when he saw me. "I thought you'd be hungry since we didn't stay to eat at Amani's."

"I am." I hadn't realized it until the garlic had hit me.

He drained a pot of pasta before he tossed it into a sauce. "Lemon, garlic, and olive oil. No red sauce. I know it gives you heartburn."

"I didn't know you could cook." In all the time I'd known him, Eric had relied on his mother or mine to cook for him. Either that or he'd gone out to eat. It was always someone else cooking, though, never him.

"Living alone for as long as I have, you learn to do a lot of things for yourself. And being a professional athlete this long—it's hard to eat right if you can't cook. Gotta fuel the body." He flipped the two steaks he had on the grill pan. "Medium well?"

"Please."

He nodded toward a bowl on the bar near him. "Can you toss the spinach?"

I nodded and took a seat on the barstool. Caramelized onions, dried cranberries, and a balsamic vinaigrette were in the bowl as well, and a bit of gorgonzola cheese. It was practically a gourmet meal he'd made for me. Nothing like what I'd expect from a bachelor.

I picked up the salad tongs and started to toss it.

"Babs texted." Picking up the empty pasta pot, Eric moved to the sink to wash it. "He's going to the Trailblazers game with a couple of the boys. Won't be back until late. That'll give us plenty of time to talk without being interrupted."

I nodded so he'd know I heard him, but I was still pretending to focus on the salad. I'd probably over-tossed it, but I didn't stop. I couldn't, not any more than I could have stopped myself from picking at my nail until it bled earlier. "That bedroom?"

He set the pot down on the counter and turned off the faucet. "I thought if you ever came to visit—with Soupy or your parents—you'd need somewhere you could feel safe. I never thought you'd come by yourself, though."

"I didn't think I would either. The stairs? You had those put in?"

"You always need an escape route." He said it in a very mat-ter-of-fact manner, as though anyone would have thought of it, would have done something like that.

I did always need an escape route. I knew that, and I knew Mom and Dad and Brenden all knew. But I didn't think Eric knew, or maybe it was more that I didn't think he would have cared enough to do something like that for me in his home. I might never have come to visit him. I hadn't once made the journey to Portland in the seven years he had been playing for the Storm.

But he'd created a refuge for me in his house anyway.

My stomach was full of flutters, unfamiliar and as uncomfortable as they were exciting. I carried the salad bowl to the table to hide my face from him.

He'd already put out two place settings. I felt him come up behind me and fought the urge to slip to the side. He didn't touch me, though. He set the pasta bowl down beside the salad and pulled out a chair for me.

"Sit. I'll bring the steaks over, and we can talk while we eat."

He pushed the chair in behind me, only touching the chair and not me. Then he pointed to my left. "Straight path to the front door. Nothing between you and escape."

I couldn't speak around the thickness of my tongue. A nod would have to suffice.

He came back a minute later and put a steak on my plate and the other on his own before sitting down across from me. Tentatively, I reached for the salad and put some into my bowl.

"So," Eric said, reaching for the pasta, "here's what I'm thinking. You'll stay here tonight, and tomorrow morning before practice I'll take you back to the airport. Put you on a plane to either Seattle, so you can visit Soupy before you go home, or straight back to Providence. Your choice."

That wasn't really a choice, though. Not a viable one. I had no intention of going back to Providence for six weeks, and my brother may love me, but this was something he couldn't help me with even if he wanted to.

I stabbed at my steak, putting all my fears into the effort of cutting through the meat. "Eric, please just consider—"

"You're not ready, kid."

Kid. There it was again.

"You think you are. I know it. And you're frustrated." He opened a bottle of red wine and poured some for both of us. "I get it, Dayana."

"No, you don't get it." I pushed back in my chair, ready to dart out that door before I recognized my response for what it was. I couldn't keep running. Running didn't solve anything. I had to stay. I had to talk to him. "When a woman flirts with you, you don't feel like there's a giant ball of fire eating you alive from the inside out. When a woman touches your hand or your arm, you don't stop breathing, your lungs don't swell up and close off until your face is purple and someone calls 9-1-1. You don't have blurred vision, you don't break out in an uncontrollable sweat, your pulse doesn't race, and your chest doesn't hurt so much you think you're having a heart attack. Don't tell me you get it."

"Fair enough." Eric sipped from his glass. "But let me tell you what I've seen since you got off that plane today. You couldn't look me in the eye when you were asking me to touch you—and stuff, as you so eloquently put it. You couldn't say the damn word. Sex. You couldn't tell me what you wanted. You jumped when I accidentally touched you when I was helping you put your coat on. You couldn't handle that waitress thinking you were my girlfriend. You tensed up when I forgot and put my hand on your back for just a second. You're not ready for this, however much you may think you are, and however much you want it."

Everything he'd observed was right, but he'd fallen short on his interpretation.

"Don't you see, though?" I kept stabbing my steak, cutting and cutting, breaking it down into pieces so small a toothless baby could eat it. "That's not going to go away on its own, no matter how much counseling I go through and no matter how much time passes."

"More time could help."

"It's not. It won't. If time could make this better, or counseling, or prescriptions...anything, I'd be past it already. I've tried it all except—"

"Except what? Except asking me to touch you, to force you to experience all of those things even when I see what it does to you? What, do you think I should just hold you down while you freak out right in front of me, because of me, because of what I'm doing to you? You might as well ask me to rape you." He blanched and pushed his plate away. "That's not going to happen, I can tell you that."

"You're not being fair."

"Oh, I'm not? Tell me what it would be if not that. Tell me how you think this will play out. I'm all ears."

"I asked you because I thought...I thought you could be patient with me. Take things at my pace."

The look from earlier was back. His eyes were so intense, so filled with anger there wasn't a doubt in my mind that if I were a man, he'd hit me. If we were on the ice, at least.

"Even better. A nice, prolonged form of torture. That'll sit really well on my conscience for the next fifty years while you lock yourself away from the world in your apartment."

He took his plate, still full since he hadn't eaten a bite, stalked back into the kitchen and tossed it all down the garbage disposal. Even from a distance, I could see the line between his brows, could nearly hear his jaw grinding in frustration.

"The cow was dead before it hit your plate," he said a minute later.

I looked down, and through my tears saw that I'd turned my steak into mush. I set the knife down and tried to eat it because I was hungry. It's not very easy to eat when you're crying, though.

I had been so sure Eric would help me.

The whole time I'd known him, he'd always told me if I ever needed him, for any reason at all, he'd do anything he could to help me. Not once had I ever taken him up on that, not really. I mean, I'd had him forge my dad's signature on my report card once in middle school, but that's not the same. That was me being a stupid kid and thinking I could sneak a bad grade past my parents without them noticing. That wasn't a real need.

He stayed in the kitchen, washing all the pots and pans, wiping down the counters, cleaning the range top. I ate until I couldn't make myself take another bite for fear it might come back up. Conflict always made my stomach nervous, and this whole day had been filled with conflict.

"You didn't eat much." He met my eyes for a second before taking my plate away. "You used to eat better. Not like a bird."

"I usually do. Eat better."

He nodded. He washed my plate, running the garbage disposal again. After he turned the water off and left the dishes in the rack to dry, he wiped his hands on a towel and came to sit opposite me again. He pushed the towel across to me. "Dry your eyes. I hate it when you cry."

I dabbed my cheeks with the towel. "I'm sorry."

"Soupy'll kill me."

My breath caught a little. If Eric was thinking about Brenden's reaction then he was considering it.

"The hockey world is small. You know that." Eric poured himself more wine, then looked at my still-full glass before returning the bottle to the table. "He'll find out you're here in no time. And he'll kill me. It'll be even quicker this year than it would have before—now that he signed with the Storm to be the captain in Seattle."

The Portland Storm's minor league affiliate in the American Hockey League was based in Seattle. My brother had been happy for the opportunity, even though it still wasn't an NHL team like he wanted to be playing for. At least it was a two-way contract, meaning he could at least get some time playing with the Portland Storm.

"First time someone gets called up or sent down, they'll be all over telling him. Hell, some of the boys who've played up there earlier this year might tell him even before that happens. They might feel like they owe it to him."

"I could explain it to him."

"Oh, yeah," he said through a laugh. "Right. You'll explain it to him as well as you explained it to me, huh? When I thought you wanted me to pay some crackpot therapist to have sex with you? Good plan. I'm sure that'll go over really well."

"Brenden trusts you. And he knows I trust you. You won't push me too hard, but you won't go easy on me either."

"This is about a lot more than just trust."

I knew that all too well.

ERIC

"Physical intimacy and emotional intimacy are tied pretty closely together," I said to her. I still couldn't believe I was thinking about going along with this, but if I was, I had to be sure she had thought about every aspect of it. "More so for women than for men, and I'm not saying that to be an ass. What happens if you start having feelings for me? This is all going to be new for you. How are you going to handle it?"

And then there was the problem of what if I started having feelings for her. But that was minor, in comparison. I could deal with my own heartbreak if it came to that. I'd gotten by before after having my heart shattered. By her, even.

But for me to be the cause of Dayana's hurt? I didn't know what I'd do with that.

"I'm not asking you for a lifetime commitment or anything, Eric. I know I might get hurt, but I have to do this. Please?"

It was her eyes that would kill me, not her brother. Soupy wouldn't like it, but I could eventually make him understand. At least I could make him understand as well as I did, which wasn't necessarily saying a lot. But fuck, her eyes! Even when she was a little girl, she had this ability to rip my heart out and squeeze it, just with those brown eyes. They'd get so big, too big for her face, and they'd fill with these massive crocodile tears. I'd never seen such big tears, building and building until I was sure they had to spill over soon, but they just kept building. When they finally did fall, it made me feel like the biggest asshole of all time because I couldn't keep her from getting hurt.

She didn't have those tears building now, but her eyes were wide enough and so full of fear and hurt and vulnerability, I knew the tears were coming.

I couldn't handle that again. Not so soon. She'd just stopped crying a minute ago.

"How long do you intend to stay?"

We were over halfway through the regular season, and the Storm hadn't made it to the playoffs for three years in a row. We were right in the thick of things, but there were no guarantees. We had to finish out the season better than we'd started, at the very least. I couldn't really afford to lose my focus right now.

But Dayana never asked me for anything, not even when she desperately needed help. And she was determined. I knew how determined she could be. It was what made her one of the best women's hockey players in the world, back in the day. It was what had kept her isolated for seven years. She was going to use that same determination now to get someone to do what she'd asked me to do.

The thought of anyone else touching her wasn't something I could contemplate. I might not be sure I had the stomach for what she wanted me to do, but if someone was going to touch her, it would damn well be me.

"I took a leave of absence from work. FMLA. I've got six weeks. I even found someone to sublet my apartment."

Six weeks. That would pretty much coincide with all that was left of the regular season. Of course it would.

"You know that my life requires me to be around the guys a lot. Babs lives here. Sometimes the boys will come over and hang out. Practice, work outs, pregame meals, games, road trips, charity events... It's not just me you'll be with. They won't touch you, but they'll be around."

For the first time all day, Dayana met my eyes—really, truly looked at me, not just in the general vicinity of me or somewhere past me, but at me.

"I know. But you'll be with me."

I heard what she said. But I also heard what she didn't say. Nothing can hurt me when I'm with you.

Did she really believe that, or was she just trying to convince herself of it?

"It'll probably be best if they think you're my girlfriend. No need for PDA in front of them, but I don't want anyone thinking you're on the market. Just in case."

Norty, in particular, needed to know to keep his mitts to himself. The guy got around, and Dayana was just his type—blond, tall, fit, and curvy.

"Okay." Dayana agreed to that too easily. That should have been a harder condition for her to accept because of what it implied. Especially considering how she'd reacted to the waitress's comment earlier.

I dragged a hand over my face, feeling the scrape of stubble on my palm. I'd have to shave tomorrow or it'd start looking like I was growing a playoff beard. I'm not superstitious, but it didn't seem like a good plan to taunt the hockey gods with something like that.

"Are you sure about this? I mean, really, truly sure?"

"Yes."

She looked so damn hopeful it made me want to punch something. How could she feel hopeful when she was asking me to torture her?

"Fuck."

"So you'll do it? You'll help me?"

"You'll have to let me tell you how beautiful you are, things like that."

Just like that, she recoiled. "I'm not—"

"You are. Beautiful. You always have been, and you always will be, and you need to hear it."

She was one of the most beautiful women I'd ever known, and it was mainly because she didn't want to be. Dayana didn't wear makeup. She didn't dye her hair. She didn't get fake nails or Botox or think about a boob job or liposuction. The thing she wanted most was to avoid men's notice, but her efforts had the opposite effect. At least on me. She was all Dayana, all natural, no additives or preservatives.

And she was beautiful.

"You have to let me tell you that as much as I want and without brushing it off. And you have to start to believe it."

She took a breath. "That's going to be hard."

Compared to everything else she wanted, letting me tell her she's beautiful was the least of her worries. For either of us. I couldn't decide if it was going to be harder on me or on her. Physically, I knew it would be worse for her. But there was a hell of a lot more going on here than just the physical.

"It's all going to be hard."

Dayana nodded. "Okay. Will you do it?"

I couldn't let her find someone else to do what should be my job. Hell, even if she didn't have the panic attacks, I wasn't sure I'd be able to stand by while knowing someone else was touching her. I didn't know what that meant, or at least I didn't want to admit it to myself. "Yeah, I'll do it." I already regretted it, and I hadn't done anything yet.

Dayana smiled, a real smile, one of the first I'd seen on her face in far too long. "I wish...I wish I was brave enough to kiss you on the cheek."

She used to do that all the time, back when she was a little girl. She would kiss her dad on the cheek, and Soupy...and after I'd been around a while, she started to kiss me on the cheek. She'd do it after I'd had a good game sometimes or to thank me for some silly thing or another. Every now and then, she'd do it for no discernible reason at all.

No one else had ever done that to me. It was so chaste. So innocent. Sweet.

She couldn't wish for it nearly as much as I did.

Chapter 3 - Breakaway

DAYANA

"Drink your wine." Eric had gone back to the kitchen, taking the half-full bottle with him. "Not enough to get drunk. Just enough to take the edge off. It'll help."

As soon as he said that, he downed the last of his glass.

He was right. I needed to calm down some after all of this. I was exhausted from all of my travel, from the emotional drain of talking to him about this—but I was also wired. It was a strange and decidedly uncomfortable combination.

I sipped on my wine, let it flow through my body until I was a little warm and tingly, in a good way.

"What...uh? Damn." He dragged his hand through his hair, mussing it up until it looked like he'd just rolled out of bed. "What do you want to do tonight?"

That question was way too open-ended. This couldn't be all about me. He had his own life to live, too. I licked my lips, savoring the sweet taste of wine there. "What would you and Kim do when you had a night off like this?"

As soon as I said her name, I regretted it. Kim had been his girl-friend for years, so long I was sure they were going to get married. They'd looked great together, just the kind of girl a professional athlete should be with. He'd even talked to me about rings one summer. But that was before he'd come home from a road trip and found her in bed with a then-current teammate who'd been left behind to rehab a broken foot.

It'd been two years since their breakup, but still. I doubted he wanted to think about her right now. As far as I knew, there hadn't been anyone since. He might still be hurting from it. "I'm sorry. I shouldn't have—"

"We'd probably sit and watch TV together for a while." Eric didn't look upset to me. He should have. It would have been easier for some reason if he were upset. "She'd lean against me and I'd wrap my arms around her, hold her close. Then we'd go to bed, and either make love or just go to sleep. That's what most of our nights in were like. Easy. Relaxed."

That sounded exactly like the Eric I knew. He was never the flashy type, never wanted to go out and party or anything. He typically got more than enough excitement from his job; he needed comfort at home.

I swallowed hard, trying not to let my panic set in about the implications of all he'd said. "We could maybe watch TV together."

I didn't say anything about having his arms around me or going to bed. I couldn't think about things like that. Not now.

"Okay." Just like that, he went into the living room and turned on the TV.

When I joined him, he'd left me plenty of space to sit beside him on the white leather couch, or if I wanted, I could sit in one of the two recliners. But that wasn't what I was here for—separating myself. I needed to push myself, to push my boundaries so I could break through them and come out on the other side, hopefully still in one piece.

I sat on the couch—not quite pushing myself up against the far arm of it but close. Eric was well on the other end. Not close enough to touch me.

I didn't know what show he'd turned on. I wasn't able to focus on that right now. Just trying to remember to breathe, to keep my pulse down at a normal level—those kinds of things took up all of my mind-capacity and there was nothing left to worry about a silly TV show.

After a while, I started watching Eric instead of what was on the screen. It was easier to think about him, anyway.

He had his right leg tucked up underneath his left, a white athletic sock sticking out beside his left knee, just like he'd always done when we were kids. I guess he'd taken his shoes off while I'd been upstairs. I hadn't noticed until now.

Every time my mom would catch him sitting like that, she'd admonish him. Not about damaging the furniture or anything like that.

She didn't really care about how much destruction we caused, or at least she knew she was fighting a losing battle with growing kids in the house. It was more about the strain he was putting on his knees and hips. "They aren't designed to turn like that," she'd say. "You could hurt your chances of playing professionally."

She was right. He knew she was right. Every time he'd straighten his legs out after sitting that way, he'd wince at the pain in his knee, but he couldn't seem to stop himself from doing it. Especially when he and Brenden would play video games. He told me once that if he sat any other way, he always lost. Eric didn't like to lose at anything. Ever.

And he still sat like that.

After a minute, he turned to me and cocked a grin. "You're making me nervous, staring at me like that."

I looked down at my lap almost immediately, watching my hands twist together. "I'm sorry." I didn't want to make him nervous. I never wanted to make anyone nervous. Not when I knew how it felt.

"Do you not watch this show? The Vampire Diaries? The married guys all say their wives are addicted. I just... I assumed. I shouldn't assume. I thought you'd want to watch."

"You can put on whatever. I don't care." I didn't. With all my heightened emotion right now, I didn't think I'd be able to watch anything and really pay attention. It would just be background noise. Something to help me get through one minute and then the next.

"You're sure? You don't mind if I put on NHL Tonight? I want to see what's going on around the league. Keep up with things."

I shook my head. Putting on something about hockey might be best, anyway. Hockey was common ground for us. It was familiar.

"Okay." Eric reached for the remote and flipped the channel. "You can take your shoes off, you know. Get comfortable."

I could, but I doubted I'd ever be able to really be comfortable, shoes or no. At least not so soon. Not being in his house. I'd planned to be in a hotel. Somewhere separate. Somewhere I could escape to when things got too intense. Still, I did it for his sake, getting up and placing my flats neatly by the front door before coming back to the couch.

He'd shifted a little, moved down a couple of inches closer to where I had been sitting. I didn't think he'd done it intentionally, but the fact remained that he was closer to my space.

I sat down anyway and, with no shoes, tucked both my feet up beside me—between the two of us. He still wasn't close enough that we were touching, I was relieved to discover...but I could feel the warmth from his body rolling over my toes.

He winked at me before returning his attention to the TV.

"With tonight's win, Colorado moves up into a tie with Portland for that eighth spot in the West," the announcer said, catching my attention with the mention of Eric's team. "Portland doesn't play again until Saturday, and by then they could have fallen out of their current playoff seeding entirely, potentially dropping as low as number twelve in the conference. It's going to be a bumpy ride getting into the playoffs in the Western Conference, as usual. There are only six weeks left in the season, and twelve teams are still reasonably in the race."

Then they cut to the arena cam in Denver to interview Gabriel Landeskog about the win. He said all the usual boring and predictable things hockey players are taught from a young age to say in interviews. "Big team win; great effort from the goalie; we left him out to dry a few times but we held on when it counted and managed to pick up a big two points in overtime." All those sorts of things. Focus on the team. Talk about what you need to do better. Don't throw a teammate under the bus even when they deserve it—that stuff stays in the locker room. Don't give any sound bites that can come back to bite you in the ass. Be as boring in front of the media as the rest of the hockey players in the world.

Hockey players weren't boring if you knew them, though. I'd never been bored being around my teammates over the years, or Brenden's and Eric's.

I stole another glimpse over at Eric but made a point not to stare this time. His jaw was set, tight. If he were facing me, I had no doubt he'd have a big crease between his brows.

He put a lot of pressure on himself to be sure the team did well. He always had. I was sure that was a big part of the reason they made him the team captain when he was so young.

With the Portland Storm missing the playoffs the last three years, and barely holding onto a spot now, this was really bad timing for me to be asking him for help. Damn it. He needed to focus, needed to pay attention to his job, to do whatever it took to get his team to succeed. Not to me.

"We have another final score for you just coming in," the announcer said. "Let's go to Nashville for the highlights."

I watched the replay of Nashville scoring five unanswered goals against St. Louis, trouncing them pretty soundly, and felt Eric's tension grow with each goal. It was rolling off of him, tightening his shoulders.

"So there you have it. Nashville pulls within a point of Portland and Colorado with this win, and they have two games in hand."

Eric ground his teeth together.

"I'm sorry," I said.

He jerked his head around to look at me. "What are you sorry for?"

"This is… It's just really bad timing. I should have realized you had more important—"

"Stop that. Stop saying you're sorry, and don't try to tell me a stupid game is more important than you."

It wasn't just a stupid game, though. It was his livelihood. Yeah, it was just a game, but it had made so many things possible for him. It was part of him, and he was part of it. I couldn't imagine what Eric would be like if he didn't have hockey. They'd always gone hand-in-hand for me.

I shivered, more from the intensity of his stare than from being cold. He got up without a word and brought back a warm chenille throw, handing it to me instead of trying to cover me with it.

"Thank you."

He nodded. "Look, I'm not gonna lie to you and tell you it's not a tough time right now. It is. We have to get back to the playoffs this year, and frankly the possibility of that happening is looking pretty shaky. But that's my job. That's for me to concern myself with, not you. I don't want you to worry about anything but yourself."

"Yeah. Okay." I unfolded the blanket and draped it over myself, carefully tucking it around my knees and feet. My toes were a little cold, actually. But Eric was full of it if he thought I would be able to worry about nothing but myself. He knew me. He knew I got anxious about anything and everything, especially if it wasn't something I could control. That was part of my charm, or so Brenden had always told me. Sure, he was probably teasing me when he said that—that's what brothers do—but still.

"Dayana." My name sounded tortured when he said it.

I met his eyes, but I couldn't read him this time.

He put his hand between us, close to me, reaching for mine.

Instinct told me to jerk my hand away, to push myself back closer to the arm of the couch, to get up and move to the recliner or run upstairs and lock myself in my room or better yet run out the front door and not look back.

I didn't.

I let him take my hand and hold it in his, resting them on the couch between us. His hand was big and warm and strong, his palm rough with a few calluses from his hockey gloves and weight machines and God only knew what else.

My pulse was racing, hard and fast and terrifying, and I couldn't take a full breath. I was hot, suddenly, so very hot. With my left hand, I ripped the throw off me and tossed it to the floor.

Eric moved to let go of my hand, but I grabbed onto him and wouldn't let go.

"Not yet. Let me see if it'll pass." I could hear the desperation in my own voice, and the fear. Always the fear.

But he stopped pulling away.

I closed my eyes, focused on taking a breath in through my nose, out through my mouth, in, out, in, out, counting them in my head and trying to ignore how hard my body was shaking.

It was no good. I couldn't ignore it. I couldn't get enough air, and my head was pounding, pounding, screaming with the pain of not getting enough oxygen until I knew, without a doubt, I'd end up with a migraine from it if I couldn't get it under control and fast.

"Dayana, I can't. I can't watch you go through this. I can't be the cause of it."

Eric tried to pull his hand away again, but I couldn't let him. I couldn't give in so fast, so easily. I dug in with my fingers so hard it hurt. I doubted it hurt him, but it was enough to get his attention. He could still pull away if he wanted to, though. He was stronger than me by a long shot.

"Just hold me. Please." Every word was torture because of the breath required. "Hold my hand."

He didn't say anything, but he didn't let go.

I tried counting my breaths again, in and out, reminding myself that it was Eric holding my hand. Eric Zellinger. Brenden's best friend. I'd asked him to do this. I trusted him.

Gradually, the shaking slowed down. The sweating stopped, but then I was wet and cold, shivering. I reached down to the floor and pulled the blanket back up onto me.

Eric didn't let go of my hand through all of it.

Once my breaths weren't quite so shallow anymore, the pounding in my head lessened and slowly went away.

"That wasn't so bad, was it?" I had to make a joke of it, make light of it, or I'd fall to pieces.

Eric didn't respond, though.

I looked up at him, desperate to hear him laugh it off, too. He wasn't laughing. I'd never seen him look so tortured, so pained, so—broken was the only word that seemed to fit.

"That was hell."

ERIC

An hour later, I didn't know if it was Dayana still shaking, or if it was me.

But I was still holding her hand.

She'd hardly moved a muscle in all that time, not to pull away from me, but not to move closer either. I wanted to twine my fingers with hers, to smooth the pad of my thumb over the back of her hand, calming, soothing, but I didn't know if she could handle that. How much was too much, too soon? Where was the line? Would she even let me back away from the line in time, or would she insist on trying to push through her attacks until she actually did stop breathing? I just didn't know.

But I didn't let go, and neither did she.

Dayana yawned. She had to be beyond exhausted. Jet lag, a day of travel, not to mention the panic attack. Those individually took a lot out of her. Combined, though?

I was about to suggest she call it a night and go up to bed when the front door opened and Babs came in, laughing. He wasn't alone. Razor was with him—Ray Chambers, one of the other rookies on the team this year.

Dayana jumped, and I could tell she wanted to pull her hand away, she wanted to run, but she didn't.

I should have told Babs about Dayana when he'd texted earlier. I should have let him know it wasn't a good night to bring anyone else in for a late-night snack or a drink or a video game, or anything. It was going to be hard enough for her to meet him tonight.

The inside of her wrist pressed against my arm. I could feel her pulse pounding, racing, nearly bursting through her veins. Damn it.

Babs went into the kitchen for a couple of waters from the fridge. "Sorry, man, she wasn't looking at you."

"Nah, bro. She wanted me, eh." Razor was oblivious to the two of us as he came into the living room and plopped down on the first recliner. "Not you. You're cute, like Bieber or a puppy or something. They want to pet you, but that's about it. But me? Girls dig me. Tell him, Zee."

Babs came back and tossed a water bottle at Razor, trying to hit him in the head with it. It almost worked, but Razor tossed up his hands at the last second and caught it.

Then he looked over at me and saw Dayana. "Oh. Sorry, Zee. I didn't... Damn, Babs, why didn't you say he had a girl here?"

Babs just gave him a how-the-hell-was-I-supposed-to-know look and then brushed his hands through his hair, trying to straighten himself up as if his mom were around or something.

Dayana, however, was strung so tight I knew she was going to blow at any moment...not in anger, but in panic.

I tightened my grip on her hand, trying to reassure her. "Guys, this is my girlfriend, Dayana. Dayana, that's Babs on the left and Razor on the right. And Razor was just on his way out."

"I—" Razor thought twice about arguing that point. Smart move. "Yeah, right. See ya in the morning, boys. See ya around, Dayana."

Babs followed him to the door and locked it behind him. He had an enormous, sheepish grin on his face when he came back. "Sorry, Zee. I didn't..." He shrugged. "You've been keeping quite a secret from the boys, there."

Dayana was squirming, and the temperature of her hand shot up fast. In no time, it was covered in sweat. She tossed the blanket off her lap again and looked at me with wild eyes.

Fuck.

"A pretty secret, though."

Babs should have kept his damn mouth shut.

Dayana jerked her hand out of mine and bolted up the stairs. I only counted to three from the moment she left until I heard her bedroom door slam closed.

"Did I say something wrong? Chicks are crazy. Maybe I should have left Razor to it, if this is what they're like."

Getting mad at Babs wouldn't help anything, but I needed somewhere to vent. Not on him, though. He didn't know better.

"Dayana isn't crazy." I picked up the throw blanket and tossed it back onto the sofa. "She's going to live here. I'll tell you more tomorrow." I went up the stairs behind her.

"Yeah... I'm sorry, Zee. 'Night."

In the morning, on our way into practice, I'd tell him more than I intended to tell the other guys. If he and Dayana were going to live in the same house, there were things he'd have to understand. But I trusted Babs. Like I'd told Dayana, he was a good kid. He'd never do anything to intentionally hurt anyone. But, he was a kid.

When I got to her door, I knocked.

No answer.

"Dayana?"

I could hear her struggling for breath just on the other side of the door, down near the floor. I dropped to my knees and pressed my ear up against it.

"It's just me. Are you...? Do you need anything?"

"I'm s-s-sorry."

"Please stop apologizing, kid."

Times like this, I just wanted to pull her into my arms and hold her until it passed. I'd done that before. When she was twelve, Soupy got hurt bad in a game we were playing. Got knocked out cold. They took him to the hospital in an ambulance, and her parents went with him and left her with me and my folks. She was terrified. We both were. She cried and cried, and all I could do was hold her tight for hours until we heard more. Until we knew he would be okay.

But I couldn't do that now. Even if she would let me in, even if she hadn't locked the door to protect herself, I couldn't. Not yet. Maybe, if she was right, if this plan worked how she hoped it would...maybe someday.

But for now, all I could do was sit on the floor by her door and hate myself for not being able to protect her from her demons.

It wasn't the first time I'd done this, sitting by her door. When Soupy and I had gone home for Christmas our senior year, the first time we'd seen her after... She couldn't bring herself to come out of her bedroom that whole break.

Her parents had tried to just go on about their lives, hoping that she'd snap out of it.

Soupy couldn't take it. He'd go to the gym for hours at a time, coming home with bruised and bloodied knuckles because he spent too long beating up punching bags.

But me? I'd sit by her door a lot, listening, waiting, hoping maybe she would tell me what I could do, ask me for help. Anything.

She didn't.

She was better by summer—at least if you considered how she is now better. She wouldn't let us hug her anymore, and she couldn't look me in the eye. There were no more kisses on the cheek or arm wrestling contests, none of the things we used to do. But she would come out of her room again.

That was progress. That was all we could really ask for, I suppose—progress.

My knees hurt, so I dropped lower until I was actually sitting on the floor instead of kneeling. I leaned my back to the wall and let my head rest against it, listening to be sure she started breathing normally again.

I had to wait a long time.

It scared me, the breathing thing. Especially since she had locked the door. I had a key, but it would just take more time if we had to get in there. I racked my mind, trying to remember exactly where I'd put the key. Just in case.

It was probably in the drawer of my nightstand, but I wasn't sure. I was debating whether I should go make sure that's where it was or whether I should stay put, making sure she was breathing, when I heard it.

"Eric?" Just a tiny voice.

"Yeah? I'm still here." I'd be here as long as it took.

"I need water to take my meds."

She sounded more normal. Calmer. She wasn't crying anymore, at least.

"Okay. I'll be right back with it."

I took the stairs two at a time. Babs had gone off to his room, whether to play video games or watch porn or sleep, I didn't know. I didn't care.

I grabbed two bottles of water from the fridge and took them back upstairs, setting them on the floor just outside her room.

"They're right here when you open the door. And there's a flashlight and pepper spray in the nightstand."

"I know." She sounded a little stronger. Less shaky. "I found them earlier. Thank you."

"Do you...do you need anything else?" I wanted her to say yes. I wanted her to need something that would force her to open the door and let me see her, let me see with my own eyes that she was better again, or at least on her way to being better.

"No, I..."

Please need me.

"I'll be fine." She sounded firm on that, damn it. "I'll see you in the morning, Eric. I'll be better tomorrow."

"All right. But wake me, whatever time it is, if you need anything."

"Good night, Eric."

Now was not the time to push. "Good night, Dayana."

I went back down the hall to my room and closed the door, and I waited. A minute later, I heard her lock turn and the door open. Then, just as quickly, she closed it and locked it again.

Instead of going to bed, though, I threw every pillow I had across the room, ripped the sheets back off the bed, and pounded the mattress.

It didn't help.

And now I had to make my bed.

Chapter 4 - Breakaway

Eric

Even after seven years in the league, standing in a locker room in clothes drenched with my own sweat while a dozen or so cameras and microphones and voice recorders were shoved in my face felt weird. There wasn't really a better word to describe it. Who the hell cared what I had to say? And why should they? I was just a guy. Nothing special. But when you play sports for a living, for some reason people give a crap whether there's anything worth saying or not.

Since I was the team captain, there was even more importance placed on the words that came out of my mouth. Was that justified? Not really. It was just the way things were.

I tried to wipe some of the sweat off my face with the towel that hung around my neck, but it wasn't really going to help much. Nothing but a shower could at this point.

"After Wednesday's loss to Calgary, how are you hoping to bounce back against San Jose tomorrow?" Mike Polanski asked. Mike was the beat reporter for the Portland Tribune. Good guy. Tired questions. He always asked inane things because he knew he'd get the same old cliché-filled answers we liked to give.

There wasn't really anything they'd likely glean from today's media session anyway. It was a practice day only. I'd never understood why we were required to have media availability on practice days. Beat reporters and bloggers have columns to fill, though, whether there was a game that day or not. Still, hockey teams like putting out answers of the innocuous variety. We're all about routines. If you had a few phrases you didn't even have to think about, you didn't have to worry about saying something stupid. The second you gave the media something interesting, they pounced on it and beat the hell out of it.

As usual, answering Mike's question didn't take a lot of thought. "San Jose's got size, skill, and speed. They are always on the attack. They're great in transition. Their D makes clean, quick passes to get the puck to their forwards. We've got to be clean in our own end and strong on the forecheck. We have to be better in the neutral zone. We've gotta take away their open ice and take the body, make it tough on them. We can't give them anything for free. They're coming into our building. We need to come away with two points and make sure they leave with none."

"Make it tough on them," a guy to my left said.

I squinted over at him through the lights shining in my eyes. Short guy. Beady eyed. I recognized him vaguely as one of the beat reporters who followed San Jose. He had a snarky look to him, especially with the way he was lifting his eyebrow. I nodded at him to go on anyway.

"I hear that a lot coming out of Portland this year. Actually, for the last several years. But the Storm haven't really been a tough team to beat. What exactly is the style of play you envision your team playing, Zee?"

That question made my blood roil. Not because he was wrong, but because he was right. I turned to face him, forcing all of the other reporters to shift around in order to make sure they got their sound bites.

"We want to be a physical team, and we want to be tough to play against. That's our style. That's what Scotty wants us to do, and that's what we do."

"Want to be. Yeah. Pesky Storm, right? That's what they're using on Twitter, your fans. They even made it a hashtag, like it's something special."

That phrase, Pesky Storm, irked me to no end. Just as much as saying we "play a physical brand of hockey" or "we want to be tough to play against" did. Those were crutch phrases used by teams who didn't really have a defined identity, didn't have a brand of play that was the core of what they were.

I should have taken a breath, taken a moment to calm myself down before I spoke. I was the team captain. It was my job to spread the message the team wanted spread.

For once, I didn't take that moment.

"Yeah, right. We're the 'Pesky Storm,' all right. We say our style is tough to play against because we have a dozen guys who haven't bought into what Coach is selling yet. Jim Sutter put together a group of guys with size and speed and skill. If there's one man in this organization who knows what he's doing, it's Jim. He brought in Scotty to be the coach because he believes Scotty is the right coach for the team he put together. Scotty preaches puck possession, physicality, getting the D engaged in the rush, and having the forwards play solid in the defensive end. Five guys working as one in all three zones. That's the kind of team we're built to be, that's the brand of hockey we're designed to play, that's the identity we ought to be believing in. But because some of the boys think they know how to play the game better, all we can be is the Pesky Storm. Pesky...aggravating. Aggravating to Jim, aggravating to the coaches, aggravating to ourselves, and aggravating to our fans. This coaching staff has over eighty years of professional hockey experience between them. Sutter played eighteen years in the NHL and has been working in front offices ever since. He's one of the most respected guys in the game. But some of the boys on the team think they know better, think they can just ignore all of that experience and do their own thing because it worked for them when they played peewee or that's how their team played in junior. So yeah, our brand of hockey is 'tough to play against.' Run with that. So is Calgary's, and they beat us on Wednesday. So there you go."

I shouldn't have let loose like that. There was a small part of me that wanted to blame my over-sharing on the turmoil brought into my life when Dayana called me from the airport yesterday, but that wasn't fair. My frustrations with the way things were going with the Portland Storm had been building for years now. I wouldn't make Dayana the scapegoat. She wasn't responsible for anything that came out of my mouth. I was.

Out of the corner of my eye, I saw Jim across the room. He was the team's general manager, the guy who decides who should be on the team—and he'd heard every word I'd just said. He raised an eyebrow at me and walked out. Fuck.

Granted, he would have heard it all later, anyway. I had no doubt it would be all over the internet, the radio, sports TV in no time.

"I think my time's up." Before they could ask me anything else, and before I could further put my foot in my mouth, I pushed through them and made for the showers.

By the time I got back into the dressing room, the media had all cleared out.

A few of the boys gave me ugly looks. Understandable. You don't call out your teammates like that. That sort of thing ought to stay in the room. They knew I was talking about them, and it hurt their pride. Maybe that's what they needed, though. Nothing else seemed to be getting through their thick skulls. I probably could have gone about it a better way, but I couldn't take it back now. By this afternoon, the hockey media would be having a field day.

Babs nodded and gave me a goofy grin. The kid was always smiling. He didn't let anything faze him. It was no wonder all the girls were going gaga over him. Teenaged girls wanted him to take them to their proms, and older women wanted to hug him and pinch his cheeks and bake him cookies. It was unreal. I'd never seen anything like it.

I was glad he was smiling at me, that his feelings weren't hurt by what I'd done. I hadn't been talking about him anyway, but he was just a rookie, still really green. He could have thought I was.

He bounded over to me like the eager puppy Razor had described him as last night. "A few of us are going to Brunetti's for lunch. Coming?"

I doubted they'd all be happy to have me with them after what I'd just said, even if Babs was. Besides, I had other things I needed to do. "Nah. I need to go talk to Sutter for a minute, and I want to see Dayana before I do my radio spot."

She'd said she'd be fine hanging out at my house this morning. That she'd find something to do with herself. I'd figured it would be good to give her some alone time, anyway. She probably wouldn't get much of it before too long, and she needed it. She always needed it. Even when she was little, before the rape, she needed her downtime to be alone and decompress. The fewer people around her, the better. Dayana was the epitome of an introvert.

And now she was going to be tossed straight into the fire of my life. I hated that for her, but she'd asked for it.

"Yeah, all right. See ya later." He pulled a baseball cap over his out-of-control mop of blondish hair and followed after Razor and

Hank, a young Swedish defenseman. The kid nearly had a bounce in his step. I hoped he never lost that enthusiasm, that wide-eyed excitement. He was going to be a big star in this league, and fame has a way of jading you. That's part of why I had offered to let him live with me. I wanted to shield him from some of the ugliness if I could.

I took a few minutes to straighten up my locker. The team had staff people who would do it, locker room attendants, equipment managers, that sort of thing. But I didn't think it was fair to leave a bigger mess than was necessary. It only took me a few minutes, anyway. Not a big deal, and they didn't make enough money to clean up after me.

I made my way upstairs to Jim's office.

Martha Alvarez, the executive assistant to the GM, looked up at me from over the top of her computer monitor. "Jim said to expect you. Go on in." Without batting an eye, she went right back to whatever she was doing before I walked up, tucking her silvery-gray hair back behind her ear and pushing her bifocals back into place on her nose. Martha was seventy if she was a day, and as organized and efficient as they come. She'd been working in the same position for over twenty years, and everyone expected she would be for another twenty if she had her way.

Everyone in the organization would be fine with that, too. She was a tough cookie, Martha. She told it like it was even if she thought it would hurt your feelings. And then she'd give you a warm, home-made cookie. It was good to have someone like her around. Lots of guys, when they first come into the league, have a hard time of figuring out the everyday parts of life. They'd never lived away from their parents. Never had to cook for themselves, never had to wash their own clothes. Yeah, they made good money, but it was a big adjustment. She made it easier.

I knocked on Jim's open door when I poked my head through the doorway.

He was smiling when he spun around to face me. "I had a feeling I'd be seeing you. Come on in. Take a seat." Jim had never looked quite right in a suit to me, even though I saw him in one every day. Gray hair and glasses couldn't hide his athletic build, just like he'd been in his playing days. He'd been a real grinder, a depth forward who had played for as many teams as he'd had years in the league. There wasn't much he valued more than hard work, and he expected just as much effort as he would have given from every guy who played for him.

I closed the door behind me and sat in the chair across from his desk. "I know I shouldn't have said all that to the press."

His narrowed eyes bored holes in me. "Why not? It's the truth."

That took me aback. Truth telling isn't really the name of the game in the NHL. At least not where the media is concerned. In other sports, when a player is sidelined with an injury, they reveal what the exact injury is. In the NHL, it's usually announced that a guy has an "upper-body" or "lower-body" injury. Nothing more specific than that. During the playoffs last year, one coach even reported that his player had suffered a "body injury." What the fuck? Supposedly, it's to protect players from other teams trying to target the specific area of injury. Whatever. The fact of the matter is that we don't like telling any more truth than we absolutely have to. The more vague, the more boring, the less newsworthy, the better.

"Maybe that's what the boys needed to hear, Zee. They haven't been getting the message from Scotty, and it hasn't gotten through to them when the doors have been closed. Maybe this will be what it takes—get it all out in the open."

"Yeah. I guess." My head was reeling, and it wasn't just because I'd lost my cool and said all that. Dayana's arrival yesterday, everything that had happened last night—I didn't feel like my feet were on solid ground.

"Did anyone give you a hard time about it?"

"Not yet. A few looks, that's all. Nothing I can't handle."

He nodded. "If you're sure."

"I made my own bed. I can lie in it." I had practice at that already after last night. I'd spent the whole night lying in a bed I'd unmade, at least. And if things went the way Dayana planned... Hell, I had to stop thinking like that. "That wasn't the only thing I wanted to see you about, though."

He took off his glasses, folded them, and set them on the desk. "You want to talk to me about Dayana Campbell, don't you?"

DAYANA

I'd been scrubbing the same spot in the oven for about ten minutes when Eric came through the garage door and made me jump out of my skin.

He stopped in his tracks with the door open and stared at me, his eyes traveling from my head to my toes. I looked a wreck. My hair was all tangled in knots, I needed another shower even though I'd had one after breakfast, I was wearing my oldest, most falling-apart jeans and a fading green T-shirt with stains that wouldn't come out, and I had giant yellow gloves on both hands. There was a bucket at my feet, and I was holding tight to a disgusting sponge covered with oven cleaner and grime.

He, however, looked like he could have just walked out of the pages of a magazine.

"I wasn't expecting you back so soon," I said, brushing my hair out of my eyes with the hand holding the sponge. Great. Now I probably had a streak of oven gunk running over my forehead and through my hair. It hadn't even been very dirty, but there were a few stuck-on spots that were driving me crazy.

"I guess this means we're having lunch in today."

Lunch? It couldn't be time for lunch already. I stole a look at the clock on the wall, and my jaw dropped. "It's one o'clock?"

"Yes, it's one o'clock. Why are you cleaning my oven?" He looked angry. Everything I did seemed to get under his skin. What was wrong with me cleaning?

"Because I finished with the toilets and it was only ten, so I figured I needed to find something else to fill some time."

Eric closed the garage door and came to stand in front of me. "Give me the sponge."

"It's covered in—"

"Just give me the sponge, Dayana. And the gloves."

He didn't have to talk to me like I was a kid. I fought away my sulky scowl, though, and put the sponge in his hand. I peeled off the gloves and did the same with them.

"Where did you even find these?" he asked. He tossed them into the sink, picked up my bucket, and dumped its contents down the drain.

"I walked down to the convenience store we passed on the way here yesterday and bought them. I couldn't find them anywhere I would have thought to put them."

"You couldn't find any because I have a housekeeper. She comes every week and brings everything with her that she needs, and she'll come more often than that if I ask her to." He washed his hands in the sink and used the sprayer to rinse away the mess from my oven cleaning venture. "When you said you'd find something to do with yourself, I figured you'd work out or read a book or watch a movie. I don't want you cleaning my house as if you have to earn your keep."

"I don't think that." I really didn't. I just had to have something to do all the time. Something to keep me moving, something to occupy my hands. I'd had this nervous energy for a long time now. If I didn't have something to do, then my mind went places I'd rather it not go.

He scowled and shook his head. "Go take a shower. I'll figure out what we'll do for lunch."

By the time I was clean and dressed, he'd put together baked mahimahi, roasted asparagus, and couscous. He set both our plates on the table, in the same positions as last night. He held out my chair for me. When I sat, he pushed it in behind me before taking his seat across the table.

He was quiet when he started eating. But it was strained. Awkward. I didn't like it.

"How was practice?" I asked, just to have some sound.

"It was fine."

Fine wasn't good. With Eric, fine was never good. It meant pretty much the opposite of fine.

He didn't elaborate.

I cut a piece of asparagus in two and took a bite. He was shoveling food into his mouth like a man who hadn't eaten in a week. He wasn't even looking at me.

I didn't know what I'd done wrong this time. I hated that. If I knew what I'd done, I could try to fix it, try to make it better. But he wasn't talking to me, wasn't looking at me, wouldn't let me make it right.

Yes, I could be neurotic. But I didn't know what I'd done wrong.

I set my knife and fork down on my plate and cleared my throat.

His eyes shot up to meet mine. Intense, green eyes. Eyes that could pierce me.

The urge to look away threatened to overwhelm me. "What did... what did I do wrong now?"

He finished chewing his bite and swallowed. He wiped his mouth with a napkin. "You didn't do anything wrong."

I blanched at the frustration in his tone.

After taking a drink from his water glass, he let out a sigh. "This isn't about you, Dayana. Not really. I just had a bad day. And I'm trying to figure out how to tell you something without—"

"Without me having a giant freak-out and locking myself in my bedroom?"

"I wasn't going to put it that way, but yeah."

It couldn't be easy for him. I'd put him in a bad position, and I hadn't given him any warning. I understood that all too well. But I needed him to start to trust that I could handle things. If he didn't believe it, how could I? I needed him to believe in me.

"Why don't you try telling me and see what happens? I'll try not to freak."

"I talked to Jim Sutter today about you traveling with the team."

Cue me freaking out. I tamped down on the urge to run and put all my focus on listening to Eric and remembering to breathe.

I hadn't factored road trips into the equation, but if this was going to work I'd have to go with him. He was right. Sometimes, he'd be gone for a week, a week and a half, maybe two weeks. How could we make any progress with my panic attacks if we weren't even in the same state, same country? Six weeks wouldn't be enough time to accomplish much if we weren't together. My trip would be a waste.

But that would mean being around the whole team, all the coaches and trainers and equipment guys—dozens of men and me—for long stretches, days on end. I couldn't do that. I couldn't handle that. Not yet.

"He's given the okay for you to fly on the team plane. Some of the boys aren't going to be happy that my girlfriend is coming along on all our road trips when theirs aren't, but I'll handle that. Their significant others probably won't be too happy about it, either, so Jim's cooking up some story. I think he's going to tell everyone that you're with us to learn what you can from the coaching staff. That you're thinking about getting into coaching women's hockey. Something like that. We're booking connecting rooms for you and me at every hotel. I'm paying for the extra room. You can keep your door locked if you want, or you can open it and come through. Up to you. Mine will be open if you need me."

I nodded so he'd know I was following along, but I could hardly process it all.

"You can take your pepper spray in a checked bag. Just not in a carry-on. And I'll be with you."

I tried to eat again, tried to make myself act normally, but I could barely get a bite of food to go down. What if I started having a panic attack on the plane? Or if we were in some strange city, and he was in the game or at practice or God only knew what and I had to deal with someone other than him? I just... It was too much.

"Dayana?"

He didn't say anything else until I looked up, until I met his eyes.

"I'll be with you. I won't let anything happen to you."

He looked so determined, so certain of himself. But that was just it: he might be able to protect me from a lot of things in life, but there were some things—things inside me—that no one could rescue me from.

"I know you'll take care of me," I said, mainly to reassure him.

"I will. I'll always take care of you." His hand twitched, like he wanted to reach across the table and touch me, caress my cheek or hold my hand. I almost wished he had, that he hadn't pulled his hand back to his side of the table. Almost. "I don't want to rush you on any of this, but I have to. The team flies out on Sunday morning. We'll be gone eleven days."

If it was going to be a short trip, a couple of games, a few days, I would have told him I would stay behind and go on the next trip. That would have bought me a little more time, given me a bit more of a chance to mentally and emotionally prepare myself for it all. But eleven days? When I'd only just gotten here, when I'd barely been able to let him hold my hand for an hour?

I couldn't lose that much time. I only had six weeks.

"Okay." My voice sounded feeble even to my own ears.

He took another bite, and I did the same. It wasn't easy to eat, not with all the thoughts swirling through my head...but I hadn't gone into a full panic attack this time. My breathing had gotten a little shallow, and my pulse had picked up, but that was all.

"I have to do a radio interview this afternoon. A call-in thing for a weekly show. It won't take too long. You've got me for the rest of the day."

"I don't— You can still have your life, Eric." I didn't want him to give up everything, to drop the things he'd normally do just because I was here. Now that I thought about it, he probably already had. Babs hadn't come home with him for lunch. He must have gone out with some of the guys. Eric probably would have, too, if not for me.

Just because he was pretending to be my boyfriend didn't mean he actually was my boyfriend.

"I know. I want to be with you, though."

He flashed me that half-grin, where the left side of his lips tilted up just a smidge more than the right side. He'd been grinning at me like that for as long as I could remember, but never once before tonight had it made me feel weak-kneed. It was a good thing I was sitting down.

Could sitting beside him last night, letting him hold my hand—was that enough to cause this sort of a change in how I saw him?

My chest felt a little fluttery, and I looked back down at my plate to keep eating. Not that I needed to stare at my plate in order to eat, exactly, but that was the excuse I gave myself. I was pretty sure I blushed, though. I was even more certain he'd noticed.

And that only made the flutters intensify.

"Will you come to the game tomorrow?"

I snapped my head up to stare at him. I hadn't expected that, although I don't know why. I should have. He was taking me with him on the road, he was telling all his teammates that I was his girlfriend...and wives and girlfriends typically go to the games, or at least the home games.

"Mr. Engels has a box that he never uses. We never see him, even though he owns the team, other than the annual Christmas party. He lets all the players' wives and girlfriends use it. It'd just be the girls. You'd be safe."

I nodded. That was something I could manage better than the road trip, at least. I was comfortable with women. And I knew Eric well enough to pull off pretending to be his girlfriend. "Do you want me to be there?"

"I do. It'll be like old times. You used to come to all of my games."

"Because they were Brenden's games," I teased.

"Yeah. But they were mine, too."

The way he was looking at me, I couldn't quite put my finger on it, but it only made me blush harder.

"Yes, I'll come."

Chapter 5 - Breakaway

DAYANA

It's a completely different experience looking down over a sheet of ice from the owner's box than it is being down at ice-level. Things move slower. You can see plays forming from above, see their genesis, things that you'd never recognize in time if you were down on ice level. At least not if you're a mere mortal like most hockey players. By the time you recognize what's about to happen, it's too late. The other guy has already stolen the puck and sent it up the ice to his teammate, and they score right around the time you recognize your mistake and react.

But up above? You can break it all apart a little easier.

That's why some coaches will bench a rookie for a few games. It's not that they aren't trying. A lot of times, rookies try too hard. So they get sent up to the press box where they can see plays taking shape with everything moving a little slower. More often than not, it helps. Plus, it pisses the rookie off, and that only makes them want to prove themselves to the coach that much more. A little piss and vinegar never hurt anyone, at least not where competitive drive is concerned.

Some very special players, though, have this ability to slow the game down and see ahead like that even when they're on the ice. They call it "vision" or "hockey sense," things like that. After you've played for a few years, you develop your hockey sense to a degree.

But those select few? They see the game like no one else does. Wayne Gretzky was one of them, and more recently, you could put Nick Lidström in that category. Players like that are always two or three steps ahead of everyone else on the ice.

As a fan watching the game on your television at home, you can't really get a feel for just what it means when the commentators talk about the vision those players have because it's about the things they do when the puck isn't on their stick. The camera follows the guy with the puck. That's who you see, plus whoever else is around him. But if you watch from the owner's box, you can follow the game away from the puck, see how guys position themselves depending on what's taking place on the ice, analyze the choices they make.

Coach Bassano had hoped it would help me after I was raped. She'd benched me more games than she played me, had me watch from the press box up above. It wasn't my hockey sense I'd lost, though. It was everything else.

But now, looking down at the Zamboni surfacing the ice in the near-empty Moda Center, I had to wonder why the expensive tickets were the ones down close to the boards. Yeah, fans wanted to feel like they were in on the action, I guess, but you can see the game in a much more complete way when you're up high.

Not once since we'd arrived had I picked up the book I'd brought with me, even though I'd been sitting alone in the box for a good twenty minutes. Instead, I'd been looking down at the ice, nearly seeing a game take place down there even though there were no players.

I didn't have a car of my own here, and Eric had suggested he ride in with Babs and leave me his. They had to be at the arena a couple of hours before game time, but there was no reason I needed to be. It was tempting, but I was afraid I'd chicken out and stay at his house if I didn't go with them when they left.

When we got here, they'd both brought me up to the box before heading down to the locker room. I'd assumed Babs would have just gone straight in to do his thing, get into his pregame routine. But he didn't.

It was only when we got inside the owner's box that I understood why. He made a beeline for the spread of food laid out, grabbed two turkey sandwiches and a banana, and then headed out. "Later, Dee," he'd called out behind him, his voice muffled around the half a sandwich already stuffed in his mouth.

I'd had to laugh. Eric had been right about Babs. I was starting to like him.

"It's good to hear you laugh."

Those words had been haunting me since Eric left me alone up there. I didn't laugh much anymore. Or smile. I hadn't for years...but I was starting to again.

A man cleared his voice behind me, and I tried to hide how much it startled me. When I stood up and turned around, I saw Jim Sutter leaning against the door. His gray hair and glasses couldn't hide how fit he still was, and neither could the black suit he wore. It'd been fifteen years or more since he'd played in the NHL, but he still looked like he could lace them up if he wanted.

"I didn't scare you, did I? I didn't mean to scare you."

I shook my head, blatantly lying.

He smiled, but it was tight. "I doubt you remember me. Played with your dad for a few years in Hartford. I haven't seen you since you were two years old. He used to put you on a sled and pull you around the ice. You had the most addictive giggle I have ever heard."

"He'd still do that today, if I'd let him."

Mr. Sutter nodded, just looking at me. "He was a good friend to me. And a great hockey player. That's part of why I signed your brother over the summer. See if he's got a little of his father's fire if given the right opportunity. He's got all the tools. I've had scouts following him for years."

That was what Brenden was hoping for, too. Injuries and bad bounces had pretty much defined his professional career. He knew he was good enough to make it, but he'd been passed around the minor leagues for years, never really getting the chance to prove himself. If you asked anyone about him, they'd tell you he was a hell of a sniper but injury prone. He never let his frustration show, though. He just kept plugging away, waiting for the day that he'd finally get a real shot at making it in the NHL—something more than just a few games here and a call-up there.

"He appreciates the chance," I said. "We all do."

"Yeah. I'm glad to be able to give it to him." He came a little further into the room, not near me, but just close enough in that he could take an apple off the table. "Anyway, I just wanted to introduce myself before tomorrow. We want to make this as easy for you as we can, Dayana. You can come to me with anything, okay? I owe it to your dad."

I wasn't quite sure what he meant about owing my dad, but I didn't get a chance to ask him about it. Three women and a teenaged girl, probably around sixteen or seventeen years old, came into the box. They breezed past Mr. Sutter without stopping their chatter.

He gave me a wink and a wave and backed out.

I kind of froze in place, not sure whether I should introduce myself or just hang back and wait for them to come to me. They talked for a few more moments and laughed...and then one of them looked over and saw me.

She had to be in her late thirties, and she was gorgeous, a real knock-out. Sleek brown hair, perfect makeup and nails, and nothing out of place. She had on skinny jeans and heels, and a silvery sweater that made her haunting, light-blue eyes pop.

Looking at her made me want to crawl under a rock. I've never been good at girly things, even though I was more comfortable with women than with men these days. When you grow up playing hockey, with a hockey-playing dad and a hockey-playing brother, things like makeup and nail appointments and gossip just feel awkward. Not to mention unnecessary.

She smiled at me, though, and whispered something to the teenager, who could have been an exact replica of her. She had to be the woman's daughter. The girl looked at me and smiled, and they excused themselves from the two other women they'd entered with to join me. "You're Dayana Campbell," the mother said. She took my hand and winked.

Women touching me had never caused the same kind of reaction that men did. I was okay with it. It didn't set off that trigger in my brain, didn't start the chemical reaction that left me a shaking, sweating, crying mess, so I let her.

"My husband asked me to keep an eye on you. I'm Laura Weber. This is my daughter Katie. My husband's David Weber." She guided me back to my seat and took the one next to me, her daughter sitting on my other side. "His sister Courtney went to school with you. Boston College. He remembers you."

Courtney Weber had been a senior on the team that year. She played defense and had one of the hardest slap shots I'd ever seen a woman get off.

The only reason David Weber, or anyone in the hockey world, would remember me was because of what happened. It had made all sorts of headlines, mainly because the aftermath of it completely derailed my potential hockey career. That and it was sensational. The media can't resist sinking their teeth into something like that.

Even if that was the only reason they were sitting with me, though, there wasn't anything I could do about it. Besides, they had come to me.

"I'm glad to meet you. Both of you."

The arena below us was starting to fill in, and the Zambonis had been put away. Some of the ice crew were situating the practice nets onto their moorings, doing a few last-minute things before the teams came out to warm up.

A couple more women came into the box. They had been laughing loudly, nearly shrieking in that mean-girl sort of obnoxious way, but they fell silent once they were in the room. I turned to see why and found them giving me the evil eye and whispering to each other.

"Don't worry about them," Laura told me. "They've just got their panties in a twist because of the comments Zee made to the press yesterday. They're going to blame you for their guys getting their feelings hurt. They're just petty and immature like that."

Those comments had been the prime subject of discussion in Eric's radio spot yesterday afternoon and had been plastered front and center of every news outlet. They were interviewing players and coaches from other teams, asking for their take on it. Should a guy have called half his team out like that? Shouldn't a team captain take it to the guys one-on-one? How would you feel if you were on the receiving end of that?

Everyone and his dog had an opinion, and a hell of a lot of them hadn't liked it. The hockey world was an old boys' club. They did things by a code. You settle your differences with your fists, in this world, and you always have your teammates' backs. Eric had broken about a dozen unwritten rules, according to pretty much everyone who had an opinion on the matter.

"But you don't?" I asked.

Laura laughed. "Honey, Dave's been in this league for seventeen years. He said it's about time someone had the balls to tell it like it is."

We watched the teams warm up. All the while, Katie pointed out which player belonged to which woman in the box with us, and she paid particular attention to which of the guys were unattached...especially the younger guys. Laura told me whose phone number I should accidentally lose, who to stick close to, who to ignore every word that came out of her mouth, who was in charge of the players' wives' charity events.

By the time all the pre-game festivities had started and the arena was full to bursting, I felt like I had a pretty good grasp on the team and their significant others, at least from Laura's and Katie's perspectives on things. And I thought I liked their perspectives, all things considered. They seemed pretty laid back. Easy. I liked that.

Once the puck dropped, most of the chatter and laughter in the owner's box fell off.

It got really quiet in our box seventeen seconds into the game. San Jose's captain, Joe Thornton, broke off a bad pass from Peter Nylund, one of the Storm's top defensemen. Thornton sent it up the wing to Patrick Marleau who was streaking in on a breakaway, his jersey flapping behind him in the breeze he created. Marleau shot off a wrister and put it just under the crossbar, glove side. The guy had gotten it off so fast I doubted the goaltender, Nicklas Ericsson, ever saw the puck until it bounced out of his net.

The game had barely started and the Storm were already fighting an uphill battle. I could already imagine the clichés they would spout off in the postgame interview. "We got behind the eight ball. We can't put ourselves in the hole like that and expect to be able to climb out of it."

There was the possibility that they could use different clichés, of course. Something like, "It was a great come-from-behind win," was certainly a possibility. They weren't setting themselves up for anything like that very well, though.

Things went downhill pretty quickly on the ice. San Jose's speed, their aggressive forechecking, it was all too much for the Storm to withstand. Portland's defensemen kept turning over the puck on passes through the middle that never should have been made, and San Jose kept peppering Ericsson with shots. He made some spectacular saves, several of them highlight-reel worthy, but he wasn't getting any help from his teammates. No one in Portland's silver and purple was having a good game. By the first intermission the Sharks were up by three. The Storm left the ice looking like they'd already lost the game, even though there were two full periods to go.

Laura turned to me with a sigh once the Zambonis hit the ice. "Looks like this one's gonna be a beating. Beer or wine, what's your poison?"

I almost told her I didn't want anything but thought better of it. Eric had already warned me we'd likely be going out with some of the guys for a postgame meal, and I doubted any of them were going to be in a very good mood if the game kept going like this.

"Wine. Red, please."

"I knew I liked you," Laura said to me when she got out of her seat. "I think I'd better make them doubles. We're in for a bumpy night."

"For me, too, Mom," Katie deadpanned. Her mother snorted. Katie leaned over and whispered to me, "I had to try."

ERIC

In my whole career, I'd never been part of a forty-minute long, players-only, closed-door, postgame meeting. When meetings like that were necessary, we usually hashed things out in five or ten minutes. Maybe fifteen when things were really ugly.

This one had been brutal.

Half the boys wanted to rip me a new one for yesterday's comments. A few thought I hadn't gone far enough, thought maybe I should have called the guys out by name. They proceeded to do just that while we were alone. No one had had a good game. Nicky felt like we'd all abandoned him, like he'd been the only one trying to play the damn game tonight. Everyone was on edge.

It nearly came to blows at a couple of different points.

There's something about having your ass served up on a nine-to-one platter that'll do that to you.

I could only hope that, after it was all said and done, maybe it would have lit a fire under some guys' asses. Mine included. My play tonight had been abysmal.

Scotty counted on me and my line to keep the other team's top offensive line in check. Jumbo Joe Thornton and his boys got five against us at even strength, and we didn't score anything to counter it. My line hadn't even put together any sort of solid attack against them at any point in the game. I don't think I'd ever been a minus-five in a game in my whole pro career. Not until tonight.

I didn't like it.

This wasn't one that I'd be keeping any memorabilia from to go on my wall. I wanted to burn it from my memory, and the sooner, the better.

By the time we'd handled all our postgame press and cleaned up, the last thing I wanted to do was go sit at dinner and look at these same ugly, beat-up, demoralized faces—but I pretty much had to. When it was all said and done, we were teammates. We were friends.

We had to protect that.

If we didn't like each other off the ice, we wouldn't be willing to fight for each other on the ice. We'd all be out there for ourselves, not the team. It had to be about the team. More than halfway through the season, we still hadn't gotten to that point.

Besides, I was the one who'd caused the rift. I had to be the one to start to mend it.

Babs was waiting for me at his locker, somehow still wearing that same goofy grin. I wished I had that kind of exuberance and innocence.

A lot of the other boys had already cleared out, picked up their wives and girlfriends, and made their way home or to the restaurant—where they went after a game mainly depended on whether they had kids at home or not.

"Ready?" I asked.

Babs got this sheepish expression in his eyes and he glanced down at my left hand. "Is it okay?"

I flexed my fingers. Winced. "Yeah. How's your noggin?"

He just nodded excitedly.

I'd been more worried about his head than my hand, anyway. One of the Sharks defensemen had hit the kid up high in the middle of the ice. Flying elbow to the head. Babs had been defenseless and went down hard.

It reminded me a lot of the type of hit Scott Stevens had always been so well known for, only Stevens never added an elbow to it. Hits like that were devastating enough on their own...and they probably ended more than a few careers way too early.

Babs was my teammate, my linemate, my roommate. He had tons of talent, and he had his whole career—hell, his whole life—ahead of him. I hadn't thought twice about dropping my gloves to stand up for him.

That's just what you do.

That was the one thing I'd done in the game that I felt proud of, that I didn't wish I could take back and get a do-over on. Frankly, this season, the Storm needed more of that kind of thing. We needed to play for each other.

By the time we made it up to the owner's box there was almost no one left. I was glad to see that Webs and his wife and daughter had stuck around with Dayana while she waited for me to finish. I was even gladder of that fact when I got closer and realized Dayana and Laura had both had quite a bit to drink. The buffet had been cleared away except for two empty wine bottles, and both Laura and Dayana had a glass in their hands. Katie was nursing a soda.

"I'm sorry I took so long."

Dayana smiled up at me, totally uninhibited. It was a smile like I hadn't seen on her face in years. "You're here now."

Before I could guess what she was going to do, let alone brace myself for it, Dayana crossed the room to me and stretched up on her tiptoes. She kissed my left cheek just under my eye, which was bruised and throbbing from my fight, swollen nearly so much I couldn't see through it. It was the same kind of kiss she'd given me when she was little. Only different, because this was Dayana now, not Dayana then.

I was so startled it almost didn't register that she was wobbling on her feet until she almost fell to the floor. I put my arms out and caught her, just in time.

She didn't recoil or break out in a sweat or hyperventilate. She fell into me, leaning until her whole body was pressed up against mine. "I might be a little tipsy."

She was warm—God, she was so warm and soft and perfect, and everything about this situation was wrong, so very wrong in every way. She fit against me. I hated myself for noticing that, for thinking about that. But she did. My arms were around her back, holding her close to me with my hands resting on her waist. I never thought I'd be able to hold her like this. Not now. I didn't realize how much I'd wanted to, needed to.

"It's my fault," Laura said. "I kept refilling her glass every time I got more for myself. We were sitting down, and she seemed fine. Until about half an hour ago, when she got up to go to the restroom and she couldn't walk straight. Katie and I had to help her get there and back."

"Does it hurt?" Dayana asked. Her breath smelled sweet like the wine she'd been drinking, and her skin smelled like the cucumber-melon-scented soap she always used. She reached her hand up to trail her fingers over my swollen flesh.

It was like I was in a dream, where none of the last seven years had happened, where she'd gone on with her life as it had been heading before those sons of bitches stole all that was light and free and whole from her, before they left her broken and timid. Guarded.

There was nothing guarded about her right now. I knew it was just the wine, that if she were sober she'd be the same Dayana I had known for the last seven years, and she'd be standing well away from me and probably shaking. But right now? She was in my arms.

"No," I somehow croaked out. It was the truth, at least for the moment. Nothing could hurt when she was looking at me like that, when her warm body was draped over mine.

"That's good. I was worried about you."

Every breath she took pressed her breasts against my chest and made it harder for me to convince myself to let her go.

Webs cleared his throat, reminding me that we weren't alone. "You, uh...you help Zee get her home, Babs, eh? Laura's sister's with the younger kids tonight. We've gotta get back."

"Yeah, no problem." The kid was practically drooling, looking at Katie.

"Good. And if you don't stop making moon eyes at my daughter like that, you won't need a jockstrap anymore."

Webs and Laura headed out with Katie trailing behind them, blushing furiously when she looked over her shoulder at Babs.

He looked at me, eyes wide. "I wasn't— I didn't—"

I laughed. "Don't plead your case to me. Besides, he probably said that more to get her to stop making moon eyes at you than anything. He knows you're not stupid, and you know she's underage."

"She thinks you're cute," Dayana slurred.

"Yeah. Like a puppy, right?" Even though Babs tried to laugh it off, he still had those big eyes. The kid had no clue. Webs would probably be thrilled if someone like Babs wanted to date Katie. Well, maybe once she was out of high school. She could do a hell of a lot worse, and there wasn't a doubt in my mind that Webs knew it.

Dayana shook her head. "No, like the Jonas Brothers. She told me when her mom wasn't listening."

Babs might not realize it yet, but that was better than her thinking of him as a puppy.

"Come on." I kept my right arm around Dayana's waist to support her and turned her around, guiding her out to the main concourse.

Dayana put both arms around my waist, squeezing me in a side-hug like I couldn't ever remember her doing before, not even when she was a fearless little girl. "Are we still going to dinner? I'm hungry."

Babs chuckled in front of us, turned around to walk backward so he could face us. "I don't think you'll make it through dinner, Dee."

Dee. He called her that again. The kid had known her for two days, and he'd already decided she deserved a nickname.

"I can too!" As soon as she said it, her knees buckled beneath her. She would have fallen flat on her face if not for me holding her up.

"Not tonight, kid." I put my left arm under her knees and lifted her into my arms. It'd be easier to carry her to the car than to drag her there—at least as long as she was drunk and oblivious to all her usual fears.

She draped one arm across my shoulders. With the fingers of her other hand, she pressed against my chin to turn my face until I was staring straight into her eyes. "I'm not a kid. And I'm not that drunk."

I had to keep calling her kid, though. It reminded me that she was Soupy's kid sister, helped me keep from admitting I wanted things I had no business wanting. And on top of that, she was quite possibly drunker than I'd ever been in my life.

Her pout was probably the most adorable thing I'd ever seen, though. Somehow, I kept myself from both laughing out loud and kissing her. "Okay. But the only thing you're going to make it through tonight is bed."

"Are you going to tuck me in like a good little girl?"

I had to fight back a groan at the thought. She was going to kill me tonight.

Chapter 6 - Breakaway

D AYANA

The Storm had their own, private airplane for travel between games. It wasn't just any old plane, either. It was all decked out,
and every seat was like first class—lots of space for everyone, cushy
leather, the works. Not that I'd ever flown first class before, but I'd
seen it as I pushed past to get to my regular old coach seats plenty of
times.

The coaches and management, the trainers and equipment guys,
they all sat up at the front of the cabin. As soon as we boarded,
they took off their suit jackets and handed them over to the flight
attendants. When you travel with a pro hockey team, you wear a suit
or you stay behind. There's a dress code for everything.

They pulled out their laptops and iPads and other gadgets, each of
them working on reviewing game footage from last night or from
the New York Rangers' last few games. They were always prepping,
always trying to find an edge and sort out the game plan.

Carrying both his carry-on bag and mine, Eric led me past them, down the aisle and toward the back of the plane. The players all sat together back there. Most of them had also removed their jackets and immediately pulled out laptops and iPads and the like. Instead of game film, theirs revealed movies and books and video games.

We passed Babs and Razor with a few of the younger guys on the right. They all had their noses buried in video games, but Babs looked up at me as we passed and gave me a big grin that brought out his dimples. No wonder Katie Weber had a crush on him. He was adorable. I smiled for his benefit, but mainly I was trying to focus on getting down the aisle without accidentally bumping into any of them.

That wasn't exactly easy to do, what with my head throbbing like it was. I'd never had so much wine in my life, let alone all in one sitting. I'd woken up sometime around three in the morning, raced into my bathroom, and puked my guts up. After the worst of it had passed, I'd realized I was still in last night's clothes, other than my shoes. Someone had thought to take those off.

Then I started to remember, only not fully. It was little bits and pieces—an image here, a thought there. But had it really happened or was it just a wine-induced dream?

I thought I'd kissed Eric on the cheek. I remembered having his arms around me, warm and strong and protective, holding me in a cocoon. The scent of his cologne was strong in my memory, and I had been high up against him and holding onto him, my arm around his neck and my hand on his cheek.

But that couldn't have happened. I couldn't have allowed him to touch me like that. And if he had put his arms around me, I wouldn't have thought it felt protective. I'd have panicked. That's what I do.

But if it hadn't happened, how else did I end up in my bed? And who would have taken off my shoes?

After my stomach had pretty much been emptied of anything and everything, I had changed into my pj's and gone back to bed, but I didn't really sleep very well after that. My head was pounding from the hangover, and I couldn't stop thinking about Eric touching me, holding me...looking down at me like he loved me.

That last part, I knew, was all in my imagination. It had to have been the wine. I mean, he loved me like a kid sister, sure. But not like a woman.

And this morning, my head was still throbbing. I felt like I needed to sleep for about a week, in order to recover. It made me regret having anything to drink at all last night, and I'd definitely think twice before having my next one.

Sitting through a five-and-a-half hour flight ought to be fun. Ha ha. I could only imagine how much worse my headache would be once we were up in the air and altitude exaggerated everything.

Eric stopped a few rows behind Babs and lifted our bags up to the overhead bins on the left. Then he moved aside so I could slip into the window seat. We'd talked about that in advance. Eric figured the window seat would be safer for me—less chance of one of the guys bumping against me as they went up and down the aisle. This way, if anyone touched me on the flight, it would be him.

The seats were plush, luxurious. I sank down into mine and immediately thought about taking a nap, trying to catch up on the sleep I'd missed from being stupid enough to get so drunk.

Fat chance that would happen, though. As soon as Eric sat down beside me, he reached for my hand, wrapped his around mine as though it belonged that way. I'd made some progress over the last few days with the whole hand-holding thing, but that wasn't saying much. I shot him a look, wide-eyed, feeling my pulse kick into high gear and my chest tighten.

"Just breathe," he said softly, leaning his head down right by my ear so no one else would hear. "Get the worst of it over now, kid, before we take off."

I nodded, focused on breathing, tried to ignore the urge to run off the plane.

By the time everyone had boarded and most of the guys had taken their seats, I'd managed to get my breathing to calm down some, even if my pulse was still racing out of control.

The plane was just beginning to taxi when Alex Peterson, a rookie who'd been called up from Seattle a few weeks ago as an injury replacement, turned around in his seat, holding his cell phone. "Hey, Zee? Soupy is blowing up my phone. Says you're not answering yours and it's some kind of emergency or something."

As he said that, several other cell phones around us started going off with text alerts.

The only emergency I could think of was that Brenden had found out I was here. It'd been three days, so I supposed that shouldn't have been too surprising. But it was awful timing.

"Fuck," Eric muttered under his breath. "I got it. I'll take care of it. Thanks, Petey." He pulled his phone out of his pants pocket, powered it on, and looked at me. "I forgot to turn it on last night after the game. I was distracted..."

The guys started to snicker as they read the messages on their phones. "Zee's got some 'splainin' to do," Keith Burns said from the seat just in front of us. He turned around, a huge grin in the middle of his dark scruff. He winked at me, but I wasn't very amused by it all.

By me, I thought. He'd been distracted by me, by looking after Soupy's kid sister. That was what Eric had left hanging. He'd been too caught up in getting me home and to bed after I'd gotten so drunk that he hadn't thought about simple, everyday things like turning his phone back on. My brother was pissed at Eric, and it was my fault.

When Eric's phone finished loading its start-up program, the text alerts on his phone went crazy. He opened the message thread and scrolled through it pretty quickly. I swallowed hard and stole a peek.

I didn't catch much of it, but I gathered that they'd shown me on TV during Eric's fight last night. The rest of it was page after page of Brenden cussing Eric out for anything and everything he could think of in as many ways as possible.

Without taking the time to read it all, because there was a lot to read, Eric texted a response:

Dayana is w/me. Safe. On the plane. About 2 take off. Will call in NY 2 explain.

He powered his phone down again.

I started to apologize, but as soon as I opened my mouth, he squeezed my hand...that he was still holding.

"Shh. Don't."

He didn't want me to apologize for everything. I knew that, and I was trying. But it was hard. If I weren't here, he'd be able to focus on his job like he needed to, he wouldn't have done anything to upset Brenden... His life would be going on like normal. Instead, it was anything but normal.

Still, I nodded.

The plane was building speed on the runway, and I looked out the window. It was easier than looking at Eric. If I looked at him, I'd probably just try to apologize again.

He was getting pretty impatient with my need to apologize. Every time I did it, that forehead crease made another appearance. Not much. Just enough for me to recognize.

After a few seconds, the nose of the plane lifted, and all the wheels left the ground. Sure enough, the pressure in my head only made the pounding in my head worse than it already was. I focused on popping my ears, trying to break down the bubble-headed sensation as it continued to build.

That wasn't so easy to accomplish, though. I felt hot, clammy, like I might get sick again. I shifted in my seat, moving closer to the window and leaning my head against the wall. It chilled my skin, but only where I touched it—I still couldn't cool off.

The heat was too much. I couldn't take it. I tried to tug my hand away from Eric, but he held me tighter.

He had to think it was one of my usual panic attacks. But this wasn't panic. This was a hangover. Headache, nausea... I pulled harder on my hand, desperate to get it free, frantic to find a way to cool my body down so I didn't puke all over him.

He wouldn't let go. "Close your eyes. It'll help block the light."

His voice was soft, soothing. Confident.

I shut my eyes. Kept popping my ears. Swallowed hard against the saliva building in my mouth, but it only kept increasing.

"Burnzie," Eric said a little louder. I cringed at the volume of his voice right beside me, even though I knew he was being quiet for my benefit. He squeezed my hand again. "Burnzie, you have an eye mask? Give it to me."

"What do you— Shit, she looks green. Hang on."

A second later, Eric pressed something into my hand. His voice dropped again. "Put this over your eyes. It'll help."

I fumbled with the mask, trying to get it to cooperate, but my headache was so intense it was making things next to impossible when they should be simple. "I can't," I said, pain and frustration making my words come out as a whine.

"Okay." He blew out a breath. His fingers fumbled with getting the mask from my hand, then he lifted it away. "Keep breathing, Dayana." It was barely a whisper. "Count your breaths for me."

Light as a feather, I felt him lowering the mask down over my head. His fingertips danced over my hair, never settling anywhere long. I did what he'd asked me to, tried to breathe in and out and think about that, not about his hands touching me. He brought the mask down into position over my eyes and gently adjusted it so it fit properly over my nose.

"Better?"

I let out a little mmm sound, terrified to do more than that. I put my head against the cool wall again, letting the chill steal through me.

There were voices around me, even Eric's. It took too much effort to listen, to really pay attention to what they were saying.

After a few minutes, he pressed a cold water bottle into my hand. I immediately lifted it to rest against my forehead. I held it there with my right hand, my cheek pressed up hard to the wall, until the nausea finally started to pass.

And then all the sweat, the clamminess I'd been experiencing, it all dropped off. As hot as I had been, now I was cold. I dropped the water bottle to my lap and brought my head back to the middle of the headrest.

Eric took my hand. I let him because he felt warm. His forearm crossed over mine, blanketing it with his heat.

I don't know how long we sat there like that, quiet, just holding hands. But he shifted his grip so that his fingers were laced together with mine and the pad of his thumb brushed lazily back and forth over the back of my hand.

This was new. This was more intimate than anything we'd done before. I should have felt panicked.

But I didn't.

His thumb kept whispering across my skin, just a little tickle, back and forth, back and forth, lulling me off to sleep.

ERIC

Dayana had been asleep for a good fifteen minutes, her deep breathing and relaxed hand proving it, before her head rolled over to rest on my shoulder.

Even though I was tempted to put my arm around her, drawing her closer, I didn't. That would have been purely selfish on my part—me wanting to satisfy my own desires instead of taking care of her. If I did that and she woke up, she'd have a full-blown panic attack right in the middle of the flight. I couldn't do that to her.

So I stayed as I was, my fingers still locked together with hers, my thumb still tracing lazy circles over the back of her hand, letting her use my shoulder as a pillow.

That was really what this whole thing was about, anyway—letting Dayana have what she needed. It wasn't about me getting anything from it, other than hopefully seeing her become healthy again, seeing her someday have normal relationships again.

I'd pulled out my iPad and was reading a book. Or I was pretending to read a book. Really, I was listening to Dayana breathe and enjoying the feel of her leaning against me. But I had a book open so that when the guys went past me to use the restroom or something, they'd leave me be.

I didn't want anyone stopping to talk. They might wake Dayana.

I supposed if there was anything good to take from all of this, it was that I'd learned something: Dayana's hangover migraines, plus a bit of panic, plus a change in altitude was an ugly combination. I only hoped that by the time we landed, she'd have slept enough of it off that she could function.

Someone bumped into my arm from behind, and Dayana's head slumped further down on me from the jolt, until she was halfway to lying across my lap. Instinctively, I shot a glare at Jere Koskinen's back as he moved on by. Costco, one of the assistant captains on the team, was oblivious to the fact that he'd done anything wrong. Bumping into a guy when you're trying to get through the aisle on an airplane isn't exactly a crime. But I didn't want anything to wake her. Not now.

Once she'd fallen over that far, though, there was nothing to stop her progress. I reached for my suit jacket and haphazardly folded it up. I set it down on my lap to give her some semblance of a pillow. It was only a minute or so later when her head dropped all the way down onto it.

Our hands were still connected underneath her. I was only able to make it a couple of minutes like that, before my hand and half my arm were asleep beneath her, tingling at first and then numb.

I couldn't stay like that, even though I wanted to.

Gradually, one inch at a time, I released her hand and dragged my arm free. When I got the last of it out from under her, she shifted just a bit, edging closer to me, and mumbled something thoroughly unintelligible in her sleep.

She looked so peaceful like this. Like she didn't have a care in the world. Like nothing horrible had ever happened to her, and she'd just gone about her life as she was meant to.

If she hadn't been raped, if they hadn't broken her like that... She might have let me kiss her, one day. I probably would have tried. Lord knows I'd thought about it more than a few times, but she was Soupy's sister. So I hadn't.

I had spent that whole semester thinking about her—about how I could go about it all without ending up with a broken face courtesy of her brother. I mean, for years she'd just been a kid. A little girl. Even when we'd gone off to Yale, she was still just in high school.

But she wasn't in high school anymore. It wasn't...weird to think about her like that anymore. It was one of those things, kind of like with Babs and Katie Weber. Right now, he couldn't let himself think about her like that. Or at least he couldn't act on it. But in two or three years? Completely different story.

That was how I'd spent the whole first semester, thinking about Dayana as a woman. Not just as any woman, but as the woman I wanted to be with.

But I hadn't done anything about what I wanted before I left for Yale that fall.

And then it had been too late. I'd missed my chance.

I couldn't let myself think like that. I couldn't linger on the what-ifs, the could-haves and should-haves and would-haves.

I couldn't.

A few wisps of her hair had fallen over her face and were brushing against her nose. I smoothed them back from her forehead. Her hair was like golden silk in my hand, softer than I had ever let myself imagine. I tucked the strays behind her ear.

Then I couldn't seem to stop myself.

Over and over again, I trailed my fingers along the curve of her scalp, letting them glide along the natural waves of her hair. My fingers kept catching on the straps holding her mask in place. I eased it off, set it aside.

She murmured something, squirmed closer. She turned her head over, so she was facing me, torturing me with how peaceful she looked. It was such a rare thing, seeing her like this. Uninhibited. Apparently, I could only see her like this if she was drunk or asleep.

I followed the line of her nose so softly I could barely feel it. Felt the rapid movement of her eyes beneath her closed eyelids. Traced her lips with the back of my forefinger.

I had to stop. I was going to wake her up.

"Nice knowing you, Zee."

Smitty's voice beside me jerked my attention away from her. My head shot up. Kurt Smith, one of our defensemen, stood right beside me with a cocky smirk.

I just shook my head in question, not wanting to say anything in case it woke Dayana.

"Listen," Smitty said, "I don't know Soupy very well, but I can tell you this. If she was my sister, you'd be a fucking dead man."

He kept walking down the aisle toward the back of the plane.

My only consolation was that we were well on our way to New York, and I knew Soupy was heading down to Austin, Texas for a game with the rest of the Seattle Storm.

No matter how much he may want to, he couldn't kill me over the phone.

DAYANA

I'd been curled up in a fetal position on the king-sized bed in my hotel room for a good half hour and still my shaking hadn't stopped.

For the first time, I thought maybe Eric was right. Maybe I wasn't ready for this. Maybe I'd never be ready.

I would have been okay if I'd awoken on the plane with him still just holding my hand. I could handle that. I was used to that. Or getting used to it, at least. I was even starting to like it.

But when I woke up, I'd had my head lying in his lap and he was stroking my hair.

I'm sure he meant it to be a soothing touch, but maybe there just wasn't any such thing, when it came to a man's touch and me.

Should I give up? New York wasn't that far from Providence. I could get home. I could stay with Mom and Dad until the woman subleasing my apartment was gone. I would be staying with them for a couple of weeks when I got back anyway, because she was staying longer than I would be here. I could go back to my job, go back to my life, go back to how everything had been for so long.

Back to safety.

Safety was starting to sound good right about now, after waking up like that.

That might have been the most intense panic attack I've ever had. Definitely the scariest. And I'd been on a plane. Couldn't get off. No escape route.

I had darted to the back and locked myself in the bathroom. That had been a bad idea, though, because it was so confined. So small. And I couldn't breathe. Couldn't get even short little tiny breaths to go down. I almost didn't open the door in time.

But Eric and the team's trainers, all the people who'd been trying to help me...they were all men. They'd been trying to touch me, trying to hook me up to oxygen, take my pulse, read my blood pressure. That had only made it worse.

I'd passed out.

When I came to, Eric had been on his knees beside me. I'd been lying on the floor in the aisle, and they'd hooked me up to an oxygen tank. A pillow had been placed under my head, a blanket draped over me. He'd made everyone else move away, far away. As far as they could go on an airplane.

It wasn't that far.

He'd been shaking as bad as I had.

We'd stayed like that the rest of the flight. When we'd finally landed in New York, it was already dark. We'd all loaded onto a waiting charter bus and went straight to the hotel.

Most of the guys had decided to go out to dinner when we arrived. I hadn't wanted anything but solitude, somewhere I could be alone and recover. I'd told Eric to go with the guys. He needed to eat. He had a game to play tomorrow.

But he hadn't gone. He'd said he couldn't leave me. Couldn't. Not that he wouldn't leave me. Was it some sense of duty he felt to Brenden to look after me? Or something else? It had to be the former, not the latter.

Even now, I could hear him in the room next to me. Pacing. Lots of pacing. My side of the connecting door was locked; he'd left his open. He'd promised me he would, and Eric had never broken a promise to me, not even once in all the years I'd known him.

I heard his voice, too. Frustrated. I'd never heard him so tense before. I couldn't make out his words. Couldn't tell who he was talking to. All I could hear was his frustration. I should never have asked him to do this. I should have gone to a sex surrogate like my therapist had suggested. Either that or I should have just accepted that I would always be like this.

But I never should have asked Eric for his help. It wasn't fair of me.

I got off the bed and moved over to the door separating our rooms. I still couldn't make out his words, not even standing so close to his room.

I had no business trying to listen in on his conversation. I tried to convince myself to walk away, tried to make myself ignore it. He deserved his privacy. I'd taken enough from him without taking that, too.

But I couldn't.

I pressed my ear all the way up against the door, straining to hear any little bit.

"Damn it, Soupy!" That was loud. Then more muffled words, too soft for me to understand.

Now that I knew he was talking to Brenden, I didn't feel quite so bad about eavesdropping. Almost. Not quite.

I was just about to give up, move away from the door, give Eric his privacy, when he shouted, "Because I made her a fucking promise."

I burst into tears and had to sit down in the nearest chair. At first, I didn't know why I was crying.

Eric was still talking to my brother in the next room, still grumbling and arguing. The rumble of his voice coming through the wall only made me cry harder, until it hit me.

He was fighting with Brenden because he intended to keep helping me. Even after today. Even after what had happened on the flight.

He wasn't ready to give up.

I had to keep fighting.

Chapter 7 - Breakaway

E RIC

I'd barely hung up the phone when I heard her voice at the door connecting our rooms. "Eric?" Just my name. Hardly loud enough for me to hear her, what with the way my blood hadn't stopped roiling through my body for even a second since she'd woken up on the plane.

Since I'd been touching her.

Since she'd almost died right in front of me. Because of me.

She had almost stopped breathing.

So had I.

I crossed the room to the door and leaned my forehead against the wall. "Dayana?"

"Can I come in?"

I'd never felt so torn in my life, between wanting to let her in so I could see her, so I could know that she was okay, and wanting to keep her as far away from me as possible. I didn't know if I could trust myself anymore. Not after what I'd done. It would have been bad enough if she'd woken up on that plane with her head lying on my lap with my hands far away from her.

But my hands hadn't been away. They'd been on her. Caressing her face. Combing my fingers through her hair. Doing all the things I'd told myself I'd never be able to do.

Well, not all the things.

But enough of them to nearly kill her from panic.

Enough that it would nearly kill me, thinking about the others.

"Eric?" she said again. Timid. Her voice was shaking.

Fuck.

"It's open on my side. You can always come in if you want to." I stepped back from the door when she pulled hers open, giving her room to come in without crowding her. I couldn't let myself get too close. If I did, I might do something stupid like pull her into my arms. The need to hold her, to touch her, was getting to be more intense than I'd anticipated.

Three steps into the room, she stopped and stared at me. "Are you... Were you talking to Brenden?"

She was still pale, so pale, with deep, purplish circles under her eyes.

I hated seeing her like that—knowing I'd caused it. I nodded. "He knows he can't really do anything to stop what we're doing. But he reserves the right to put me in an early grave if he sees any reason to do so. If you—"

"I can't get worse than I already am."

That only confirmed my fears; she didn't intend to call it quits.

Even though she'd made progress—being able to let me hold her hand, that sort of thing—I wasn't entirely sure I could keep doing what she asked of me. Not after today.

There was no way in hell I would let her go to someone else, though. If any son of a bitch was going to touch her, it would be me. Only me.

I didn't see much point in trying to deny it to myself anymore. I loved her. Absolutely. Completely. Head over my fucking heels in love with her. She may not love me in return, but that was okay. I couldn't control that. All I could do was be what she needed me to be, do what she needed me to do. Always. As long as she'd let me.

Later, once she went back to Providence and left me behind, I could lick my wounds in private. That was what I'd done when I started dating Kim, back in the day. I knew I would never be able to be with Dayana, not the way I wanted to, and so I'd tried to find someone else.

Kim had deserved better. It wasn't that I didn't care for her. I did. It had just all been about me. As a professional athlete, there has to be some of that. You have to do the things required to earn your contract, and that takes a lot of sacrifice. But I'd taken it too far. There was a part of me I'd kept to myself, when I should have given it to her. I couldn't give it to anyone but Dayana, though.

I shouldn't have been surprised when I came home and found her in bed with Chris Powers. He'd always paid her more attention than I had. But for some reason it had surprised me. And it had hurt.

But it had only hurt my pride. Not my heart. That was why Kim had deserved more.

"You should eat," Dayana said to me. She came further into my room and tucked her hair behind her ear. That only made me think about how I had been doing that very thing on the plane. "Order room service or something," she added.

She was right. I'd thought about it before calling Soupy, but I didn't really think it was such a hot idea to eat at the moment. I had still been so worked up over how her face had been turning blue when she came out of the bathroom on the team plane, I didn't know if I could keep anything down.

But now, with her here—pale but not blue—I could probably eat.

"Okay. What do you want, kid?" I still needed that reminder of who she was—who she had to be—to me. It was getting harder and harder to remember I needed to think of her as a kid sister when I wanted her to be so much more.

Dayana shook her head. "I'm not—"

"You have to eat. Something. Soup. Something."

She'd been sick all day. She was weak. I needed her to eat.

"All right. Soup."

I knew she was just trying to appease me, but I'd take what I could get. I went to the phone by the desk, called the operator, and placed an order. When I turned around again, Dayana was sitting on the foot of my bed.

My heart stopped for a second and then went into overdrive. Looking at her on a bed—I couldn't. I couldn't go there.

I turned my head away and took a seat behind the desk, a good ten feet from her. Not only did that put some distance between us but a desk, too. Something big, physical, solid.

"Jim's telling the boys, tonight at dinner." I kept a close eye on her face as I told her, trying to gauge her reaction. "After what happened on the flight, he figures they need to know the truth of it."

He'd tried to convince me of that when we'd first talked about Dayana. He'd said they would figure it out anyway, but I didn't want them to know if they didn't need to. I guess I'd been trying to convince myself that something like that wouldn't happen. But Jim knew. Babs knew. Webs knew at least some of it because of his sister.

By now, they all knew—what had happened to her so many years ago, what it was still doing to her today, why she was with me now. They knew it all.

At least I wouldn't have to worry about any of them touching her in some innocent way without knowing any better, and then having to pick up the pieces.

Dayana nodded. "That's probably for the best." She accepted it a lot easier than I had. She leaned back on the bed, propping herself up on her elbows, and crossed one leg over the other.

I couldn't stop myself from looking at her legs. I should have, but damn. Long. Lean. Too damn gorgeous for my own good...hell, for my sanity.

She was wearing a royal-blue wrap dress—simple but perfect. It came down to just below her knees, but with the way she was lounging, a triangle came open just a little bit above her knee.

She didn't have any idea how sexy she looked like that. If she did, she'd be sitting up straight in a chair, legs perfectly positioned so as to reveal as little as possible.

It was weird for me, to see her in a dress. Back when she'd played hockey, she had to dress for game days, but I hardly remembered thinking about seeing her in dresses back then. She was just a kid. That was just how it was.

Now it was something to notice. And I did.

Most sports required dressing for games. The hockey community was even stricter about dress codes than most other sports, though. In the NHL, the dress code for travel to and from games is written into the Collective Bargaining Agreement, and most teams take it a step further than the CBA requires. With the Storm, a suit and tie are required on your way to and from every game, and slacks and a polo shirt are the bare minimum for any team event. No jeans. No T-shirts. No shorts. For Dayana to travel with us, she had to be in dresses or pantsuits pretty much at all times, even though she wasn't actually a member of the team and was just posing as a coaching intern.

I didn't mind that, getting to see her in dresses. It was nice. It kept her from hiding herself away too much.

A knock sounded at the door, and I got up to let the waiter in with our order. As soon as she heard the knock, Dayana immediately sat up, straightened herself, pulled the skirt of her dress back into place. It was a shame.

He set the food up on the small table next to the window. I signed the receipt, gave him a twenty to go with it, and he left.

Even though she had been all ready to tell me she wasn't hungry, she ate her soup.

Thank God. I worried about her enough as it was. I didn't need to add the possibility of her starving to the list.

DAYANA

The few days I'd spent in Portland hadn't been nearly enough to reset my internal clock to West Coast time, but between that and all the travel I'd done in such a short amount of time, my body's idea of sleeping time and waking time was a wreck. After spending half the flight yesterday asleep, and considering that we were back on the East Coast, it shouldn't have been all that surprising that I woke up well before dawn.

It still surprised me, though. Mornings weren't really my thing, usually.

Breakfast wasn't until eight. The team would all come together in the big conference room for it, and then, afterwards, everyone would travel together to the arena for the morning skate. Both Eric and Jim Sutter had made it clear that since I was traveling with the team, it meant I was part of these things. It wasn't optional for the players, so I had a feeling it wasn't optional for me, either. Well, I wouldn't be involved in morning skate, but I had to be there with them.

Breakfast was a couple of hours away, though, and nothing at all would happen until after that. I needed to find something to do to pass the time. Sitting alone in a hotel room would drive me crazy in no time.

I didn't want to wake Eric up. He was used to West Coast hours, and he had a game to play tonight. He needed his rest. I was pretty sure the hotel had a gym somewhere downstairs, and I hadn't had a good workout since leaving Providence. I should have plenty of time to do that and still get back upstairs and shower before breakfast.

After putting on a pair of yoga pants and a long-sleeved T-shirt, I headed for the elevator. The gym was nearly empty when I got there. The only other person was Cam Johnson, one of the guys on the team. He'd shaved his head, maybe because he was starting to lose his hair. That was how it looked, at least, but maybe he just liked it that way. The man was solid muscle, too. Big. Hulking. Intimidating. The shaved head only intensified that effect.

He was a winger and a tough guy, but the type of tough guy who could still be competitive at this level. He wasn't a goon. He wasn't just there to fight, even if he would never back down from one. Most seasons he scored as many goals as he had fights, which was a rarity in the league.

Most of the fighters would fit more in the goon category, strictly enforcers. They got to play maybe five minutes a night, just long enough that they could work their way onto the score sheet with a fight.

The last few games, Johnson had been sitting in the press box as a healthy scratch, though. He'd just come back from an injury, and the coach was making him work his way back into the lineup.

He was busy using some weight machines, working hard enough to have a good sweat going. I decided to leave him to it. I didn't really want to bother him, and I really didn't want him to bother me. I made my way over to the elliptical machine and got to work.

After twenty minutes, it was time to change it up. A punching bag was hanging near the wall. That had always been one of my favorite ways to work my arms. I found some gloves on a shelf near it and strapped them on. When I was ready, I started my routine.

I'd been at it for a few minutes when I realized Johnson had stopped his workout. He was standing off to the side, watching me. He was keeping a reasonable distance, though. Not too close.

He caught me looking at him and looked away. "Sorry. I didn't want to startle you. I was just watching your form."

I nodded and kept punching the bag. I didn't particularly want to think about him being in there with me, about the fact that we were alone. There was no reason for me to panic.

There was nothing wrong with him watching me. I didn't think he meant me any harm. Not really. Tough guys, enforcers, they tended to be really sweet guys off the ice. Teddy bears. Quiet and respectful, deep thinkers. But my breathing still got wonky, damn it.

I bent over, my hands resting on my knees while I tried to smooth out my breathing.

"Shit. I'm sorry, I didn't—" He took a step closer, but it was more to move fully into my line of vision than it was to get closer to me. His hands were in the air, out in the open where I could see them. "I just... Have you ever taken any self-defense? Kick boxing? Karate? Tai Chi? Anything like that? Or is it just for exercise?"

I shook my head. "It's only something I do to work out."

"Not anymore." He went over to the same shelf where I'd found the gloves and picked up some target pads. "Hit me instead of the bag."

He was crazy. But then again, he had to be. Part of his job was going out on a shift specifically to start a fight with some other crazy guy. But seriously, the man was massive, and he was all solid muscle. He had to be six foot four, easily 240 pounds.

"I can't."

"Yeah, you can. I do this all the time with my sister back home." He had the target pads in place on his hands and held them up for me. "Come on. Just like you were doing with the bag, only aim right for my nose."

"I don't want to break your nose."

"I don't intend to let you."

I swallowed hard, but I settled into a proper stance: left foot forward, right back, knees bent slightly, toes facing front. I pushed forward with my right hand but I didn't have much behind it. He easily moved one of the targets into place, and my fist landed against it with a thud, not a solid smack like I'd been getting against the bag.

"You can do better than that. Move your left foot closer to me and bend your knees just a little more. Put some more force into it, and push straight forward like you mean it."

I reset my stance and tried again. Better connection this time. I could feel the difference.

He nodded. "Good, but don't bend your wrist. And keep your left hand up."

"I didn't bend my wrist."

"Yeah, you did. Watch me." He took the targets off and took up a position like mine and mimicked what I'd done. "I want you to do just like this. Pay attention to the position of my arms, the angles, what muscles I'm using." He repeated the motion several times. His muscles were so well defined, it was easy to see them contract and release, to recognize how he was moving through the space.

When he put the targets on again and I struck, I could feel the difference in my next punch.

For the next half hour, he stayed with me. At my gym back home, when I would try to instruct someone on proper body positioning for a new exercise, I would usually end up touching them. I would move their arms and legs into the position they needed to be in to properly work the muscle.

He didn't ever do that with me. If he wanted to correct my stance, my swing, whatever, he took the time to show me by doing it himself. He let me learn by observing and repeating. No touching.

By the time I went back upstairs to shower and get dressed, I had a pretty good left jab. At least, I did according to Cam Johnson. If anyone knew a good left jab, I figured it would be him.

ERIC

It was a tie game heading into the third, knotted up at two apiece. That was saying something at Madison Square Garden. The Rangers' home crowd always seemed to give them a little extra jump, that added boost they needed to deflate anyone who tried to come into their building and steal a couple of points.

They weren't going to give us any open ice, and we knew it.

I skated out to center ice for the face-off. Babs was lined up to my right, and Jakub Gazda to my left. Gaz had just joined the Storm after a trade a few weeks ago. He was still trying to find his groove with us, but he could drive the net like nobody's business. He had a knack for getting to the crease and staying there, no matter how much abuse the other team's goaltender and defensemen decided to dole out on him. That was a handy trait to have in a linemate.

The linesman dropped the puck, and the game was back on.

I managed to tie up Brad Richards's stick and kick the puck back to our D with my skate. I shook free of him and headed for the line. Burnzie made a sharp pass over to Gaz, who was already heading into the zone.

He charged the net like a bull with his nose down and got a quick shot off. Lundqvist made the save, but the rebound went straight to Babs. Wicked wrister, in close. It clanged off the cross bar and shot out of the zone.

Richards must have smelled something in the air. He was waiting to pounce on it in the neutral zone. Turned on his jets and flew toward Ericsson. Only Peter Nylund had any chance to catch him, but Richards had a good two steps on him. Ny made a diving play for the puck but missed and got his stick caught up in Richards's skates, tripping him.

Penalty shot.

Not what we needed less than a minute into the third period of a tie game.

Richards skated in, deked, shot it stick side into the net.

The red light flashed, the goal horn sounded, and MSG erupted like it was a playoff game.

"One shot, boys." Scotty paced behind the bench, making sure everyone heard him. "That's all it'll take to get us back in this. Keep your head in it. One shot."

He sent Sarge's line out next. Sergei Ivanov was a fucking Russian magician. He could do things with a hockey puck that most people couldn't dream of, deking and dangling, all sorts of insanity. But that kind of genius takes some special players to be able to feed off him.

Scotty had been changing up the line combinations lately, trying to find the right way to utilize Sarge's gifts without making the line a defensive liability. Tonight, he had Costco and Pasha out with him. Costco could be a candidate for the Selke Trophy as the best defensively minded forward in the league, at least if he was playing on a team that was good enough around him, not like us. And Pavel Spanov...well, the kid had a ton of skill, but he'd been moved all over the lineup since he came into the league. He'd never found just the right fit.

Sarge took the faceoff, but he lost it. The Rangers tried to immediately push into the zone, but Smitty laid a hip check on their puck carrier along the boards. Another Rangers forward rushed in to grab up the puck. He thought he had it, too, but Costco poke-checked it free. It went straight to Sarge's stick, but Sarge was surrounded by four blue sweaters.

He spun around, twisted past one Rangers defenseman, did a zig and a zag, and somehow got by all of them still with the puck on his stick.

Pasha and Costco were waiting for him at the line. Once they were in the zone, they cycled the puck down low, passed it around like a tic-tac-toe game. Sarge got Henrik Lundqvist to bite on a deke and pull himself out of position, then passed it over to Costco who was waiting by the side of the net for an easy one.

Just like that, the game was tied, and Scotty had found his new top line.

Our whole bench was on our feet. We tapped our sticks over the boards in celebration. Babs looked over at me, gawking. "How the hell did Sarge do that?"

"He just tried something fucking crazy and it worked."

Never mind the fact that the guy put in about a million hours in the gym, came early and stayed late at the rink. But still. Most of the truly amazing things Sarge did on the ice were things he'd never tried before. Sometimes they worked. Sometimes they failed miserably.

Once Babs really had an understanding of that, the sky was the limit for this kid. He was only nineteen, and I'd already seen him do things that left me gawking just like he was now. But the next game, he'd make some boneheaded rookie mistake (they're called rookie mistakes for a reason), and then he'd let doubt creep back in. He just had to learn to let the mistakes roll off his shoulders.

Screwing up one minute doesn't mean you can't be amazing the next. You just have to learn from your mistakes. Go in and try something different next time.

Maybe I needed a dose of my own medicine where Dayana was concerned. She wasn't ready to quit. She wanted to keep going with her plan.

I had screwed up, and she'd had the worst panic attack I'd ever seen. But what was stopping me from trying something different?

Only my own doubts.

Just like Babs.

"Heads up!" Smitty shouted from down the bench.

I barely registered it in time. At the last second, I ducked out of the way of the puck that was flying straight at my face.

Would have served me right for thinking about Dayana in the middle of a hockey game.

Chapter 8 - Breakaway

DAYANA

I had a mouthful of oatmeal when Jim Sutter sat down across the table from me.

"You're coming with us today, aren't you?"

Today was a practice day for the team, a day between games. We were staying in the same hotel in New York after last night's overtime loss to the Rangers because tomorrow the Storm would play the Islanders and a game against the New Jersey Devils was up on Thursday. Three games in four nights wasn't exactly unheard of in the NHL, but it was never an easy stretch to get through, particularly on the road.

At least they'd managed to come away with a point last night by getting to overtime. The guys weren't satisfied with that, but it was better than nothing.

I nodded. Since I was playing the part of a coaching understudy—even though the guys knew what was really going on—I had been taking part in just about everything the team did, at least in terms of being present. "Unless you don't want me to come."

Jim winked at me. "We want you there. Go back up to your room and get some clothes you can be active in. We're doing something a little different today.... It's not going to be a normal practice."

Before I had a chance for that to sink in and question him on it, he got up from our table and moved on.

I darted my eyes over to Eric, giving him a questioning look.

He just shrugged, a how-am-I-supposed-to-know expression on his face.

He was supposed to know because he was the one who had been playing in this league, on this team, for years. I wasn't even officially a part of the team, so I couldn't imagine what this whole something a little different might be, or why I needed to be involved in actuality instead of just in name like I had been so far.

After I finished eating, I went up and got the workout clothes I intended to wear tomorrow morning for my session in the gym. The ones I'd worn today were still damp with my sweat. Jonny, as Cam Johnson had insisted I call him, had really put me through my paces before breakfast. But I was getting more confident with everything he was having me do. I tossed my clothes into a small duffel bag and headed out.

By the time I got back down to the lobby, the guys were already starting to load onto the team's charter bus. Eric was waiting for me. He took the duffel from my hands and slung the straps over his shoulder. With his free hand, he reached for me.

I took it. My pulse kicked into gear, but it wasn't my usual panic. It was more of a tingly sort of thing, like anticipation. Excitement. Nervous excitement, definitely, but not panic.

The change, or maybe it was more my realization of the change, had my face filling with a different kind of heat as we got onto the bus and took a seat about halfway back.

"You're blushing," Eric said. He was leaning down near me, his voice barely more than a whisper close to my ear. He sounded amused, and maybe just a little amazed. Probably just amused, like Brenden would be.

Still, it only made me blush deeper.

As the driver led us out into the New York traffic, Eric shifted his grip on my hand. His fingers twined with mine, like they had the other day on the plane. It was like a surge of electricity jolting through me. I sucked in a breath.

"I like it when you blush."

"You used to try to embarrass me all the time. You did it on purpose."

"I've always liked it when you blush."

When we were kids, I'd thought he was doing it to be mean, to pick on me like Brenden always did. It had felt familial, like he was my brother. It felt different now. I let that sink in, wash over me and fill me up. But it couldn't really be different, could it? We didn't talk much during the rest of the bus ride. We just sat there together, holding hands while all sorts of new sensations flew through my body and unfamiliar thoughts peppered my mind.

I'd thought we were on the way to a gym of some kind since Jim wanted me to be involved, but when the bus came to a stop we were at Central Park.

Scott Thomas, the team's head coach, stood up at the front of the bus. "We've reserved the ice at Wollman for the next couple of hours, boys. Let's get out there and have some fun."

All the sort-of-pleasant-but-more-exciting tingly sensations I'd been experiencing melted away, and it felt like a fist of ice had gripped my lungs and was squeezing. They wanted me to get on the ice.

To skate.

I hadn't put a pair of skates on in a very long time. I'd tried to go back to school that year, to get myself back into playing hockey. But every time I'd put my skates on, I'd thought about all the things that had happened to me. About what they'd done to me.

I'd still been in my gear when they grabbed me. The girls and I had been on our way back to the dressing room after the game when I realized I didn't have my locket. It was something Eric had given me years before, just a silly little thing. It had a picture of a hockey goal inside, not of him or anyone else.

I hadn't been wearing it during the game. I didn't like to wear it when I played because the silly plastic chain would get tangled with my hair and pull. It distracted me. Anything I could do to limit distractions, I would. But I always had the locket on the bench with me during games, sitting on the inside of the boards where we kept water bottles, and I'd accidentally left it there. I knew that if I didn't go back to get it right away, I'd never see it again. The arena crew would probably put it in the trash. It was cheap, not real gold or anything. Just a throwaway locket he'd gotten out of one of those vending machines with the eggs filled with toys.

I'd never made it back to the bench.

I'd never gotten my locket back.

After playing in a few more games that spring, I had dropped out of school and never played hockey again. I'd never put on a pair of skates again. I hadn't even gone out on the ice in my shoes, or to let Dad pull me around on a sled like he had when I was a little girl.

I just couldn't.

And now, these guys expected me to get out there like nothing had ever happened. Maybe they didn't expect me to, but they wanted me to.

The whole team had gotten off the bus, all but Eric. He was still sitting beside me holding my hand. Staring at me. I could feel his eyes on me, feel his concern, but I couldn't look at him. I could only stare at the back of the seat in front of me and try to get through one minute so I could make it to the next.

"You don't have to do this, Dayana." It was Jim's voice. "No one is going to make you do anything. Scotty's going to have the boys do some scrimmaging, a little outdoor three-on-three shinny game. We're using a tennis ball, not a puck. No hitting, nothing physical or too intense. We're just going to get out there and enjoy ourselves. Do a little team building, bonding. That sort of thing. I thought if you wanted to try, it would be a good opportunity. The coaches, all the front office guys...we're all going to play, too. Just for fun." He made his way off the bus, leaving me and Eric alone.

"Do you want me to play?"

For some reason, I felt like I needed Eric to tell me what to do. Or maybe I just wanted him to. I wanted someone else to make this decision, not me.

He didn't answer. Not right away. He took the hand he was holding and turned it over so my palm was up. Then with just the tip of his finger, he traced the lines of my palm, causing a resurgence of the tingles and a flutter in my belly.

"I want you to be the Dayana I knew before all of this happened, kid. I want you to laugh and smile and be free with your hugs. I want you to be fearless. I want you to do what you love." He let go of my hand and got up. "What I want doesn't matter. Do what you want to do, Dayana. It's not every day you get to play pond hockey. I have to get out there. The boys are waiting for me."

Do what I love? I'd spent the last seven years doing what was necessary to function in a sort of half-life state. I wasn't sure I knew how to do what I loved anymore.

I wasn't even positive if I knew what that would be.

ERIC

An excited crowd had gathered around the rink by the time we all started to head out to the ice from the dressing room. Most NHL teams have open practices, where people can come and watch, but this was different. This was a team playing around on a pond, out in public. Even though nothing had been announced in advance, it didn't take long for word to spread around the city.

I wouldn't be surprised if some of the people who saw us coming in had taken to Facebook and Twitter to announce it to the world. Things like that tended to go viral.

I stole a glance over to the bus, trying to see through the tinted windows. It didn't look like Dayana was still in there, but I couldn't be sure.

Even if she wouldn't get on the ice, I hoped she'd at least get off the bus. Come and watch. Whether you're playing or watching, a game of shinny hockey on a pond was pretty hard to beat. That was why so many people were gathering around. That and maybe the hope that they'd get something signed by one of the players.

I made my way over to where Allan "Drywall" Tierney, the head equipment manager, was setting out everyone's sticks. Don't ask me why he was called Drywall. In my rookie season, someone told me a crazy story about how he could only skate a hair faster than the speed of paint drying. He was a big, lumbering sort of guy, so that could be true. I didn't know if that was the real meaning behind his nickname or not, but I'd been calling him Drywall as long as I could remember.

He sorted through the bag of sticks pretty quickly and pulled out a few of mine. "She's all set with one of Norty's sticks, Zee. It's a little longer than she needs, but it'll do. And her skates got to the hotel this morning. Overnighted from Providence. I guess Jimmy put in a call to her dad or something."

I didn't want to seem surprised, but I was. "Yeah?" I tried to brush it off, like I'd been expecting it. But I hadn't been. Not in the least.

Dayana was proving to be one surprise after another right now. It left me feeling like the ground was moving beneath my feet.

I couldn't decide if that was good or bad.

Just yesterday, I'd had the shock of my life when she came up to the room before breakfast and told me she'd been learning boxing techniques from Jonny. Now she was going to get back on the ice. I didn't quite know what to make of it all.

"Yeah," Drywall said, still sorting through sticks and helmets, never slowing down in his movements. He had a system of doing things, an order. It wasn't a good idea to try to help him because he'd just redo whatever you'd done the way he wanted it. Equipment guys can be like that. "She looked at those skates real funny when I gave 'em to her. Stared at 'em a long, long time before she went to get dressed."

I could only imagine. I didn't know for sure but I bet she thought they'd been given away years ago, donated to a family that couldn't afford hockey gear for their kids or something.

"Yeah. Thanks, Drywall." He had other guys coming for their equipment and he hadn't finished sorting things the way he wanted, so I took my sticks and moved on. I found a group of the boys sitting on a bench near the ice, taping their stick blades, so I took a seat and did the same.

A minute later, she came around the corner from the dressing room. I'd never seen anything as beautiful as Dayana walking toward me in sweat pants and a baggy T-shirt, her coat on but hanging open, and her skates tied together by the laces and hanging over her shoulder. She didn't look at me other than to give me a tiny nod.

She sat down beside me and bent over to put her skates on. She had both her feet inside the boots, but she sat there for a minute with the laces undone, staring down at the skates.

I didn't want to say anything, to push or whatever. This was a choice she had to make for herself. So I kept quiet, focusing on getting the tape just right on my stick.

Dayana kept staring.

Jonny came over and sat on a bench right across from her. "Dayana." He didn't say it loud, but there was a no-nonsense, authoritative tone to the way he said her name.

Her head shot up.

"They lace up the same way as your sneakers. Same as they always have. You haven't forgotten anything."

She still just sat there.

"It's just like riding a bike. You'll be fine once you're on the ice."

"Yeah." She nodded, but it was like she was trying to convince herself he was right. Then she said it again, only more convincingly this time. "Yeah, right." A minute later, her skates were on tight and she was ready to go.

I caught Jonny's eye and gave him a nod. He didn't respond at all, just kept taping his stick.

In very little time, everyone was ready. We went out on the rink, and everyone tossed their sticks in the middle. Dayana had taped hers in purple, so she could tell the difference between it and the one Norty would use. He was the only guy on the team close to her height, but he still had a couple of inches on her.

Scotty asked some random person from the crowd watching us to come in and separate the sticks into two equal piles.

Once the pile had been fully divided, we were separated into the teams we'd play with. Dayana was on the other team, but I wasn't worried. Not too much, at least. She would be with Jonny and Babs, and Jim was on that team, too. She had guys she knew, guys she felt at least a little bit comfortable with.

And I could be sure no one on my side touched her when she went out on the ice.

Scotty set our tennis ball in the middle of the rink, and three guys for each side went out. There wasn't any particular order to who played when or with whom, and we didn't have goaltenders. Nicklas Ericsson and Jack Boyle were going to be skating instead of guarding the net, trying to score and defend, just like the rest of us. Who knew how long it had been since either of them played any position other than goal? It could be interesting. We put some trashcans on their sides at each end of the rink and designated them the goals.

Then the game was on.

The second Dayana got on the ice, I did, too. She was out with Babs and Ny, so she was surrounded by the type of high-end skill she could really make use of. Back in the day she'd been a play-making winger, kind of like Ray Whitney. She had tons of creativity and a true goal-scorer's touch.

I had Smitty, a veteran defenseman of the stay-at-home variety, and Boyler, our backup goaltender. Boyler was in his goalie skates, even. Not really the best kind of skates to wear for something like this, but it was hard to get used to the change. I figured he was better off as he was than trying to play in skates he wasn't familiar with.

It didn't take much brainpower to figure out that if the three of us had any hope of generating any type of offensive pressure during this shift, it was all going to be on me. More likely, we'd just be trying to stop Dayana's trio the whole time we were out.

Babs had the ball and was heading up the ice with Ny only a step behind him. Boyler and Smitty were skating backward and defending against them, so I stayed back some, waited to see what Dayana would do. She skated over to center ice a little timidly. I backed into the zone, staying close to her but giving her room to move if she needed to.

I'd never seen her timid on the ice before. She was always active, hungry. When the neighborhood kids would get together to play, it had never mattered to her that she was three years younger than me and Soupy and a lot of the others. She'd thought she could hang with us, and she got out there and proved it. Being shorter wasn't important—she'd just skated faster. Weighing less didn't matter—she'd just learned how to evade us. Being physically weaker was irrelevant—she'd just worked on her shot until she could beat us that way, too. She'd always found a way to turn what should have been weaknesses into some of her greatest strengths.

By the time she passed the center of the rink, she looked a little more comfortable on her skates. Her strides lengthened, looked smoother.

I could see in her eyes, though—she was thinking about skating right back off the ice and not coming back.

Before she could escape, Ny passed the ball straight to her. It was a perfect pass, like he always gives me, right on the tape, hard enough for her to do something with it but not too hard to handle.

Dayana took one look at me, and I recognized the competitive gleam the moment it lit up her eyes. She took two good strides, circled around, and passed it behind her back with a no-look pass to Babs, who had worked himself a step ahead of Smitty. He shot it. Smitty tried to get his stick in there to foul things up, but it was no use. The ball rolled into the trash can for a goal.

Babs and Ny almost pulled Dayana in for a hug to celebrate before they thought better of it.

All the players on both sides went off the ice and let another group come on to play.

I spent the whole shinny game watching Dayana instead of paying attention to the action on the ice. It was easy to tell she hadn't played in years, at least it was for me; she'd lost a lot of her skating speed, half her passes were just a shade off the mark, and she always deferred to someone else instead of shooting it herself. But the more she got out there, the more it looked like she belonged.

On her fifth shift or so, by the time she was skating back to let someone else come on the ice, she had a grin on her face. All the guys were smiling, too, relaxing, enjoying the day. But it still took me aback to see her smiling.

After an hour, the ice was chopped up pretty badly and needed a good flooding from the Zamboni. Scotty called it a day, giving us some free time to enjoy the city.

We still had a game tomorrow and another the day after that. And then we had to travel down to Raleigh before finishing off our trip in Dallas.

But for the rest of the afternoon, we could do whatever we wanted.

I wanted to be with Dayana. I wanted to take her to see something on Broadway or to visit Times Square. Whatever she wanted to do. I just wanted to be with her.

I was about to skate over to her and see what she was thinking when Burnzie clapped a hand on my back.

"We need to get all the boys together and do something this afternoon. Do some sort of team bonding to carry on with what Scotty had us doing this morning."

He was right. Damn it. Burnzie was one of the assistant captains on the team, part of the leadership core. I didn't want to admit he was right on this, though, because it would mean I couldn't follow through with my plan to spend the rest of the day with Dayana.

I let my gaze travel over to her, settle on her. She was still smiling, laughing while she took off her skates on the bench with Babs and Jonny.

But I'd already dropped the ball on this part of my job way too many times since she had come back into my life. It wasn't fair to my teammates to leave them in the dust. I had a responsibility to them.

"Yeah," I said. "Got any ideas?"

"Monty suggested a private yacht company. They used it some-times when he played for the Islanders to get the guys together for a day in the city."

"All right. Get on that." I had to go tell Dayana that I couldn't spend the day with her. Not that I'd promised her I would, and she'd already told me several times I needed to go about my life like I normally would.

But I still wanted to be with her instead.

Chapter 9 - Breakaway

DAYANA

By the time we flew from Raleigh to Dallas, I was totally and completely baffled by how these guys could handle this lifestyle: flying from city to city, never staying in one place for more than a few days at a time. Sure, the team takes care of all the details and logistics, but no amount of planning could really prepare a person for something like that.

I'd only been on the road with them for about a week, and I was beyond exhausted. Not just tired—bone-achingly tired. All I wanted was to crawl into my bed and not get out for a week, but we still had three days to spend in Texas, including one with a game, before we could fly back to Portland. It would probably be well after midnight by the time we landed after the game that day. Talk about insanity.

In New York, the Storm had managed to pull off a win in a tight game against the Islanders, but they'd lost in regulation the next night to the Devils. Against Carolina, they'd come away with a point by taking it to the shoot-out. A win against the Stars would help a lot with how this road swing looked, but that was still a few days away.

When we got off the plane at Love Field and walked across to board the waiting bus, I expected Eric to reach over and take my hand. That had become almost second nature between us in the last few days, and I was getting to the point where I not only expected it, but I liked it. I knew it was different for him, though. His arm did come across to me, but he didn't hold my hand. He put his hand on the far side of my waist, drawing me closer to his side than he'd ever done before.

My breath caught. He wasn't touching me anywhere other than where his hand met my waist. There was no contact between the lengths of our bodies, none where his arm fell across my back. But I could feel the warmth of him everywhere, surrounding me and enveloping me in a cocoon of comfort.

It felt so much more intimate than when he held my hand, so much more...well, just so much more. I couldn't even begin to describe the things it was doing to me.

Even though my first instinct was to pull away, I held back the urge. I allowed the sensation of his possessive hold on me to pour through my limbs, let the emotions it roused swirl through my body and settle in my core.

Yeah...possessive. It felt like he was staking a claim on me. Marking me as his. The heat of his hand was almost enough to brand me.

That couldn't be, though. It was all in my head, maybe because subconsciously that was what I wanted him to do. The thought almost made me laugh, but it was a nervous sort of laughter—mainly because I couldn't decide if I liked it or was disturbed by it.

Babs had been walking beside us, but when he saw how Eric was holding me, he gave me the most adorably sheepish look and raced ahead.

It felt weird with my arm hanging between us, not having his hand to hold onto while we walked. I didn't know what to do with it. There was nothing that made me feel more idiotic than not having something to do with my hands. It kept bumping into my side because I was trying to keep it from accidentally moving too close to Eric and bumping into his side instead. But that just seemed stupid, like I was trying too hard to avoid something I didn't really need to avoid. I knew it wouldn't bother him if I touched him in such an innocent manner. The only person it might bother was me, and I couldn't know if that would be the case unless I actually let myself touch him.

I reached behind him a little more tentatively than I would have liked and let my fingers rest on the small of his back.

As soon as I made contact, his head whipped around and he looked down in my eyes. The heat of his gaze, green and electric and tortured, scorched my skin. The tortured part of it had to be because this was hell for him, me being Brenden's sister.

"You're okay?"

I nodded. I was okay if you considered having crazy nervous energy zinging from one extremity to another being okay. But I knew what he was really asking. My breathing came fast and shallow, and my pulse was roaring through my veins...but it wasn't panic. This was the same sort of experience I'd had when he'd traced the lines of my palm the other day, exciting and a little bit terrifying but not something I wanted to end. At least not yet. I wasn't sure what to do with it, how to respond. All I really could do was let it run its course, allow myself to feel what was happening.

When we got to the bus, Eric let me go on ahead of him, his hand still settled casually against my waist as he followed close behind. He didn't take it off me until I reached an empty row of seats and moved into it, settling into the chair next to the window as had become our habit.

He took my hand when he sat down, his fingers automatically moving to thread between mine.

We were some of the last to get onto the bus. A minute after we were settled, everyone else was on board, but Jim had another announcement.

He stood up in the aisle at the front and cleared his throat to get everyone's attention. "I know it's late, and I know you're all anxious to get to your beds, but I wanted to give everyone a heads-up about tomorrow. On the official schedule, all it says about what we're doing is 'Team Building.' Even though we've had a late night tonight, it's going to be an early morning tomorrow—earlier than I think any of us will like, but we can't avoid that. Breakfast is at six because the bus is heading out at seven. We'll be traveling to a camp near Fort Hood. Bring athletic clothes and shoes. Some retired soldiers are going to put you through your paces."

A few of the guys around us groaned. I knew, from talking to them over the last few days, that most of them had been hoping we'd be going to a golf course or something equally relaxing and enjoyable for the day. Winter in Texas usually wasn't too bad. When the plane had landed, the temperature was easily in the fifties even though it was late February. You couldn't ask for more perfect golfing weather at this time of year, and there's not much most hockey players like to do on a nice day more than work on their golf game. Going to a camp to be 'put through their paces' was pretty much the opposite of what they wanted.

I looked over at Eric, but his expression was inscrutable. It didn't matter if he was happy about what they were doing tomorrow or not. He was going to support management on this, put on his game face for the guys. He'd just suck it up. That was what he always did.

Jim took his seat, and the driver pulled out to take us to the hotel.

When we got there, a tray of envelopes waited for us at the front desk, just as I was coming to expect. Each envelope had a name on front and contained our room keys.

Eric picked up the two marked with his name and mine, and he led me to the elevators. Like before, his hand was resting just at my hip. He'd taken to wheeling my suitcase behind him with his carry-on strapped to the handle. I still always reached for my bag out of habit, but he somehow got there before I could. He let me carry my purse myself, but that was pretty much all.

It was just something he did, kind of like opening doors for me and pushing my chair in for me at meals. It was the kind of thing I'd expect him to do for his mother if she were traveling with the team. Yet another reminder that I was just a kid sister to him.

About half the guys on the team got onto the same elevator as us. They were talking, laughing. Comfortable. Even though it was a little crowded, none of them bumped into me or pushed into my personal space. None but Eric, but I oddly didn't mind him being in my space. Not anymore. That was a change that had happened faster than I'd ever expected, and I still wasn't sure how to process it. He kept his arm around my waist, holding me so close that I was almost pressed right up against him.

Almost.

We got off on the twelfth floor, and a few of the other guys did, too. They turned left; we turned right.

At the end of the hall, just before a massive wall of windows looking out over the city, he stopped. He leaned the suitcases against the doorframe as if he didn't want to let go of me just yet, and used my key card to open the door.

The doorway itself wasn't wide enough to let us through side by side, so Eric followed me into the room. He lifted my bag to the rack where I could easily get into it.

"Thank you." I wasn't sure exactly what I was thanking him for. It went so far beyond carrying my luggage and opening doors for me.

He just smiled at me, the type of smile that made me feel like I could melt into him...if I could let myself get that close. My heart stuttered, fluttering inside my chest like a thousand butterflies fighting for space, like I'd just chugged four espressos, one right after the other.

He set the envelope and my room key down on the dresser. "The door on my side will be open."

He told me that every night. Just a reminder.

For just a second, I thought he was going to reach out and brush his knuckles along the line of my jaw. For just a second, I thought I wanted him to.

But he didn't. He turned to where he'd left his carry-on bag just inside the door and picked it up. "Good night, Dayana."

"Good night." I almost said something else. Even though it was on the tip of my tongue, nearly spilled over, itching to come out, I didn't even know what it would have been.

He walked out into the hallway and pulled the door closed behind him. I went to it, turned the deadbolt and secured the internal safety lock. But I stood there for a moment, leaning my head against the doorframe, letting the light, clean scent of his cologne trail over me and wrap around me.

When I got myself together again, I went to the windows and made sure they were fully closed and secured. I took the pepper spray and flashlight from my suitcase and set them on the nightstand, right beside the bed where I could easily reach them.

I heard Eric move into his room. As soon as he was inside, the unmistakable sound of him unlocking the connecting door between our rooms filtered through to me, just as he'd promised he would.

It was almost one a.m., and I knew it was going to be an early morning and a very long day tomorrow. I had to get to bed. Sleep was a precious commodity these days, not something to pass up when the opportunity presented itself.

I changed into my pj's, an oversized and overly worn T-shirt and a pair of yoga pants, and got into bed. Two minutes later, I turned on the light and got up again. I rechecked all the locks and made sure I'd put the pepper spray and flashlight where I thought I had.

Nothing had magically moved. Everything was as it should be.

I got back into bed and turned out the light.

It was probably only five minutes before I was up again.

This time, I remembered I hadn't taken my meds. I went into the bathroom and filled a glass from the tap, dug my pills out of the suitcase, and swallowed them. I got back into bed, determined to stay there.

I couldn't. I only made it a few minutes.

There was just...something. I didn't know what it was. Couldn't put my finger on it.

I went to the door between our rooms and unlocked my side. I still wasn't sure what it was I needed to say to Eric, but I had to see him again.

I nearly jumped back in shock when I opened the door on my side and found him staring back at me in concern, his large body leaning against the doorframe similar to what I'd done after he'd left my room a short while ago.

"Are you okay?"

"I..." I took a half-step backward to regain my bearings. "I just needed to...see you."

He nodded. His eyes roved over me as he straightened away from the door, like he didn't trust my word and wanted to verify it for himself. "I— You seemed to be more anxious tonight than normal. You kept getting up. I was worried."

"I'm okay." I definitely couldn't say everything was normal. Nothing felt normal, whatever normal might be, but it wasn't a bad feeling. "Do you usually listen through the door like this?" With anyone else, it would feel creepy and stalker-like. With Eric, it just felt protective.

"I know I shouldn't. I just need to reassure myself that you're okay sometimes."

He was always looking out for me in that big brotherly way.

"Okay." I nodded. The butterflies beating a path in my chest hadn't slowed down at all, and now they multiplied, an exponential explosion of tiny wings beating inside me. I swallowed hard. "Is it—" I cut myself off, immediately regretting that I'd ever gotten up this last time. "Never mind."

Eric reached out and took my hand, stopping me from turning back into my room and closing the door between us. "Is it what?"

One of his fingers was resting against the inside of my wrist. He had to be able to feel how insane my pulse was going, how rapidly the blood was pounding through my veins. Everything in me was screaming to pull away from him, to close the door and lock it and forget that I'd ever thought it was a good idea to open it in the first place.

With his left hand, he tipped up my chin. Only one of his fingers touched my face, just enough contact to get me to raise my eyes and look into his. The bruising from his fight last week was almost gone, just a small yellowed mark now. He was looking at me with such concern, but with something else too. I swallowed again, so very tempted to turn my head toward his hand, to rub against it like a cat searching for more contact, to urge him on to caressing my cheek.

All the contradictory needs and emotions racing through me left me shaking, terrified.

"Is it what?" he repeated.

I licked my lips but immediately wished I hadn't. His eyes followed the path of my tongue and stayed on my mouth.

I closed my eyes and blurted it out. "Is it all right if I leave the door open tonight?"

He was quiet, so quiet for so long, I wanted nothing more than to dig a hole in the sand somewhere and bury my head in it.

Just when I was going to open my eyes again and give in to the desire to close the door between us, I felt his lips on my forehead. So soft. Gentle. Terrifyingly sweet. His five-o'clock shadow scratched my skin, a stark contrast to the tenderness of his lips pressing lightly against me.

I gasped at the contact and grabbed the first thing I could reach with my free hand to support myself.

It was his biceps.

He tensed beneath me, his hand holding mine firm and sturdy. Steadying. Calming. "I'm sorry. I shouldn't have—"

I shook my head. "Don't." It was just a whisper.

"I won't do it again. I'm sorry, Dayana, I wasn't thinking."

"No."I needed him to understand, but I wasn't sure I could speak enough to explain.My thoughts were racing, too fast to grab hold of them. I swallowed, reachedfor words in my mind like a hand groping in the dark. "Don't apologize."

ERIC

I couldn't sleep.

I lay in bed for hours, listening for signs of Dayana panicking in the next room.

She didn't make a sound.

Twenty minutes or so after she'd gone back into her room and turned off the light, I could hear the deep, even breaths that meant she was asleep.

How had she been able to fall asleep so easily? She'd been as electrically charged as I was. I could feel it in the rapid pumping of her pulse beneath my fingers. I could sense it in her ragged breaths. Her eyes had been wide and so dark they were nearly black with intensity and fear and need and every other emotion under the sun.

But she had fallen asleep, and I was still lying here in the dark, desperate to touch her again.

She was just in the other room. The doors—both of them—were open between us. I could get up and go into her room, sit by her bed, and watch her sleep. But I didn't trust myself not to touch her again like I had on the plane. The urge to slide my fingers through her hair, to kiss her forehead, or her eyes, or her nose, or her lips—God, her lips—it might overwhelm me.

I couldn't let myself slip up like that again.

She'd already done so many things I'd never imagined she would, allowed a level of intimacy I'd been certain she wasn't capable of. I couldn't cause her another setback. I couldn't.

But I also couldn't stop thinking about how it had felt earlier, when I'd put my arm around her waist and pulled her close to me. When I'd kissed her forehead and she'd gripped my arm.

This was all getting to be too much. Too intense.

I didn't think I was strong enough to do what she wanted, what she needed. More than that, I was beginning to doubt I had the strength to let her go.

Dayana wanted me to help her learn to touch and be touched. To learn to accept a lover's touch. And then she was going to leave, go back to her life where she'd find someone else to do the touching.

The thought of anyone else holding her hand, kissing her, in her bed—it all left me blind with the most intense jealousy I'd ever experienced and made me nauseated beyond belief. But that was what she'd asked me to do. I knew, when I had agreed to do this, that she'd walk away in the end. That was still off in the distance for now, something that was on the horizon but not close enough that I should worry about it.

I couldn't help myself.

The more confidence she gained, the more beautiful she became.

The more she smiled, the more I allowed myself to hope.

The more she let me touch her, the less capable I felt of stopping.

I needed to sleep. Tomorrow would be hell, and going into it without at least a few hours of rest would be insanely stupid.

But I couldn't.

I threw back the sheets and went to stand in the doorway between our rooms. Dayana had left the curtains open. Moonlight poured over her in her bed, bathing her in an unnatural glow. She was on her side, her head nearly hanging off the edge of the bed. Her arms hugged a pillow close to her body just like she used to do with her teddy bear.

It was like nothing had changed.

I knew better. Everything had changed.

It was still changing, faster than I could keep up.

Chapter 10 - Breakaway

DAYANA

For the first time since my arrival in Portland, the Storm's players were really, truly working together as a team.

That wasn't a good realization, considering I'd witnessed a handful of their games already—most of them losses, even if in a few of them they'd managed to scrape together a point in overtime or a shoot-out. Points are important for the standings, but wins are more important for the psyche. Athletes don't like losing, and to make it to this level in any sport, you have to be ultracompetitive.

But this afternoon, Sergeant McDougal presented them with something they couldn't successfully complete unless they worked as a single, cohesive unit. Work as one, or fail. It was that simple and that complex, all at the same time.

The military obstacle course was as elaborate and seemingly impossible to navigate as anything you could imagine. It was designed as a rescue mission unlike anything I'd ever seen before.

At the start, most of the team had to crawl through the thick mud under a rope net. When they got everyone through, they had to retrieve a ring of keys that was hanging from a ten-foot-tall post. The keys unlocked the cell that three guys were trapped in. Once they were out of the cell, all of them had to go back through the mud...but the "prisoners" had their hands bound and were attached to a rope that spanned the entire obstacle course, making it impossible for them to veer even just a little bit off the designated path.

Scotty had initially suggested I participate, like I had joined in on the ice at Central Park—that maybe I could be one of the prisoners since I weighed less than any of the guys and would be easy to lift and carry. Being locked up in a cell with my hands bound while surrounded by a bunch of men didn't sound like such a good idea to me.

Eric agreed with me, although he went about stating his case in a grouchy, authoritarian sort of way. He'd told Scotty there was no way in hell that was going to happen, so he could just forget about the idea entirely.

When he looked at me afterward, fierce protectiveness mingling with something softer in his eyes—which had giant, exhausted bags underneath them—my legs had felt like mush. I couldn't stop thinking about how he'd kissed my forehead last night, how I hadn't run away in panic.

How I wanted him to do it again.

The way he had looked at me made me wish I could be braver. I was curious, almost painfully so, about how it would feel if he kissed me on the lips. What if he'd done that last night? The thought of it made concentrating on the team's progress through the obstacle course nearly impossible.

At the other end of the mud pit, they had to scale a twelve-foot vertical wall by using nothing but a single rope attached at the top and their ingenuity. This was the first time they really started to gel on the course, to work as one instead of twenty-three disparate parts. In order to reach the rope, they had to either make a running jump for it or give each other a boost.

It was difficult enough to accomplish for the guys who had full use of their arms, but they also had to get the prisoners whose hands were bound up and over the wall. Sorting out the best way to accomplish it didn't seem to go well. They had guys trying different things, but they weren't really working as a unit. Everyone did his own thing, pretty much. Eventually, Eric and a couple of the other guys who weren't bound got up to the top, and they lifted the prisoners up and over while the guys on the ground pushed from below.

This was yet another reason I couldn't have participated. If I was able to jump up to the rope and pull myself over, that might have been okay. But with my hands bound? I didn't think I could have even let Eric pull me over like they were doing. I had let him hold my hand and put his hand on my waist, sure. I'd let him brush his finger over my chin and kiss my forehead. But to have some of those guys below me, pushing up on my legs, trying to lift me? No way. Not now. I couldn't do that.

The team got past the wall, but that only put them halfway through the course.

On the other side of the wall, they had a pool of water waiting for them with posts sticking up at intervals and a few landing platforms all the way across. The platforms were large enough that the entire team could stand on them at once. They'd been given planks of various lengths. The goal was to find a means of using the planks to move the entire team from one end of the pool to the other without anyone falling in.

They'd only been working on this portion of the course for a minute or so when the arguing started. Each of the guys seemed to think he knew what would work and that none of the others had a clue.

Since I'd stayed behind, I was with the coaches and management, and Sergeant McDougal was at the starting line. I shot a glance at Scotty, who was talking feverishly with his assistant coaches. Jim was watching them, too...just as concerned as I was. This wasn't good. The team needed to come together. They needed a leader to step forward, whether it was Eric or someone else. Someone had to step up and take charge.

Eric seemed to be one of the most talkative, one of the surest his way was right. That surprised me. He's usually not very vocal. He just does what needs to be done. But in all his arguing, he didn't seem to really be taking charge. He was just yelling. Trying to make himself heard. He wasn't leading.

It was pandemonium. The clock was ticking (they were competing for the best time against a high school ROTC group), but they couldn't stop fighting amongst themselves long enough to even try anything.

Finally, Jonny had had enough and did what I would have normally expected Eric to do.

He took the first plank, laid it out between two posts, and carried the next plank across with him. At first, the other guys just stopped and stared. But when he put the second plank in place and turned back for another, Razor was already halfway across the first one to hand it to him.

Eric was just watching, his arms crossed over his chest. From a distance, I couldn't quite make out the expression on his face, but I had the sense he was frustrated with himself more than he was with his team. He was letting it all get to him.

No, he was letting me get to him. If I hadn't come and asked him for help, he'd have his focus where it needed to be.

They set up an assembly line of sorts, working through what was essentially a maze over water. I'm sure it took them longer than they would have liked, but eventually they got the whole team across so they could move on to the final stage of the obstacle course.

Here was where it really got interesting. The rope attached to the three prisoners was wound around posts, up and over, down and around again, twisting and turning in a tangled mess. The guys who were free would have to work their prisoners through this headache of a rope knot, managing the slack so they could pull the guys through it. And pull was definitely the right term. Once again, like with the vertical wall, they had to lift the prisoners up and over or dig a hole in the ground and drag them beneath a log—all sorts of crazy things.

I nearly started panicking while watching this part of it, just thinking about being in the middle of it all.

There wasn't so much arguing during this portion of the obstacle course. They split themselves into three teams, each group working to get one prisoner through. It didn't take long for them to decide who was best at doing the heavy lifting, who should be in charge of the rope slack, and who should untie knots. The prisoners were able to help at least a little bit by throwing their bodies into the task, using their own strength where possible to aid their rescuers.

By the time they freed the prisoners from the rope course and crossed the finish line, most of the guys collapsed into a heap on the ground, sucking in huge amounts of oxygen to recover. They'd spent the whole morning on a hike with the ROTC students. Well, a hike was what Sergeant McDougal had called it. I would call it a torture run. He'd had them put on military gear and packs, and their pace had been more of a jog than a walk. I was fairly certain they'd each carried an extra seventy-five pounds or more of equipment. They'd asked a lot of their bodies today.

They'd only been finished for about thirty seconds when Babs started laughing. For whatever reason, the players had decided to have all three of the rookies on the team be the prisoners, even though those guys weren't necessarily the smallest or the lightest.

They weren't even necessarily the youngest, though in the case of Babs, he was. The rookies were just the newest. It probably hadn't been the team's brightest decision.

Babs was six foot two and, considering his age, most likely still growing. He had to weigh over two hundred pounds. He couldn't have been the easiest teammate to pick up and toss around like they'd had to do. He was covered in scratches and bumps and bruises by the end, but he was laughing. Almost hysterically.

Eric said something to him. I couldn't hear what they were saying from my vantage point, but whatever Eric had said, a few minutes later they were all laughing.

It was good to see. There hadn't been a whole lot to smile or laugh about, lately. Not when it came to things they'd done together as a group.

They'd only won a single game in the whole time I'd been with them. It was a skid they had to find a way to end, and fast. That wasn't going to happen unless they started acting like a cohesive unit. Today's experiment was certainly revealing where that stood. They'd come together in the end. But not like they had needed to.

I stole a glance at Jim and the coaches. It was hard to read them, but I got the sense they were more than just a little concerned with what had just taken place.

A few minutes later, the team came over to where we were. Eric came straight to my side. For a second, I thought he was going to touch me with his muddy, sweaty hands. I moved away, laughing while I shifted forward and to the side.

He gave me a grin that, were he not covered in grime, might very well have crumbled my wall of defenses.

Good thing he was filthy.

After that, it was incredibly difficult to focus on the ROTC students competing against the Storm to complete the same obstacle course. I tried to watch, and a few times I was able to recognize that, in general, the students were operating as a much more focused unit than the Storm had, even after they'd come together. I had a hard time concentrating, though, because every few seconds, Eric would creep a little closer to me.

All I could think about was the massive amount of mud caked on him and how to avoid getting it on me.

Sergeant McDougal brought the students over to us after they'd completed the course, and he announced the completion times. The Storm had finished in twenty-six minutes and twelve seconds. The students beat them pretty soundly with a time of nineteen minutes and forty-seven seconds.

Another loss. This one didn't count in the NHL standings, but I knew it had to sting the team's pride.

Then Scotty said a few things, something about great teamwork and that they should be proud of what they'd accomplished once they'd decided to work together—things that didn't really line up with the looks he and the coaches had given each other earlier.

I didn't really catch much of what he said after that. Eric had moved even closer still, until his mud-caked hand was only inches away from me. I took another step to the side, but I nearly bumped into Babs, so I jumped back.

Eric reached out and caught me, both his hands gripping my arms and spreading his mud all over me. I had to stifle a squeak of indignation.

He let me go pretty quickly, but I was almost as coated in grime as he was. "Sorry," he whispered in my ear, but I could hear the laughter in his tone. He wasn't sorry at all.

I shot him a glare. Then I took a couple of steps forward, putting some space between us, pretending to really listen to what his coach was saying.

A few minutes later, Scotty finished his speech, and the guys started to disperse to go clean up before we made the bus trip back to Dallas.

I spun around to tell Eric just what I thought about his getting me dirty. I noticed the mischievous glint in his eye a nanosecond before he smeared a handful of mud on my cheek.

"Aaahhh!" I couldn't stop myself from squealing like a little girl.

I also couldn't stop myself from laughing like a lunatic.

The look Eric gave me nearly knocked my knees out from under me. "Didn't want you to feel left out." He winked at me just before he walked after the rest of the guys.

We hadn't played around like that in so long and never without Brenden taking part in it, too. Maybe he was just reminding me I was still a kid in his eyes.

I stood there for a second, debating whether I wanted revenge more than I wanted a shower and trying not to think too hard about what all these new looks from Eric meant. Before I'd made up my mind what to do, Babs came up beside me. He'd hung back from the rest of the guys, almost like he'd been waiting to talk to me. Even underneath all his mud, I could make out those adorable dimples and sheepish grin.

"You didn't panic, Dee." He brushed off some of the caked-on mud from his forearms. "Zee held your arms and stuff, and you didn't panic."

I blinked and thought about it for a second. Babs was right. Eric had grabbed both my arms and touched my cheek. And I'd squealed and squeaked and laughed, but I absolutely had not panicked.

I walked beside him toward the showers. There had to be a women's locker room somewhere near where the guys were all headed, and I definitely needed one. "No, I didn't."

Huh. I didn't panic.

ERIC

After we got back to Dallas, Dayana had gone to dinner with me and a group of the boys. I'd spent nearly the whole time we were out with my arm around her waist, my hand resting just over her hip.

I liked the feeling of having her close to me, probably a little too much. Or a lot too much. I never knew anymore just how far was too far. Her do-not-cross line was moving every day, maybe even every moment.

I got the feeling that even she didn't know where it fell at any given point in time.

It was confusing for both of us.

I had a few beers at dinner, even though I knew I shouldn't. I didn't really drink too much during the season. I preferred to put better things than that into my body, so I could get better productivity out of it. But after the beating we all went through at Fort Hood—and after I'd touched Dayana in new ways and she'd allowed me to—I really needed a drink.

If I was being honest with myself, my need to drink was more about Dayana and less about the obstacle course. I'd been exhausted and not thinking clearly. And when I'd teased her, when I'd acted like I was going to cover her with mud, she'd reacted just like I would have expected a decade ago. It was like Dayana then, not Dayana now.

So I'd touched her. I'd covered her with mud, and she'd giggled.

Even now, hours later, I could still hear that laugh as clear as it had been when it had happened.

I'd do just about anything to hear her laugh like that again.

When she'd laughed, I'd nearly lost my mind and pulled her into my arms, mud and all, and kissed her as long and deep and hard as I had been dreaming of. I'd barely stopped myself in time.

That was why I had a beer. One led to a second, and then a third. And considering that I'd only had about an hour of sleep the night before, if that, the alcohol affected me a lot more than it normally would have.

I was holding Dayana a little closer than I would typically dare when we walked back to the hotel, my arm wrapped around her waist and pulling her near enough to my side that she was pressed against me some. It felt good. Too good. It felt even better because she wasn't pulling away.

She had her arm behind my back, her hand resting just over my waistband. Casual. Not tense.

The boys were walking along beside us, talking like guys tend to do, only not. They all seemed to be guarded with Dayana around. I had kind of hoped that since she's a hockey player, too, and since she'd been around so much, they'd get used to her. Be themselves. They weren't. They were acting almost as if their mothers were with us.

She responded to them every now and then. More often than I did. But mainly she just walked beside me and let me hold her.

All I could do was watch her, in awe that she was letting me touch her like this.

Burnzie asked me something in the elevator, but I didn't know what. I only knew he asked anything at all because Dayana answered him.

"I think we're just going to call it a night."

Calling it a night sounded perfect to me.

I followed when Dayana moved to exit the elevator, never relinquishing my hold on her.

"'Night, Zee. 'Night Dayana." The boys snickered as the elevator doors closed behind us.

I didn't care.

She pulled her key card out of her purse and opened the door to her room. I started to follow her inside but thought better of it and stopped just outside.

Dayana turned around after setting her key down on the armoire. "The door between the rooms is still open, you know. You can come in." She slipped off her shoes and jacket and then got onto the bed, sliding backward until she was propped up against the headboard with the pillows behind her back. She tucked her feet up under her and off to the side.

I didn't need any more invitation than that. I closed the door behind me. For a moment, I debated sliding onto the bed beside her so I could hold her hand but decided against it. I didn't trust myself to be on a bed with her and not touch her in ways she wasn't ready for. I went to sit in the armchair by the window.

She flipped on the TV and scrolled through the channels, but she didn't really seem all that focused on it. Her eyebrows were furrowed, just pulled together enough that I knew she was upset about something.

I'd almost made up my mind to ask her about it when she set the remote control down on the nightstand and turned to me.

"You have to spend more time with the guys. At least on road trips."

I don't know what I had expected her to say, but that wasn't it.

"I spend plenty of time with the boys." Even as I said it, I knew it wasn't true. Not lately, at least. But I didn't know how I could be what the guys needed me to be and still do what Dayana needed me to do. It wasn't working.

"If I weren't here, you'd be with them a lot more. And you'd be present when you are with them. Back in Portland, they'll be with their wives and girlfriends, too. We can be together more when we're there.

But on the road, it's supposed to be guy time. Team bonding. Not hang-out-with-my-pretend-girlfriend-and-ignore-the-guys time."

She had me there. Half the time, I didn't know what they were talking about anymore. I couldn't keep my mind clear. All my thoughts kept going back to her. Even when we were supposed to be team building, I was thinking about her, worrying about her. I couldn't seem to stop myself.

"But you are here."

"I know." Dayana started picking at the fingernail on her left pinky, her eyes fully focused on that. "But I can't take over your whole life."

It was too late for that. Not that it was her fault. She hadn't asked me to give up everything and think of nothing but her. She wouldn't want that. She'd specifically told me not to do that, and on more than one occasion.

But I probably had been doing too much of it lately.

She drew her legs up and wrapped both arms around them, propping her chin on her knees. "You guys all have the day off tomorrow. You need to spend it with them."

I'd been thinking about things I could take her to do and see. I'd been making plans, almost like putting together a real date to take her on. "But what about—"

"I can find something to do. I'm a big girl."

I let out a frustrated sigh and scraped my hand down my face. The scratchiness of my stubble was getting a little out of hand. "The whole point of you coming along on the road is so we can practice touching. How the hell am I supposed to touch you if you're not with me?"

"I can be with you here."

Here. In her hotel room. With her sitting on her bed, the last place my mind needed to go was to touching her.

"That's not the—"

"You touched me when we were in the room last night."

I hadn't been able to get that out of my mind for even a moment the entire day. I kept seeing flashes of her eyes, of how she'd clung to me when I'd kissed her forehead. Every moment was filled with thoughts of so much more.

"It's not a good idea." I almost called her kid again. I really needed that reminder, more so than ever before. The line between what she was and what I wanted her to be was blurring more and more each day. Each moment.

Dayana straightened her legs out and scooted to the edge of the bed. "None of this is a good idea." She stood up and crossed over to me.

Out of instinct, or maybe need, I reached out for her hand.

She let me take it, hold it in mine. Just like last night, her pulse was pounding at a crazy pace. I pulled her hand closer to me and turned it over, laying her palm out flat. Her fingers curled upward, almost beckoning me.

I traced the lines of her palm with my finger, reveling in the feel of her shivering from my touch. I followed the third line, the one that curved around the fleshy part at the base of her thumb, past where it ended at her wrist, trailing over the sensitive skin there.

I lowered my head and lifted her wrist, bringing them together so I could place a kiss where my finger had just been.

She sucked in a sharp hiss of breath. The sound was more erotic to my ears than any moan could ever be, like a shot of adrenaline straight to my baser needs.

I wanted to pull her down onto my lap and draw thousands of those breaths through her lungs.

She was more addictive than crack.

Chapter 11 - Breakaway

DAYANA

After he kissed me, the rough scratch of his stubble rubbing against the sensitive skin on the inside of my wrist made a shiver race up my spine.

He instantly lifted his head and looked at me, concern making his eyes the deep green of moss. "You're shaking."

"It's okay." I didn't want him to stop. I wanted him to touch me more, push me further, test my boundaries.

He shook his head, and he dropped his hold on my hand. "It was too much. Too soon." His eyes took on that tortured look they had so often, like everything I was asking of him was too much to expect, since he thought of me as a kid sister.

I didn't want him to stop, though, as selfish as it may have been. "No, I..." I lifted my hand to his face and ran my fingertips along the prickly surface of his jawline. I shivered again. "Don't stop."

He let out a groan, soft and strangled in his throat. But he turned his head toward my hand and pressed his lips against the inside of my forearm again.

My pulse was roaring, so loud in my head and so frantic in my wrist.

Slowly, torturously slowly, he placed a series of tiny little kisses up my arm all the way to the inner bend of my elbow.

A wave of dizziness crashed against the backs of my knees. I put my left hand on his shoulder to support myself so I wouldn't fall into him.

He kissed me there, again and again until he'd covered every minuscule patch of flesh inside my elbow with his lips multiple times. His fight for air was rough and ragged like mine. The rise and fall of his chest lifted his shoulders, pushed my supporting arm up and dropped it down with each breath.

Then he moved higher, his lips blazing a fiery path along my inner biceps.

I couldn't think. Could barely breathe. Needed more. I released his shoulder and moved that hand to fist in his hair behind his head, pulling him closer.

The side of his face brushed against the outside of my breast. That was when all the pleasant tingles turned to full-on panic.

I ripped myself away from him, fear clawing at my lungs. Flew around to the far side of the bed. Grabbed the pepper spray and held it out in front of me as I crumpled down into a ball in the corner.

"Fuck!" Eric was up from his chair and coming toward me, but he stopped halfway across the room and turned back. "Fuck. I'm sorry." He paced, running his hands through his hair, over his face.

I was shaking so hard I worried I would accidentally spray him. But it was him. It was Eric. I'd asked him to do what he was doing. I wanted it. I wanted him.

Keeping my head pressed back into the corner so my lungs were open and I could get as much oxygen as possible into them, I reached up with a shaky hand to put the pepper spray back on the nightstand. It clattered around for a second before I dropped it.

Eric spun around to me, his eyes wild. "No. Pick it up again." He marched to the door and I heard the locks of the main door click into position before he moved to the passage between our rooms. "Pick it up, and come lock this door behind me."

"Eric?" His name, nothing more than that, was almost too much for me to get out.

"I'm sorry. I— Just pick it up and lock the door, Dayana." He was standing just inside my room, looking more haggard and pained than I'd ever seen him. "Please."

Nausea was roiling in my stomach. I swallowed, trying to force it down and keep it at bay. "Stay with me." Even saying that much nearly released the bile building in my throat. But I needed him to stay. I needed him to fight through my panic as hard as I was fighting.

For a minute that felt unreasonably long, he stared at me. But he returned to my room and paced to the chair he'd been sitting in. He sat down hard, never moving his eyes from me. He barely blinked.

I stayed where I was until I felt confident I could get up off the floor without collapsing. I wobbled a bit, but I eventually got myself back onto the bed.

The shaking still hadn't stopped, but it was usually the last thing to go. I pulled my knees to my chest and leaned my head against the headboard, wishing the pulsing of blood in my temple would slow.

There was so much fear in Eric's eyes, fear and guilt and self-condemnation and things I'd never be able to name. I hated that. I hated that he felt at all responsible for my panic.

I swallowed past the lump in my throat. "You didn't do this to me." I needed him to understand that much, if nothing else.

"Dayana..."

He didn't get it. As much as he knew, and as much as he thought he knew, he really didn't understand.

"You didn't do this to me." I said the words more slowly, punctuating each syllable as though that would hammer it into his head somehow. "You weren't there. It wasn't you and your buddies who grabbed me in that hallway. You didn't drag me, kicking and screaming, into a janitor's closet. You didn't rip my clothes off me, slap my face, hold your hand over my mouth and nose until I was blue and thought I was suffocating, just so I'd shut up, so no one would hear me scream. You didn't hold me down, and you didn't rape me. You didn't look down at me and laugh afterwards while I was bloody and crying and scared and confused. You didn't do any of this to me."

He couldn't have looked more surprised if I'd sucker punched him.

"You've never talked about it before. With me."

I hadn't talked about it before with a lot of people. Mainly just my counselor, but I'd talked about it ad nauseam with her over the years. "It's not really something that comes up in polite conversation."

"No."

"You didn't do this to me, Eric."

He was quiet. Too quiet. And he wasn't looking at me anymore. I felt better when he looked at me. When I could see his eyes, know that it was him and that I was safe. It hadn't been his eyes looking back at me that night. They'd been cold and dark and mean and empty. Terrifying. His eyes were nothing like that.

"But I am now." His voice cracked as he said it, and it was like my heart cracked right alongside it.

"No. You're helping me."

His eyes shot up to meet me. "Is that what you call it? Helping? When you're in a fetal position in the corner and shaking and you can't breathe? Yeah, that's a big help."

"You're helping me retrain my body, to learn that all touch isn't bad. That some can be good. Exciting. Healing."

All he did was shake his head, bloodshot eyes boring through me. He got up and went to the connecting doorway, stopping just before he passed through. "You're asking too much of me, Dayana."

He was right, and I knew it. But he was my only chance.

He slipped into his own room and closed the door, but he didn't lock it.

He would never lock me out. Not even if he should.

ERIC

I spent the whole day off with the boys.

Smitty found a golf course not too far from the team hotel, and all piled into a few cabs. A couple of the guys were nursing some nagging injuries and stayed behind, but otherwise we all went.

Dayana didn't come. After our conversation yesterday, after she'd told me in no uncertain terms that I had to start hanging out with the guys again and leaving her behind, I'd asked her to come with me.

But she wouldn't.

Even though I knew she was right, that I needed to focus on getting the team to really gel together and make a push for the playoffs, it stung. It felt like she was pushing me away and going off to hide in the corner with her pepper spray when all I wanted to do was love her.

I knew that wasn't fair of me, to put it all on her like that. But that was how it felt. I didn't like it.

The guys seemed a lot looser when she wasn't around, though. I knew they were holding themselves back from saying and doing things they normally would just because she was with us, but it had never been more evident than today. Crass language and locker-room humor ran rampant all afternoon.

I knew I was doing the right thing for my team—for my team-mates—but I still couldn't get my heart into it. Not fully.

I kept thinking about Dayana.

In less than two weeks, she'd become like an obsession.

I made it through an afternoon of golf, through dinner, even through a few beers with the guys before I excused myself. I wanted to get up to the room, see what she'd done today. See if maybe she was ready to let me touch her again. Just a little—I wanted to hold her hand or something simple like that. Last night, I'd gone too far. I wouldn't do that again so soon, but I didn't think it was a good idea to go very long without touching at all.

Why had I told her she was asking too much of me? There was nothing she could ask of me that I wouldn't give her, even if it left me an emotional wreck in the aftermath. I could never deny her anything.

When I got to my room, though, she was gone. The connecting door was open, all the lights were out, and Dayana was nowhere to be found.

That deflated me more than it should have. More than I should have let it.

I took a shower and changed, putting on a T-shirt and a loose-fitting pair of athletic shorts. She still hadn't returned by the time I finished with that. I thought about calling her, but that seemed too pushy. It didn't matter that we were pretending she was my girlfriend. We both knew she wasn't really. All the guys knew it, too. She had every right to go out and do whatever she wanted to do. She didn't have to answer to me.

It wasn't even that I expected her to answer to me. Not at all. I just wanted to see her.

But she might interpret me calling her in any number of different ways.

Maybe I could text her. Just something casual. Not pushy. Hey. I'm back. How's it going?

A text message would be okay.

I'd almost convinced myself to pull out my phone and send her something when I heard her putting her key card in the door to her room. She set her purse down before she poked her head through the open doorway between us.

My breath hitched at the sight of her.

She'd pulled her hair up and back, so it was off her neck in a haphazard twist with the ends hanging out. The dress she had on today, like all her dresses, kept her pretty much covered up. The warm brown fabric didn't reveal even a hint of cleavage and came down to just above her knee. She had on flats, plain and entirely unremarkable, not the sort of shoes that would make you sit up and take notice.

But I sat up and took notice anyway. "You look beautiful." That didn't even come close to how she looked, but sometimes words weren't anywhere near enough.

"I was..." She blushed under my attention. I probably looked like I wanted to devour her whole.

That might not have been too far from the truth, now that I thought about it. I had to get myself in check.

"Jim Sutter took me to dinner tonight."

I nodded. Jim had a special interest in Dayana and Soupy because of his years playing with their father. He'd told me when I first talked to him about Dayana that he'd help me look out for her.

It was a relief to know she hadn't been alone all day long. And that she'd spent some time with a man I trusted.

"I went golfing with the boys."

She already knew that. I don't know why I told her.

She smiled, a gorgeous, shy smile. The kind of smile I don't think she ever gave anyone but me. It made me want to hoard them, keep them locked away to comfort myself with after she left me, even though I doubted they would comfort me at all. They'd drive me insane with wanting her.

"Did you do well?" She stepped into my room. Just a tiny step, so small she was barely on my side of the door.

I laughed. "Horrible. I'm sure Babs will be thrilled to tell you how awful I was." I was too busy thinking about Dayana to focus on my stroke.

I'd been too busy thinking about Dayana to focus on much of anything lately. Anything but her.

"He'd never say a bad word about you. He thinks you're the best thing since Playboy." She took another step, pulling away from the doorframe. "Can I...?" She gestured toward me.

I nodded. It was only when she crossed the room and sat down beside me that I realized my mistake.

I was on the bed. Scratch that—we were on the bed. She was sitting close enough that I could feel the heat of her body. Even though it had been hours since she'd showered, the cucumber-melon scent of her soap was still strong, and it was wrapping over me, around me.

The simple act of sitting side by side had her breathing heavier than normal. I watched the rise and fall of her chest. Hated myself for doing that. I was only making this harder on myself than it needed to be, making myself want things I had no business wanting.

I couldn't seem to help myself. I reached down and took her hand in mine, threading my fingers through hers. I lifted it to my lips, turning her hand over so I could kiss the backs of her knuckles.

She sucked in a breath, but she didn't pull away.

But where was the line today?

"What did you and Jim talk about at dinner?" I wanted to get her mind on something else, see if having a different focus would help her to fight any panic she might feel from being so close to me.

She shook her head. "Not a lot."

I lowered our hands to my lap and brought my other hand to close over hers.

"He told me some stories about his days playing with Dad. That's all." She turned so she was facing me, but she didn't pull away. I looked down into her eyes, the brown as rich as melted dark chocolate. She licked her lips. I wanted to do the same to her. She took a breath. "I wanted to ask you something."

I nodded, keeping quiet so I wouldn't say anything that might fray her nerves or cause her to shy away.

"I..." Her tongue darted out to wet her lips again, which nearly drove me insane. "Will you kiss me?"

DAYANA

He released my hand and bolted off the bed as soon as I asked the question. "I already kissed you."

Now he was just being intentionally obtuse. "You've kissed my forehead, my hand, my arm. I want you to kiss me."

He shook his head, like he couldn't believe what I was asking him. I almost couldn't believe it either.

"You just had an attack last night," he said. "I can't put you through that again."

"Damn it, Eric. You didn't do that. You didn't do anything to me."

"It's too soon."

"It'll always be too soon. Please." I crossed over to him, reached down to take his hands in both of mine. "I need to know."

His eyes were searching mine. I could feel his desperation, how he was trying to find a good reason to avoid doing what I'd asked.

Now I'd really asked too much of him. Kissing me had to be like kissing his kid sister. He'd been able to hold my hand, but I'd asked him to cross a line he shouldn't ever have to cross.

It wouldn't be like that for me. I knew it. There was something in the way my heart fluttered and my skin tingled anytime I was near him. How I viewed him had changed. He wasn't just Brenden's best friend anymore, not in my head. Not in my heart.

My counselor had warned me about this. She said that even with a sex surrogate, people tend to fall a little bit in love with the ones who are helping them. That it's normal, just a part of the healing process. That it's to be expected, because like Eric said to me that first night when I'd asked him to do this, physical intimacy and emotional intimacy tend to go hand in hand, especially for women.

I knew I was going to end up with a broken heart over this. When I went home, when I returned to the everyday grind in Providence, I knew I would have to put the pieces of my life back together without him. That was okay. I'd find a way. And I'd make sure Brenden didn't take it out on Eric, because it wasn't his fault.

Eric couldn't make himself see me as a woman and not as Brenden's kid sister. I'd crossed a line in asking him to kiss me.

I released my grip. "I'm sorry. I shouldn't ha—"

With both hands, he cupped my ears, the heels of his palms resting against my jawline and the tips of his fingers brushing against my hair. I shivered.

"What do you want me to do when you panic?" he asked.

When I panicked. He hadn't said if. There was probably good reason for that.

I swallowed hard, fighting to calm my breathing, but everything in my system was going haywire. I could get away if I needed to. His hands were firm but as gentle as he'd be with a newborn baby.

"I— Just hold me." I'd always been able to get past my attacks faster if Mom would hold me, if she'd wrap me in her arms and hold me tight and not let go. My counselor said that was normal. That there's something about human touch, a hug, the close contact that can help to repress the body's panic and return to order.

"Hold you?" he repeated.

I nodded. "Don't let me go."

He stared down at me for what felt like forever. Minutes. Hours. His eyes were so dark and intense, so raw. "I won't let go."

Then he kissed me.

His lips were strong and tender, moving over mine with focused purpose. He still hadn't shaved, and his stubble scraped against my chin. I gasped from the sensation, my nerves a warring jumble of heightened awareness.

When my lips parted, he took my lower lip between both of his. The tip of his tongue slid over it like I would do to wet my lips, and he suckled against it, drawing it into his own mouth.

Every new touch, every new sensation was a shock to my system.

All too soon, he pulled away, but he left his hands holding my head. He leaned down, until his forehead touched mine. His ragged breaths flitted over my face, warming my cheeks. With the pad of his right thumb, he traced the lines of my lips.

"You're okay?" he asked once he could speak.

I couldn't even come close to speaking. I was so out of breath it was like I had just run a marathon, and every nerve ending in my body was alive and electric and desperate for more. I wanted to move closer to him, to have our bodies touch in so many ways. The heat was intense, too much, but I needed more. To brace myself, I raised both arms to his shoulders and put one hand at the nape of his neck. His muscles tensed beneath me, jerking to life where I touched him.

I nodded, my head bumping against his. There wasn't an okay bone in my body, but I didn't want him to stop.

His thumb tugged my lower lip down, opening me for him. He angled my head and came back to me, his tongue sweeping into my mouth to explore.

My blood was hammering through me, throbbing in my veins. He slid one hand down to the side of my neck, resting over the madness of my pulse.

I ached everywhere, all over, a desperate, needy sort of ache that I'd never felt before and didn't know how to relieve. Even back in high school, before I was raped, I'd only gone on a date here and there, nothing serious. My focus had been entirely on hockey, not on boys and dating and kissing and sex. I leaned into him, the length of my body resting against his, my curves finding a home against his planes.

Eric recognized the shift before I did. Even as the panic started, he stopped kissing me. He moved both of his arms around me and held me, close, tight, not letting go even though I fought against him. It rose up through me, strangling me, choking me, but I tried to fight it off. I didn't want this to end.

It was no use.

He had my arms trapped between us. I almost kicked, almost let the training I'd done with Jonny come into play, but finally I heard Eric's voice in my ear.

"I've got you. I won't let go. I've got you." Over and over and over again. He ran his hands up and down my back, calming me, soothing me. He didn't stop until I collapsed against him and gave up my fight, and even then he kept holding me tight to his chest.

I put my arms around his waist, drawing myself even closer than before. I let my head fall into the curve between his shoulder and neck, breathing in the scent of him.

He brought one shaking hand up to cup the back of my head, to brush lightly over my hair. We stayed just like that, wrapped up in each other until we were breathing as one.

Chapter 12 - Breakaway

- -

E RIC

I was just about to leave the practice rink and head home to
Dayana when Bergy stopped me. "Scotty wants a word before you go,
Zee. In his office." You could barely hear his Swedish accent anymore
after all the years he'd spent in the NHL, but there were still faint
traces if you listened for them.

It was the first year Mattias Bergstrom was playing the part of an
assistant coach, but he was just as intimidating as ever. He'd just
retired as a player after last season. I was still more familiar with him
trying to push me out of the goal crease than coaching me. He'd been
a real bruiser of a defenseman in the league. Big body. Strong as an
ox. He'd always had a real mean streak and played just on the edge.

Even though it was nice to not have him cross-checking me all the
time anymore, I kind of missed playing against him. He had this way
of bringing out the ultracompetitive nature in anyone. The better

you were, the more he wanted to beat you and the harder he pushed you.

"Yeah, I'll be there in five."

I'd been expecting a meeting, at least somewhat.

Not only had we lost the game last night in Dallas, but we'd lost several players at least for the near future.

Boyler, who was our backup goaltender, had tweaked his groin in the pregame warm-up. He was going to have to sit and rest it for a week or two, minimum. Boyler had more than his fair share of experience with groin pulls.

Ny broke his leg while blocking a shot in the game. That meant our number one defenseman would probably be out at least six weeks, maybe eight. That's a hell of a long time to be without a guy like Ny, who excelled in every aspect of the game, particularly when a team is struggling like the Storm have been lately. He wouldn't be back until the playoffs, and whether we would make the playoffs or not was still very much up in the air.

Petey, who'd been centering the fourth line and making a name for himself as a solid penalty killer, broke his face on Stars captain Jamie Benn's fist. Well, technically he broke his orbital bone. But Petey wouldn't be back for at least a month, probably longer. When he came back, he'd have to wear a cage just like Burnzie had been wearing. Essentially, we would be without him for the remainder of the regular season, too.

And then there was Steve Matthews. Matty had been taken off the ice on a stretcher with a concussion. There was no way of knowing when he'd get back with us. He had gone in for a hit on Benn, but he came out on the worst end of it. Fell awkwardly. Hit his head hard on the ice. The impact snapped off his helmet, and his head bounced up before smacking back down again. It was pretty ugly.

That was when Petey had dropped the gloves with Benn. He'd been up ice and hadn't seen it happen. He'd just turned around and saw Matty down on the ice, not moving, and Benn standing over him. Made an assumption. Went out to stand up for his teammate. And broke his face.

I couldn't fault Petey for doing that. I probably would have done the same thing if I'd been out there. But now we were down four more bodies. Even with the guys who'd been sitting in the press box lately, we wouldn't be able to put a complete team on the ice for tomorrow's game without bringing in some call-ups from Seattle.

When I finished cleaning up my locker stall, I set my duffel on the bench. I made my way to Scotty's office.

He wasn't alone. Both of his assistant coaches, Bergy and Daniel "Hammer" Hamm were seated at the round table in the middle of the room, and Jim Sutter was looking out the window, both hands in his suit pockets. He turned and smiled at me when I came in.

No one else was smiling.

I couldn't blame them. We'd been playing like shit lately, the guys were dropping to injury left and right, and we'd just finished one of the worst practices of my professional career. I didn't feel much like smiling either.

"Have a seat, Zee." Scotty finished up whatever he was doing on his computer and made his way to the table in the center of his office. He sat next to his assistant coaches.

I took a chair across from them, and Jim made his way to join us.

Then everyone was quiet.

That was never a good sign with Scotty. If he goes quiet, that means he's really taking the time to weigh his words so he doesn't spout off with something he'll regret later. It means he's pretty much at the end of his rope.

I met his eyes, but I couldn't stop feeling like a kid sitting in the principal's office after shooting my mouth off at a teacher or something equally juvenile.

After a minute, he cleared his throat. "So here's the thing, Zee. The team's floundering. A trip like we just went on usually does one of two things. It either solidifies a team, brings everyone together so they're all on the same page and working toward the same goal, or it can be the straw that breaks the camel's back."

He fell quiet again, but there wasn't any reason to wonder which result he thought we'd achieved. I didn't entirely disagree. Sure, we came back with a handful of points off that road swing. But we'd only won a single game. That was unacceptable. That wasn't going to get us to the playoffs. Not even close.

Bergy scowled and shifted in his chair, and Hammer took another sip of his coffee.

"You know the trade deadline is next week," Scotty said.

I immediately tensed and shifted my gaze to Jim, but he wasn't looking at me. Fuck! They're trading me. He'd look at me if he wasn't going to trade me.

Maybe he'd done it already.

I immediately started trying to figure out what I'd do about Dayana, but how could I plan without knowing where I was headed? And Babs would have to find his own place, or maybe he could go live with Webs and Laura. No, they wouldn't let him with Katie still at home. Maybe Jonny, though. Jonny had an extra room or two.

"Jim's got a real tough decision ahead of him, whether he should hold on to the guys we've got or if we need to make some changes."

"And I don't want to have to make changes," Jim cut in.

Okay, so maybe I hadn't been traded yet. Maybe I was jumping to conclusions.

"But the fact is he'll have to if things don't turn around, and pretty quick." Scotty leaned forward, both his elbows on the table between us. "As it is, he's going to have to call up some more of the boys from Seattle, but they won't exactly be an upgrade over what we're missing. They know our system, but whoever he brings up is still a new face. A new voice in the room. Our guys aren't really coming together as it is yet, and we have to make more changes. And that means we need more from you."

"I'm doing everything I can out there—"

"Bullshit," Bergy interrupted. "I played against you. You're not bringing it, not like you can. You're coasting, relying on your skill to get you through. You're not battling."

I was already feeling defensive, but this only made it intensify. That pissed me off.

"The fact is," Scotty said, "you're distracted. Look, we all know what you're trying to do for Dayana. We get it. We don't blame you for it. Frankly, I admire you for what you're doing. But we need you to start acting like the team's captain again. We need you to leave your personal life at home, and lay it all out on the line when you're on the ice."

Jim stood up and headed for the door, but stopped just before leaving. "There's a reason Ben Carter put that C on your shoulder, Zee. It's time for you to remind everyone why. There are some call-ups on the way. I'm counting on you to make sure everyone gets settled in with the boys." Then he left.

Ben Carter had been the GM before Jim. He'd pulled me into his office during training camp before my second year and told me I was already acting like the captain, so I might as well be the captain. He'd told me he believed in me. He'd said the team was bound to be great under my leadership, bound to accomplish big things.

The next year he was gone, and two years later we missed the playoffs for the first time in over a decade. We hadn't been back since. Some leader I'd been.

I sat there fuming in my chair. I felt like I was being attacked, but even more than that I was mad at myself because I knew they were right. They were just calling me out on something I'd been trying to ignore.

"Are we done here?" I asked a minute later. Sitting still after hearing I wasn't doing my job well enough wasn't really working for me.

Scotty scowled. He hadn't liked saying what he'd said any more than I'd liked hearing it. "Yeah. Get out of here."

I didn't waste any time. I went back to the locker room and grabbed my duffel bag, but Jonny stopped me before I got out to the parking lot.

"Hey, can I get Dayana's number? I need to see when she wants to get together again. I know she'll be busy with the St. Patrick's Day baskets the wives are putting together for charity."

I hadn't even thought about St. Patrick's Day being right around the corner. With Dayana playing the part of my girlfriend, she had to really play that part. She had to get involved in all the charity events the players' wives put together. It would give her something to focus on other than what we were doing. That was a good thing. Especially if I was going to have to start redirecting my attention back to the team. I took out my phone and pulled up her number for Jonny.

"You planning to keep working with her while we're home?" I asked him.

She'd slept in this morning instead of making her now-usual trip to the gym, and I hadn't had the heart to wake her up. Road trips are exhausting even if you're used to them. I couldn't imagine what it was like for her, especially since she didn't have the adrenaline of playing in a hockey game every other night to help her push through the wall of jet lag once it hit.

Jonny finished saving her number in his cell. "If she wants to. She's picking it up well."

She'd always been a fast learner, especially with anything physical. I nodded. "Thanks for that."

He just looked at me. "I'm not doing it for you. I'm just doing what needs to be done."

"I know." I shifted my bag to the other shoulder. I didn't expect anyone else to understand that doing something for Dayana was doing it for me, in the end. "But thanks anyway."

"Yeah. See ya, Zee." He went back down the hall and turned toward the gym. He'd been working out a lot lately, trying to keep himself in shape since he hadn't gotten back into the lineup yet. That should change tomorrow, with all the injuries we'd had. I doubted he'd stop the extra workouts, though. Maybe he'd cut back a little. The guy worked as hard as anyone I'd ever known, never expected anything he hadn't earned. I had to admire that.

He made the league minimum and had never made a dime more than that; Jonny would never be one of those superstars in the league making millions upon millions each year. He hadn't been drafted. He just kept pushing, kept improving, kept working on his game and conditioning, making it harder and harder for anyone to overlook him, even if he only got fourth-line minutes. Jonny never let any of that get to him, though. He didn't wear it like a chip on his shoulder—more like a badge of honor.

I made my way out to the parking lot, to my car, and headed for home.

Seeing Dayana wouldn't help me be a better hockey player or captain, but maybe it made me a better man. No matter what it made me, I needed to see her, to be with her.

I needed to touch her again.

She made me feel like I could do anything, be anything. She believed in me more than I believed in myself anymore.

When I came through the door, she was by the coffee pot in the kitchen, still in her pj's from last night. Her hair needed to be brushed so bad it was ridiculous. The right side of her face was still creased with lines from her pillow.

She couldn't have been out of bed more than five minutes. It was almost one in the afternoon. I'd never seen anything more adorable.

"Did you sleep well?"

She took a sip from the cup of coffee she'd just poured for herself. "I feel like I got trampled by a herd of elephants." She glared at me. "How do you look so rested and put together?"

"Practice fooling people."

"Brenden called. That's what woke me up."

I went to the fridge and started looking for something to make for lunch. "What's Soupy up to?"

"He's on his way to the airport to come here. Jim Sutter called him up."

I froze. Never in my life, not one single moment, had I dreaded seeing my best friend. Not until now.

DAYANA

Eric decided to wait in the car. He didn't think it was a good idea for us to be together when Brenden got off the plane. We didn't really know what to expect from him when he arrived. He hadn't talked to either of us much lately. Nothing more than the one phone call with Eric when word got out that I was in Portland and a very brief call this morning. I'd wanted to give him time to sort out how he felt about it, and he hadn't made the effort to call me.

My brother wasn't smiling when he arrived at baggage claim. He always had a smile when he saw me, but not today.

Unlike Eric, Brenden's dark hair was cut neatly and he was clean-shaven. He and I had the same long nose and brown eyes, but that was pretty much where the similarities ended. He was six foot three and 225 pounds of lean, solid muscle. He and our dad had very defined, square faces that gave them an almost aristocratic feel. Elegant was the word that always came to mind when I thought of them. They looked more like movie stars than hockey players.

You'd think that the opportunity to have an extended tryout with an NHL club would have been enough to get past his anger or whatever he was feeling toward Eric. Or me. I couldn't be sure which it was, or maybe it was both of us.

Today, Brenden had a cut along his left cheek that looked like it had probably been caused by a skate blade to the face, but it didn't make him look any less handsome than usual. Just a little more rugged.

He looked me over from head to toe, like he was trying to convince himself I was okay.

I hated that he wasn't saying anything. Even earlier, when he'd called me, he'd only said the bare minimum. Just enough to tell me he was coming and see if we could pick him up at the airport.

"Did you have a good flight?" I asked, trying to break the tension.

"I'm going to break his nose. And you're not going to try to stop me."

A little laugh came out, but tears started pooling in my eyes at the same time, which pissed me off. I'd been holding myself together pretty well lately, considering all the crazy emotions that had been flying through me. "He wouldn't try to stop you, but I can't let you do that. I've missed you." I lifted up on my tiptoes and gave him a tiny kiss on the cheek like I used to.

He had a weird look in his eye when I backed away, but I didn't have long to think about it. Jim Sutter joined us and shook Brenden's hand.

"Zee said you'd be staying with him, so you won't need a hotel room like the other guys."

With the recent rash of injuries, the Storm had called up four players from the AHL to fill in. Brenden was only one of them.

"Yeah." Brenden didn't take his eyes off me. "That's the plan."

Jim nodded. "Good. I'll leave Dayana to get you settled in, and we'll see you in the morning. I'll be sure Drywall gets all your gear sorted out."

"Thanks for the opportunity, Jim. I really appreciate it."

"Show me on the ice." With that, Jim went off to greet the other players who'd come on the same flight.

Brenden picked up a suitcase off the conveyor to go along with the smaller carry-on he had with him. They must have told him to expect a lengthy stay for him to have brought that much.

I tried to take the smaller bag, but he wouldn't let me. He gave a little nod, urging me to lead the way, so I started walking.

"Later, Soupy!" one of the guys with Jim called after us. He was a tall, gangly kid with bright-red hair and a face full of freckles.

Brenden didn't respond. Once we were out of hearing distance, he said to me, "I told them that if I catch them even looking at you funny, I'll make sure they can never look at a girl again."

I couldn't really say anything to that.

We got out to the parking lot and I turned toward where Eric had stopped to let me out. We walked along for a few minutes without saying anything. I could feel the tension rolling off my brother in waves.

"He's helping me, Brenden," I said finally. "He's only doing it because I asked him to. He didn't want to."

He let out a derisive laugh. "You've always been sheltered and innocent and all that, but I never thought you were naive." He pushed ahead of me.

I had to nearly jog to keep up with his long legs.

Eric was standing outside his SUV when we got there. I tried to put myself between the two of them preemptively. They just scowled at each other like only men can do. After a minute, Eric opened the back for Brenden to put in his bags.

Eric didn't help with them. Instead, he took my hand and pulled me around to the passenger door. He opened it for me.

The last thing I wanted to do was get in the car while they were both out of it. I shook my head.

"Get in the car, Dayana," Brenden said, still putting his suitcases into the back. "I have no intention of facing assault charges for hitting him at the airport in front of dozens of witnesses."

Eric looked down at me and raised a brow. I got in, and he shut the door after me.

Then he went behind the car and shut the trunk, making it impossible for me to hear what they were saying to each other. I knew they were talking, because otherwise they would have both climbed in and we'd be driving back to Eric's house.

I watched in the side mirror, but I could only see Eric, not my brother. He wasn't bleeding. That was about the only positive I could come up with. His shoulders were tight, and even from this distance I could see the crease between his brows.

A few minutes later, they both got into the car.

Neither said a word the whole way. But halfway there, Eric reached across the armrest between us and took my hand.

I could practically hear Brenden grinding his teeth in the back.

This was going to be hell.

ERIC

She was talking to Babs and putting together a salad when I came back from getting Soupy settled in a room. He'd insisted on having the room right next to hers, like he thought I'd try anything with her while he was in the house. Then he'd laid out in explicit, excruciating detail exactly what he'd do to me if I hurt her, made her cry...whatever.

Soupy still didn't get it. He thought I was just trying to get in her pants, to do anything I could whether it was good for her or not.

Out of all the people in the world, I thought he would understand. I thought he'd know that I loved her. That I would never do anything to hurt her.

I don't think he really had a grasp of just what we were doing, though. How could he? We'd barely talked that night on the phone. Not enough for me to really explain it. Hell, I didn't even understand it back then, and I wasn't a hundred percent positive I understood it now.

But I would never hurt her. That Soupy believed I would irked me.

Babs was leaning over the island on a bar chair, his elbows propping him up. He had the goofiest grin on his face when I got close enough to see. "I couldn't do that. I'd never hear the end of it from the boys."

"Hear the end of what?" I plopped down on the stool next to his.

He blushed. The kid had no clue what that would do to girls. Or maybe he knew exactly what it would do to them. Either way, he didn't answer me.

Dayana reached for a carrot and the vegetable peeler beside her. "I told him he should take one of those girls to her prom—the ones with the signs at the games. He'd have his pick. You guys could maybe auction him off for charity or something."

"That," I said enthusiastically, "is an excellent idea. In fact, we've got a silent auction coming up at Casino Night. I'm sure Jim would be thrilled to add a prom date with you to the docket in exchange for the right donation to the Storm Foundation." I stole a cherry tomato from the bowl Dayana was assembling her salad in; she shot me a look but kept peeling the carrot.

"You wouldn't." He looked panicked, but in a way that made his eyes wide. Yet another point to earn him favor among the Sweet Sixteen set. Those big eyes were lady-killers. "Don't tell him, Zee."

"Don't tell who what?" Soupy came in to join us and took up a position beside Dayana as though to guard her from me. He had his arms crossed in front of him, his chest puffed out. I don't even think he was intentionally trying to intimidate. He just didn't know he was doing it.

"Nothing," Babs said a little too desperately.

"Don't tell Jim that Babs wants to put himself on auction for prom dates." Dayana put down the peeler and picked up a butcher's knife. She hadn't finished peeling the carrot yet. I was pretty sure she was using the butcher's knife as a warning, but I wasn't positive if it was meant for me or her brother. Maybe it was for both of us. Either way, she started slicing the carrot with gusto. "I think you should do it, Babs. I bet you'd raise a ton of money. It's for a good cause. Sara Thomas was just telling me all about the charity work you guys do this afternoon."

Scotty's daughter hadn't wasted any time in recruiting Dayana's help. I was glad of that because it would give her something to do when I wasn't with her. And based on my meeting with Jim, Scotty, and the other coaches today, I was going to have to start spending an awful lot more of my time away from her, whether that was what I wanted or not.

Having Soupy here playing babysitter was really going to put a wrench in things. Dayana and I would only have limited time together to work on her issues. It hadn't been a big deal, having Babs here. He was pretty good at taking a hint and finding something else to do with himself. Even if he didn't catch on that we wanted privacy, I could tell him to scram, and he would.

Soupy, though? The way he was acting, I didn't know if he'd let me have two minutes at a time alone with Dayana. He'd even admitted to me, once Dayana had gotten in the car, that he could see a difference in her. But in practically the same breath, he'd warned me away from her, said he would do anything he possibly could to keep me from touching her while he was here.

That wouldn't be good for her progress, and it would be hell for me.

Chapter 13 - Breakaway

DAYANA

I never thought I'd be unhappy about having my brother around, but over the last ten days I'd come to absolutely hate it.

Brenden hadn't hit Eric like he'd threatened to, not even in practice or anything like that. He was just making it impossible for me and Eric to continue what we'd started.

Instead of sitting up like a normal human being when we were all hanging out in the living room, he would sprawl out on the sofa, taking up the whole thing all by himself, making sure Eric and I had to sit apart from each other on the recliners. He'd started escorting me to my room at night and waiting by my door until he heard me click the lock, apparently to keep Eric from touching me or something like that. He had even rode shotgun in the car if we all went somewhere together, making certain Eric and I couldn't even do so much as hold hands for that brief time.

It was driving me insane. He was driving me insane.

Worse than that, I couldn't understand it. Not really. Brenden had told me a few times how shocked he was that I'd kissed him when he'd gotten off the plane in Portland. He kept talking about how baffling it was that I was able to hang out with all the guys on the team without starting to panic. He'd even touched my arm a couple of times—whether on purpose to test me or on accident—and I hadn't panicked. He knew it, knew I was doing better. There was no other reason for my improvement if not for the work Eric and I were doing. Brenden had to see it, even if he didn't like it.

It had been so long since the two of us had been able to touch in nearly any way that I'd jumped this morning when Eric put his hand on my waist. I was in the kitchen getting a cup of coffee, and Brenden had just gone off to take his shower. That was pretty much the only time we got to be alone anymore, when Brenden showered.

Eric didn't pull away even though I'd jumped. "Okay?" he asked quietly.

I nodded, but I set my coffee cup down on the counter. I didn't want to risk burning either of us if I started shaking too much. I had no way of knowing if I would regress after not continuing with what we'd been doing. How far could we take things before the next panic attack would start?

He pulled me closer to him, turned me in his arms so I was facing him, and used his other hand to caress my cheek.

He was going to kiss me. I knew it. I could see it in his eyes, in the way he was lowering his head down to me. It had been so long, I'd felt so distant from him, that my whole system immediately went into overdrive.

How was it possible for something so simple to cause my body to freak out like that? My heart kicked into a gallop and I couldn't take a breath to save my life. I didn't want to, if it meant putting an end to this fluttery, vulnerable sensation.

I never let myself be vulnerable. Never.

Not for anyone but Eric. Even though it was nearly enough to paralyze me with fear, I couldn't stop myself from letting him in, past my wall of defenses and into the areas where he could hurt me.

I lifted my head some, watching his lips move closer to mine.

His hand dug in a bit at my waist, pulling me closer, almost lifting me off my feet. With his other hand, he knotted his fingers in my hair and tipped my head back. It felt like he was preparing to ravish me, to kiss me hard and deep enough to make my toes curl.

I almost wanted him to.

But instead, when his lips touched mine, it was just a breath of contact. Nothing more than a whisper and a shiver.

My whole body was alive, pulsing and aching for more. I leaned in, tried to deepen the kiss, but Babs cleared his throat from the hallway. "Incoming."

Just like that, Eric backed away from me and I nearly collapsed against the counter.

Brenden came into the kitchen, half-dressed and with wet hair. He glared at Eric, grunted at Babs, and came over to get a cup of coffee. The tic in his jaw was going crazy. He'd seen us.

He and Dad had both always had this jaw tic thing, kind of like Eric's crease between his eyes. It was their tell, the way I could read them even if they were trying not to let me see that they were upset.

When Brenden turned to me, his eyes were wild in a way I couldn't remember ever seeing him. He swallowed hard, moving his gaze over me from head to toe. "No panic?" His voice cracked on those two words.

I shook my head. "No panic."

He nodded.

Two minutes later, the three of them were on their way to the arena for the morning skate, and I was heading out with Sara Thomas and Laura Weber to plan for St.Patrick's Day baskets for the players' wives' charity raffle.

ERIC

Even though we had a bunch of rookies and guys filling in for injured players on the team right now, we'd finally started to pull together and edge out a few wins. Between that and getting some points in overtime on the road trip, we were still right in the thick of the Western Conference playoff picture. The problem was, so was nearly everyone else.

Still, it had been enough for Jim to hold pat at the trade deadline. He hadn't pulled the plug on me or anyone else. That didn't mean we were safe over the summer. If we didn't keep it up, didn't get to the postseason like he expected us to do, it wouldn't be surprising if he decided to make sweeping changes to the makeup of the team. I had two more years on my contract, but I didn't have any sort of no-trade or no-movement clause. He could move me anywhere he wanted, and I wouldn't have any say in it at all.

With all the injuries we'd had, Scotty had been toying with the lines again, switching the wingers around, messing with defensive pairings. Other than Sarge's line, which had been the same three guys for a couple of weeks now, the rest of us usually didn't know who we would be going out on the ice with until he sent us over the boards. At least it seemed that way. He was rolling out new combinations nearly every period of play and almost every practice.

It was halfway through the third period, and we were tied at two with Edmonton. They were right behind us in the standings, so we couldn't afford to let them get out of our building with an overtime point. Beating them in regulation was the only option.

The Oilers didn't always play up to their potential, but when they did, they could really fly. They were young, big, fast, and insanely skilled. That's what happens when you get a number one draft pick a few years in a row.

Tonight? They were playing as well as they ever played, and it was taking everything we had to keep their young guns off the scoreboard.

After one of the television timeouts, Scotty sent me out to take the face-off against Nugent-Hopkins. This time, he sent Babs and Soupy with me. They're both usually right wings, but Soupy went over to my left. He's never liked playing on his off-wing, but it was what Scotty wanted him to do.

He'd done a lot of things he didn't particularly like to do since he'd been called up. And he'd done them well. That was why he was still with us and they hadn't shipped him back to Seattle for some other replacement. He'd scored his first NHL goal last week, and he had a few assists to go along with it now.

I figured Scotty was hoping some of our old chemistry would show up tonight when he put us out there together. Why else make that decision? Soupy had been serving time on the third and fourth lines so far in his stint with the Storm, and he hadn't really earned a place on a higher line yet. Not according to Scotty's usual standards. It would be nice if our chemistry made an appearance, but I wasn't sure tonight was the best night for it. Not after Soupy had caught me kissing Dayana this morning.

Still, that was the line Scotty wanted on the ice, and that was the line he got.

Nugent-Hopkins beat me on the draw. Babs and Soupy both tried to crash in and help steal the puck, but the Oilers managed to control it.

They went flying into the zone, and we had to scramble to get into good defensive position. They kept passing it around, tape-to-tape. It was like Cirque du Soleil out there. Shot. Rebound. It kicked back out to their D, and they just managed to keep it in the zone. I could feel a slapper from the point coming, so I dove to block the shot. It hit me right in the chest, knocking the wind out of me. By the time I got back on my skates, the Oilers had controlled the puck again and were cycling it down low. We were all exhausted, needed to get off the ice for a change, but they had us hemmed in.

Burnzie managed to get a stick on it, force it away from them. Soupy grabbed it and passed it up to me to get over the line. I missed it. It landed right on the tape of one of the Oilers' defensemen. As soon as he had it under control, he slapped it again. This time it was Soupy diving to block it. It glanced off his hand and knocked his glove off. The puck ended up in the corner. Babs went into the scrum and kicked it out to me. I iced it because we had to get a whistle.

Since we were the ones guilty of icing it, the Oilers put a fresh line out there. We all had to stay. I skated over to the face-off dot to Nicky's left. Soupy had picked up his glove and was flexing his hand.

"Anything broken?"

"Nah. It's fine." He put the glove on, then bent over and sucked in as much air as he could.

I nodded and got Nicky's attention. "I'm pulling it back to you. Be ready for it."

He glared at me, but he nodded. Goaltenders don't really like it when their teammates try to win a draw back to them. It could accidentally go in. But that was why I'd warned him. If I got it back to him, he could control it and send it up the ice to Babs or Soupy, and we could get it out of the zone cleanly to get our change.

The linesman dropped the puck. I won it clean, pulled it straight back on Nicky. Soupy had gotten past his man and was streaking up ice. Nicky flipped it up in the air hard. It fell right in front of Soupy's skates. None of the Oilers defensemen were going to catch him—it was just Soupy and the goaltender.

He deked and pulled it to his backhand. Five-hole. In the net. We had a lead.

Now we had to keep it.

DAYANA

"I could take care of Babs's basket," Katie Weber said quietly but emphatically, trying to interject herself into the conversation I was having with her mother and Sara Thomas.

The Storm had won the game tonight, sealing the deal with an empty-net goal from Keith Burns in the dying moments of the game. We were waiting for the guys to finish cleaning up and dealing with their media responsibilities so we could go home. Since we had some time to waste, we were having an impromptu meeting to continue the work we'd done earlier, trying to sort out who would be responsible for the raffle baskets for the players who didn't have a wife or girlfriend around to do it for them.

Laura raised a brow at her daughter and shook her head. "I don't think so, hon. You've got your glee club competition coming up next week, not to mention tests in Pre-Calc and History. No time."

The sulky look on Katie's face was priceless. "I know more about him than you do," she muttered.

With the number of young guys on the team and all the recent call-ups, there were a lot more significant-other-less players than usual. We were trying to make sure everyone got covered, and preferably by someone who knew him at least a little bit.

The baskets were supposed to be filled with things representing the players. Of course we would put in signed jerseys and pucks and all those sorts of things, but it needed to go further than that. We wanted to put in a CD by the player's favorite band, something from a movie or TV show they liked, a book they had enjoyed, an item from their home country...something more personal.

"I'll take care of Babs," I said, and I winked at Katie. "You can give me some good ideas at the next game your mom lets you come to."

"Not on a school night," Laura put in.

"But you're already doing the baskets for both Zee and your brother," Sara said to me. "No one else is doing more than two. That's a lot of work for you."

"I don't mind." It'd give me something to do. I hadn't had much of that lately, and I was starting to get antsy. I'd always prefer to have something to occupy my mind, if not my hands. Having too much time to think allows my mind to take me places I'd rather not go. "Besides, I'm living with all three of them. It only makes sense."

"You're right. It does." Laura made a couple of notes in her phone and put it away. "I think that should take care of all the guys, then. We just have to get all the girls together the day before the Vancouver game and make sure everything is done."

I ran through the team's calendar in my head. The Vancouver game was the second night of a back-to-back, and the first half of it was on the road against Chicago. "I'll have to get mine together early and leave them with one of you. We won't be back in time."

"See, Mom? You should just let me do Babs's basket."

"Glee club. Pre-Calc. I don't want to hear any more about baskets from you."

Katie rolled her eyes, but I didn't get the feeling she was really all that upset. She just wanted an excuse to spend some time with Babs, even if it was just a little bit.

Sara reached for her glass and took a sip. "Well, that gets us past St. Patrick's Day. I guess the next thing on the schedule is Casino Night."

Laura's eyes lit up. "Which means shopping. I think David's going to buy me a hot little red dress I've had my eye on this time."

"You mean David's credit card," Sara said, laughing.

"Of course." She finished off her glass of wine and immediately looked for the bottle to refill it.

I pulled mine out of her reach preemptively. I had learned my lesson the first game we'd watched together. I hadn't let Laura Weber near my wine glass since then.

"So," Laura said, attempting to sound casual but failing miserably, "what are you going to wear that night?" She raised her brows at me suggestively.

"Something that'll make Zee do a double take," Sara said. She had a sly grin on her face, too.

I got the feeling they were double-teaming me. I shook my head, trying to put them off the hunt. "I'm sure I've got something—"

"Oh no." Laura set her wine glass down with authority. "You're not pulling the I-have-something-nice-in-my-closet routine with us. Unless you're hiding a slinky minidress and some kick-ass heels, you're going shopping with us on Monday."

"Yes!" Katie did a little fist pump. "Shopping."

Laura laughed. "You'll be in school, so don't get too excited."

I couldn't really afford to go shopping for a dress and shoes and all that right now. I hadn't been working for weeks, and my savings were only going to hold out for so long. And I couldn't ask Eric to pay for that. He was paying for too much already, letting me live in his house, feeding me, taking care of all my travel so I could stay with him.

I supposed I could ask Brenden, but he wouldn't be too happy about buying me a dress that Eric might ogle me in. Not that I thought Eric would ogle me, but that was what Brenden would think.

Before I had a chance to sort it all out in my head, Eric, Brenden, and Babs showed up in the owner's box. My heart immediately flipped when I saw Eric. He had on a charcoal-gray suit tonight with a bold green shirt that made his eyes pop. He'd slicked his still-wet hair back from his face, and his jaw was still scruffy, as always. All I could think about when I looked at him was how he'd kissed me this morning, how much I wanted him to kiss me like that again. How much I wanted him to kiss me like I'd initially thought he was going to.

He might have, if Brenden hadn't interrupted us when he did.

I shivered, just remembering how it had felt.

Laura started talking since I couldn't seem to find my voice. "Perfect. You boys each need to give Dayana a couple hundred dollars to fill your St. Patrick's Day baskets. And Zee, she's going to need your credit card so Sara and I can take her shopping for Casino Night."

I blinked hard. I couldn't help it. I was fine with her telling the guys I needed money for their baskets—they had been expecting that. But Eric's credit card so I could go shopping?

I shook my head. "That won't—"

"You've got it," he interrupted. He met my eyes, but I couldn't be sure what the look on his face meant. "Do you girls need her any more tonight, or can we steal her from you?"

"She's all yours," Sara said. "I'll pick you up Monday morning after Daddy leaves for practice."

"Webs and Scotty should be done any time now," Eric said. He angled his head toward the door. The other two guys were already on their way out.

"Yeah, all right." I gathered my purse and followed my brother and Babs into the concourse. "Good night," I called behind me.

Their giggles followed us out of the owner's box.

Babs and Brenden were up ahead. When I caught up with Eric, he reached out for my hand. I let him even though Brenden might see. He'd caught us kissing this morning and he hadn't done anything. Maybe he was starting to ease up on us a little bit.

"You had a good game tonight," I said. "It looked good with Brenden on your line."

"Yeah. It felt good."

He shifted his grip on my hand so that our fingers were laced together. I took a breath, trying to keep myself from getting so caught up in sensation that I couldn't think. He had a tendency to do that to me, and I wanted to talk to him. At least at first. I wouldn't mind if the flutters came later.

"You don't have to give me your credit card."

"Yes, he does," Brenden called from ahead of us.

I rolled my eyes. "Would you mind your own business?" He was always sticking his nose in where it didn't belong. I slowed down a little, hoping he and Babs would get farther ahead of us so he couldn't hear us anymore. "You don't," I said to Eric. "I'll buy my own dress. You've already done too much."

"You know I make a lot of money, right? I'm sure I can afford a dress." He was laughing, making a joke of it. But it wasn't a joke to me. It didn't matter that he made millions.

"That doesn't mean you need to spend your money on me."

"What if I want to? Have you thought about that?"

"I..." No, I hadn't thought of that. There was no good reason for him to want to spend any more of his money on me.

"Are you going to buy shoes, too? You should. Something totally impractical, not like anything you'd normally buy. Just for fun." He gave me a half-smile, and my knees nearly buckled. "You should get them to take you to get your nails done, too. Pamper yourself a little bit."

I didn't know how to pamper myself. I doubted I'd like it. The thought of it felt so foreign. Even if I did, though, I didn't want to do it with his credit card.

We'd made it out to the parking garage, and Brenden and Babs were waiting by the car for us.

Eric unlocked the doors, and Brenden opened the front like he was going to get in. Instead, he held it open for me.

"Thank you," I said quietly. Then I got in.

He didn't close the door right away, though. I looked up, wondering why.

"If he's going to kiss you like that, he's going to buy you a fucking dress. And a lot more, if I have anything to say about it."

He closed the door and climbed in behind me.

Was he not going to try to stop us anymore? It seemed that way, but I didn't want to get my hopes up.

Eric got behind the wheel and started the engine. After he pulled out and got on the highway, he reached for my hand again.

"Don't think I won't still rip your fucking heart out through your ass and shove it down your throat if you hurt her."

"I'm counting on it," Eric said.

I stole a look over at him. His jaw was set, but he turned and winked at me. That wink was exactly what he'd do when we were kids and he was picking on Brenden—letting me in on the joke. Another reminder that I was just Brenden's kid sister to him. I tried not to let my heart sink at the realization.

"Just to be clear," Babs said from beside Brenden, "my heart isn't in jeopardy, right? Or my ass?"

I laughed and turned to look at him. "Not until you think about asking Katie Weber out on a date. I have a feeling her dad might have something to say about that."

He turned bright pink. I shouldn't have teased him, but then both Brenden and Eric got in on it, too. The rest of the drive home, I don't think Babs's face went back to its normal color. At least he was laughing.

We all were.

Chapter 14 - Breakaway

E RIC

"I'm calling it a night. See you two in the morning." Soupy got up from the recliner, stretched his arms over his head, and flexed the hand he'd blocked the shot with earlier.

Even a few hours later, after we'd had a postgame meal with some of the guys and come home, it didn't look like he'd broken any bones. It was definitely bruised and swollen, even after he'd iced it for a long time after the game. A bruised hand like that could be a bitch for a hockey player to deal with. Makes it hard to really grip a stick, and that makes it next to impossible to get anything behind a shot. He didn't act like he was going to let it keep him off the ice, though. I'd be shocked if it did. He'd spent enough time rehabbing injuries in his career already. Short of an injury bad enough that the doctors would pull him, he was going to play.

For the first time since he got here, Soupy was heading to bed without making sure Dayana was closed away in her room with the door locked. Thank God. When he got to the foot of the stairwell, he looked over his shoulder, right at Dayana. She gave him a little nod and said, "Good night, Brenden," and he kept going, even though he had a look of pure conflict on his face.

As soon as he disappeared up the stairs, I could feel her anticipation kick into gear. At least I hoped it was anticipation and not fear.

Not panic.

It had been way too long since I'd been able to touch her.

It was late, but I didn't want to pass up the opportunity to spend this time with her while I had it, even if it meant being tired at practice tomorrow. It had been a fairly big group at dinner of the guys and their wives and girlfriends—the ones who didn't have to rush home to relieve a babysitter, at least. Postgame dinners after a much-needed win tend to be really loose and make for some late nights. Tonight had proved to be no exception to that rule.

Babs had gone off to his apartment not long after we got back to the house. He had some video game competition going with Razor and Harry, one of the call-ups who'd arrived with Soupy, and they were going to play for an hour or two tonight.

So, now, we were alone. Really alone, like we hadn't been in over a week.

Dayana was beside me on the couch, just close enough that her hand was in mine and I could feel the heat of her leg next to me. She looked up at me with a shy smile that threatened to tear my restraint to shreds.

"Can I kiss you again?" I asked, not sure what I'd do if she said no.

The way she sucked in a breath, like she was already gasping for oxygen before I'd even done anything to cause it, had my blood rushing straight to places I wished it would avoid. The more I touched her, the more I found myself needing to touch her...needing her to touch me. I wanted her in ways that were becoming torturous.

It would kill me if I had to stop myself. When she looked at me like that, her eyes lidded so she had to peek at me through her lashes, her cheeks pink, I couldn't think of anything but touching her in as many ways as she would allow.

"I was hoping you would," she said.

I reached for her to pull her closer, but she was already moving. She propped herself up on her knees, facing me at a right angle that lifted her head up higher than mine and had her looking down at me.

I couldn't resist lifting my hand and letting my fingers trail through her silken hair, especially since it might help me keep from touching her in ways she wasn't ready for. But I would let her take control of what we'd do tonight. I waited for her to kiss me, to initiate how this would go.

Her breathing was already in tatters before she lowered her mouth to mine. She moved her lips tentatively at first, testing and teasing like she was trying to learn what felt good. It all felt good to me. I knew she hadn't kissed any man but me, at least not since she was a teenager, dating boys who could never have come close to deserving her. Her inexperience made every awkward peck all the sweeter.

But then she got bolder, and the tip of her tongue pressed against the seam of my lips.

I groaned when I opened for her, and groaned louder when her velvet-soft tongue slid against mine. The pulse in her throat was frantic against my palm when she changed her angle. Mine was just as intense, my blood roaring just as fast through my veins.

Dayana lost her balance, falling against me. She put both hands on my shoulders to support herself but broke off the kiss.

I didn't even think about what I was doing. I lifted her, drew her over me so her legs were straddling my hips. The wrap skirt of her dress parted over my lap, gave me a glimpse of her panties. White. Cotton. Totally sensible. That turned me on more than any sexy little thong could have done because it was perfectly Dayana.

Those panties, my slacks, and a tiny bit of space were all that were between us. All that kept me from being inside her. God knows I was hard enough it would take no time, otherwise.

My mouth felt dry, and I forced myself to look away, to look up at her face.

She was flushed—I hoped as much from arousal as from embarrassment. She had her head turned away from me.

Both my hands were still on her waist from when I'd lifted her onto me. I moved one hand up, cupped her cheek, and turned her to face me. She still wouldn't meet my eyes.

"Do you want to stop?" My voice hitched when I asked.

"No."

Thank God.

"Dayana?" I let the pad of my thumb slide down her jawline, felt her tremble from my touch. "Look at me."

Inch by inch, gut-wrenching moment by gut-wrenching moment, she raised her eyes to meet mine. Hers were nearly black, frantic in a different way than I was used to seeing her. There was a little panic in there, but there was more. She was just as turned on as I was. If I touched her panties, I had no doubt they'd be wet with her need.

And that was the last thought I should have allowed myself to have right then.

One step. We had to move this forward one step at a time. Putting my hand on her sex was about seventy-three steps beyond the point we were at.

"I'm sorry," she whispered. "It's just so much."

I knew that all too well. Every nerve in me was frayed; every inch of my body was zinging with awareness. I could only imagine how it must be for her, when she didn't have anything to compare it to other than when she'd been raped.

I kissed her chin. I had to kiss her somewhere, to touch her somehow. "You make me want things I have no business wanting."

"Like what?"

I didn't know if she was whispering so Soupy and Babs wouldn't hear or if that was all she was capable of. I didn't care. It was sexy as hell, her breaths warm and moist, washing across my face.

With one hand, she toyed with the hair at the nape of my neck, twirling it through her fingers. I wished she would fist her hand in it, tug on it hard, use it to guide my mouth where she wanted it.

I couldn't think while she was doing that.

"Like what?" she repeated a minute later.

"I want to touch you, Dayana."

"You are touching me." Her hand stilled, though. She knew what I meant.

"I want more."

Just a tiny nod. "So do I."

I let my hand on her face drop down. With just the backs of my knuckles, I grazed the side of her breast.

Her whole body started shaking, the panicky type of shake, not the good kind.

I tried to pull my hand away, but she grabbed my wrist and held me tight.

"Don't stop. Not yet."

There was a tear pooling in her eye, one of those big crocodile tears she'd always shed as a kid. I brushed it away with my free hand. She pushed her head into my palm, like a cat searching for more contact.

"Tell me when to stop."

She nodded.

I was shaking as hard as she was, but I moved my hand back to her breast. I traced my fingertips over the curve of its underside. Even through the fabric of her dress and her bra, her nipple peaked into a rock-hard pebble. I couldn't tear my eyes away from hers, even when I cupped her with my palm, letting the tight nub graze against my flesh.

Her back arched a bit, pushing her further into my touch. I groaned again and put my other hand on her other breast.

She hissed in a breath, and her hips dropped down onto me. I nearly came in my pants from the feel of her pressed against me like that.

Dayana jumped again almost immediately, tensing her thigh muscles to lift her body up and away from me. Her eyes were huge. Panicked.

But she didn't climb off me. She didn't run away.

I dropped my hands to my sides, forced myself to keep them there.

She lowered her forehead to mine while she fought off the attack, but she stayed with me, her hands resting on my shoulders.

Once she wasn't shaking as bad anymore, she lifted herself off me and sat down beside me again. I reached for her hand. She let me wrap it in mine, pull it closer to me so our joined hands were resting on my thigh.

"I'm sorry," she said after a minute.

It killed me that she was still apologizing.

I rubbed the back of her hand with my thumb, needing to touch her in whatever way I could. Something she'd said to me a while back kept pressing at my mind. She'd said she needed to retrain her body, to learn that not all touch was bad.

"Do you...?" My voice cracked, and I had to clear my throat and start over. "Have you ever touched yourself? It just— It might be easier for you if you've had at least some positive touch to associate with...with another touch." With my touch.

She didn't get tense or run away. She just sat there with me, letting me hold her hand. After a minute, she said, "My counselor suggested that a while back—seeing if I could handle it. I tried some."

Tried.

"It didn't feel good?"

She shrugged. "It didn't feel like when you touch me."

I understood that better than I could ever tell her. "Did you ever try anything to help?"

"Help?"

She was so fucking perfect and sweet and innocent.

I just shook my head. "Never mind. Not now." I didn't think I could handle talking about vibrators if I couldn't touch her again.

I didn't let her go. I held her hand in mine, stroking the back of it with my thumb. I kissed her forehead.

All I could think about was how she'd never had a positive sexual experience of any kind, not even something she could do for herself. She'd never been touched and had it feel good.

She'd never had an orgasm.

I wanted that for her, more than I could remember wanting anything in my life.

But would I ever be able to give her a gift like that?

DAYANA

It was only lunchtime, and I was exhausted. Sara had arrived at the door to pick me up at what felt like the crack of dawn.

I'd been getting up early and going to the gym with Jonny most days, but he'd tweaked an injury in the last game and needed to take a few days off. After last night, I didn't think I could get up early, anyway. The emotional sort of exhaustion was so much more intense than the physical sort, left me feeling more drained than I knew what to do with.

From the time we'd met Laura at the mall—the very moment the mall opened—until now, they'd had me trying on every dress they could find.

They both seemed especially fond of putting me in dresses I'd never be caught dead wearing in public. Some of them were too low-cut on top, others too short, almost all of them too form fitting. These dresses left nothing to the imagination. Considering the fact that I would almost always prefer to be wearing yoga pants and a T-shirt, just putting me in something more than a basic wrap dress was already enough to push my limits.

Laura reached into the middle of the table and took a piece of bread from the basket. "I think we need to go back and get that blue one. The one that shimmers? It was the best you tried on by a mile."

"Not a chance." I shuddered, just thinking about the dress she was talking about. It had hugged every curve I had, and I'd felt like I was going to spill out the top if I sneezed. Or took a step. Or breathed.

"Two against one," Sara said. "We overrule you. But we've got to find the right pair of shoes to go with it. Something to really show off your legs. You've got insane legs, and that dress makes them look even more amazing somehow."

The last thing I wanted to do was show off my legs. Or any part of me, really. I didn't like to be on display. I didn't want to draw attention. I just wanted to blend in with the background.

I felt safer that way.

"Why don't we go back and try on that kimono-type dress again?" I asked. Out of all the dozens of dresses they'd put me in, I had felt the closest to comfortable in it. The hem came down to around my knees, and it covered my chest all the way up to my neck. It had a cutout in the back, so it didn't completely cover me up, and it fit close to my body without making me feel like I was as good as naked in public.

"Bad color for you," Laura deadpanned.

"I have blond hair and brown eyes. I'm as vanilla as they come. Vanilla goes with everything. There's no such thing as a bad color for me."

"No, but there are good colors for you," Sara said. "That gray fabric didn't pop on you. If your hair was more of a silvery blond, maybe, and if you had blue eyes. But the blue shimmery dress? That one popped."

I rolled my eyes, but it didn't seem worth fighting over at the moment.

"I wasn't thinking at the game," I said to Laura, changing the subject so that maybe we could get away from the whole discussion of my dress. "I probably won't see Katie again before the St. Patrick's Day raffle. I have to leave with the Storm for a quick road trip, and we'll only be back for a couple of days before heading out again."

"Oh!" She set down her fork and reached for her purse. "She already thought of that. She gave me a list to give you."

After fishing through her purse for a minute, she came out with an envelope and passed it over to me. I opened it and pulled out three sheets of paper filled with bubbly writing. They were covered front and back with Babs's favorite things, at least according to Katie Weber.

I laughed. "She was incredibly thorough."

"She can't help but be thorough," Laura said. "She's in puppy love. Just think how thorough she'd be if she loved Babs the way Zee loves you."

I smiled and laughed but inside I could only cringe. Eric didn't love me—not like that—and I had no business wishing he did. He loved me like a kid sister, and everything we were doing was torture for him. That was the only explanation for how pained he looked when he would kiss me, touch me. I was only setting myself up for an even bigger heartbreak when I had to leave, because I was falling and couldn't seem to stop myself.

The waiter brought our salads and set them in front of us.

"So how have things been since the other night?" Sara asked. "You looked...I don't know, exhilarated...when I picked you up this morning."

That was probably because not two minutes before she had rung the doorbell, Eric had pulled me into the hallway and kissed me senseless.

I blushed.

It wasn't that I didn't want to talk to them about it. I'd told both of them at least bits and pieces of the truth, about why I'd come to Portland and asked Eric for help. I'd had to talk to someone about it because I was so frustrated after Brenden arrived and kept getting in the way of things. They both seemed to think there was something deeper forming between us, though. That Eric loved me the way I was coming to love him, and not as the kid sister I knew to be how he really saw me.

I knew they didn't mean any harm, that they were only teasing me. Honestly, I was glad for their teasing. It helped me to laugh off my embarrassment over my own inexperience. We never talked about anything related to my time with Eric when Katie was around—she didn't need to be exposed to this type of thing—but otherwise they'd become my confidantes.

"Exhilarated?" Laura raised a brow at me, a grin touching her lips. "Has your brother finally backed off?"

My face felt hot, so I knew I was blushing. At least it was just for the two of them to see. Well, the two of them and a restaurant full of strangers.

"He has!" Laura almost shouted. People at nearby tables turned to stare at us. She dropped her voice. "Tell us. Details. Has Zee done more than kiss you yet?"

I must have blushed even deeper.

Sara had a knowing smile. "He has."

I looked down at my salad. If I looked at them, I'd see all the people in the restaurant, and I wouldn't be able to talk. "I just... He just touched me...some."

"If he'd held your hand or something like that, you'd be able to tell us. So..." Laura gave Sara a knowing look. "Clothes on or off?"

"On!" I said under my breath. I couldn't believe we were having this conversation in public. "We were kissing, and I kind of fell onto him and then he—" I pressed my eyes closed, couldn't believe I was talking about this in a public place "—he touched my breasts."

"Too bad he had his clothes on," Sara said, wiggling her brows at me. "I bet he looks good with his clothes off."

Laura took a bite and swallowed. "Did you like it?"

"Too much. I haven't been able to stop thinking about it. About him." I pushed my plate away from me a bit. My stomach was doing flip-flops, reliving the previous night with the girls.

"Honey, that's how it should be when you're in love—the thinking about him all the time. At least in the beginning."

"I'm not—"

Laura dropped her chin and hitched her brow, her dubious expression more than enough to stop me.

"Okay. Fine." If I couldn't talk about it with them, who could I talk to? "I think I love him, and it scares me to death because when this is all over I have to go home. I have to leave. I knew I might start to have feelings for him, I knew it was a risk I was taking, but I don't think I really understood how much it would hurt."

"I don't know," Sara said. "I don't get the feeling he's going to be too keen to let you go."

Laura leaned forward. "You're driving yourself crazy with this because you don't think he loves you."

"He doesn't," I said. "I mean, okay, he loves me, but he's not in love with me. It's different. He still thinks of me as a little sister."

I ignored the dubious looks they gave me. I wished I weren't falling in love with Eric. It would be easier because he was still only doing this as a favor to me. How could he change how he saw me so quickly? How could they be right, when every time he kissed me or touched me it looked like pure torture for him?

They were both giving me these pitying sorts of looks. I hated that. I didn't want their pity. I knew I'd been asking for heartache when I'd asked Eric for help. I'd just never had a broken heart before, so I didn't really understand just how deep the knife could cut.

"Anyway," I said, trying to change the subject again, "I wish I could let him touch me more. It feels good, at least when I'm not freaking out."

"Really good, I'd bet." Sara leaned in, propping her left elbow on the table, and rested her head on her hand. "Did you panic?"

"A little." I nodded. "Not too bad this time. Not as bad as I would have expected, considering..." I'd been doing really well having his hands on my breasts. He was so gentle with me, so careful. And it felt so good. Too good. I still didn't fully understand how a simple little touch like that could make me ache everywhere, how it could make me feel so needy.

I would have been able to let him keep touching me for a while if I hadn't let my hips drop down. But then I'd felt him, hard and hot, beneath me. For just a split second, I'd been back in that janitor's closet. The terror hadn't lasted long, but it still took me a while to recover. Longer than I'd wanted.

And when I'd gone to bed that night, I'd still felt achy and needy.

I'd tried touching myself again, since we had talked about it and it was at the forefront of my mind. Maybe I just didn't know how to go about masturbation, but it didn't help. It didn't feel good. It just made me wish Eric were still touching me, because when he touches me I feel alive and electric. When I touched myself, I didn't really feel much at all. Definitely not anything to make the ache go away.

"Good." Laura's no-nonsense tone was back. "That's progress, right? You two can do some over-the-clothes petting while you adjust to that, you can finish yourself off with your B.O.B. afterward, and you can gradually move up to the good stuff."

I nearly spit out a mouthful of water. "I don't have a vibrator." I couldn't believe I'd said the word out loud. I couldn't believe we were talking about it. "Even if I did, I wouldn't have the first clue what to do with it."

Both Laura and Sara were staring at me with their mouths hanging open slightly. Damn. Now I felt even more awkward than I already had.

Sara picked up her napkin and dabbed at her mouth. "Well, I guess we know where we're going after we get the shimmery blue dress and some amazing shoes."

I was afraid to ask.

Chapter 15 - Breakaway

E RIC

Instead of going off to find his room once we got to the hotel in Phoenix, Soupy followed me and Dayana up to her room.

He had been accepting of the fact that she and I were kissing, holding hands, and maybe a little more as long as we were in Portland, but he didn't seem to be sold on the idea of Dayana being in a room that connected to mine. It didn't matter that he knew we'd already spent an entire road trip with that setup and she'd been just fine. Better than fine, actually.

For whatever reason, this was different in his mind.

I couldn't really blame him for thinking that way. The truth was, there was something different about being on the road with connecting rooms. We could go into our rooms and shut the door, and we didn't have to worry about Soupy or Babs walking in on us. That made it more special, somehow. It definitely gave us more freedom to explore whatever area of touch she wanted to explore.

I unlocked Dayana's door and let her go in ahead of me. Soupy followed. He left his bag near the door and headed straight for a chair near the window. He kicked his feet up onto the ottoman in front of him and made himself right at home.

This wasn't how I'd envisioned the night going.

I lifted Dayana's suitcase onto the luggage rack, trying to busy myself with mindless things like that so I didn't lose control with Soupy. Things had changed between us since Dayana showed up in Portland. He was still my best friend, had been for most of my life, but it was different now. It might always be different, even after Dayana left me.

Dayana wasn't as tactful as I was trying to be, though. She sat down on the foot of the bed and turned to her brother. "I'm tired. It was a long flight. You need to go."

I stole a glance over at him, still trying to make myself busy with Dayana's stuff. I knew she'd need her meds before bed, and the pepper spray and flashlight, so I started digging through the outer pockets of her bag to find them.

He scowled and pointed across at me. "He needs to go, too, then."

"No, he doesn't."

I found the pill organizer with Dayana's meds and pulled it out, but the flashlight and pepper spray weren't in the same pocket so I kept looking.

In the next pocket, what my hand landed on was definitely not her pepper spray. Or her flashlight. Holy shit.

Soupy made a strangled sound.

I could concur with that sentiment, considering what was in my hand and all the places it made my mind go.

"Dayana—"

She cut him off. "Unless you want to sit here and watch while he gets to second base, you'd better get off your ass and leave."

Now I was the one who felt like I was being strangled. I couldn't look at Soupy. I couldn't look at Dayana, either, without potentially doing just what she'd threatened her brother with.

A minute later, he got up and left, cursing under his breath as he walked past me.

Dayana followed him to the door and locked it behind him. She stayed there for a minute that felt like an eternity to me.

"Were you serious about me getting to second base tonight?" I tried to sound casual about it, but my voice cracked on the words. The last couple of nights, we'd mainly just kissed. I didn't want to push her. But God, I wanted to touch her again. "Or was that just to get Soupy to leave?"

"I wanted him to leave."

"Yeah. I figured." That felt like a kick in the balls.

She came over to me and picked up the pill organizer I'd set on the armoire beside me, turning it over in her hands. "I wanted him to leave because I hoped you'd want to try again."

My heartbeat stuttered, tripped. "Dayana, there's not a moment in any day I don't want to touch you."

She blushed and set the pill organizer down, then reached for me.

Too late, I remembered I still had her vibrator in my hand. It was one of those little bullet types. She touched it, looked down, and backed away more red-faced than I'd ever seen her.

"Fuck," I said beneath my breath. I set it down and moved over to her, tried to pull her into my arms, but she pushed me away.

"Don't." She turned her back to me and covered her face with her hands. "Oh, God."

I put mine in my pockets so I wouldn't try to grab her again. I watched her. She wasn't shaking, wasn't breathing crazy. No panic. Just embarrassment.

I could deal with embarrassment.

After a couple of minutes, she was still trying to hide herself from me. I couldn't take it anymore. I moved in closer, put my arms around her from behind, wrapping them around her waist. I tugged until her back was flush to my front. She didn't fight me this time. She even leaned her head against my chest a little and turned it to the side so her cheek was pressing against me.

"I'm sorry," I said quietly. "I didn't mean to embarrass you. I was just trying to find your pepper spray."

"I don't even know why I brought that. I should have left it in Portland."

I let my chin drop down to rest on the top of her head. "Where did it come from?"

"Shopping with Laura and Sara. They thought I needed one."

I agreed wholeheartedly. The thought that she had girlfriends here, though—girls she could talk to about this sort of thing—it made me much more comfortable with everything we had been doing since she didn't have her counselor here.

"Have you tried using it?"

"Mmm-hmm."

She didn't elaborate.

"Did it feel good?"

Her chest was rising and falling with her breath. I tried not to focus too much on her breasts, but from my vantage point the lure of them was inescapable.

She swallowed hard. "It felt nice. Not as good as when you touch me."

If only I could touch her where it had been.

She turned around in my arms, pressing her body against me and putting her hands on my back. She felt so fucking good like this, her breasts pillowing against my chest. I tipped her chin up so I could kiss her.

Our lips had barely touched when she sucked my lower lip in between both of hers. I groaned, and she did it again. She lifted up on her toes, put her arms up around my neck and held on.

I changed the angle of her head, took the kiss deeper. She let my tongue in right away, no hesitation at all. Her heart was pumping frantically, pounding against my chest. She kept trying to get closer, rubbing up and down in a way that I knew I wouldn't survive for long.

When I broke it off, she fell toward me.

I took her hand, pulling her toward the bed. She hesitated.

"Just second base, like you said," I said. "You can stop me anytime, just like always."

But maybe she was smarter than me this time. It probably wasn't a good idea to lie down on that bed with her.

Dayana looked at me with those big, brown eyes, though, stared into my eyes with so much more trust than I deserved. She stepped out of her shoes. She sat down on the edge of the bed and scooted over toward the middle.

The way she moved across the mattress tugged on her dress, a sea-green shirtdress with buttons down the front and a belt at her waist. One of the buttons nearly popped open, and she lifted her hips off the bed to ease the pull on the material.

While she was getting settled, I took off my jacket and tie, setting them on the nightstand, and slid my shoes off. Her eyes followed my every move.

I waited until she stilled, waiting to see how she would position herself. This could go badly in a hurry if I pushed her into what I wanted, instead of letting her set the pace, determine what she was ready for. She had some pillows behind her back, propping her up just a little bit into a lounging position. Crossing her legs at the ankles, she bent her knees and tucked her feet beside her on the far side.

I sat down on the edge of the bed, not too close to her at first. Not until she reached for me. I moved in, lying on my left side with my elbow bent beneath me for support.

Her eyes were bigger than ever. Terrified. I knew she wasn't scared of me, that it was the fear of what had been done to her, but I hated seeing that in her. I brushed her hair back from her face, just using the tips of my fingers to sweep it to the side and tuck it behind her ear.

She shivered when I touched her on that spot just behind her lobe.

I watched the trail of my fingers as I moved them over her, tracing the line of her jaw and down the length of her neck. The pressure was feather-light, just enough to tickle. Everywhere I touched, her skin jumped, the muscles coming to life beneath my exploration.

When I followed the line of her collarbone out to her shoulder and back across to the other shoulder, skimming over the soft fabric of her dress, she rolled toward me a bit. I met her eyes again. They were dark, intense, but not nearly as full of fear as before.

I dipped my head down and kissed her nose. "Okay?" I knew my efforts were having the desired effect, but I needed her to say it, needed to hear it from her mouth.

DAYANA

"I'm okay." My voice shook. I wasn't anywhere close to okay, but I couldn't bear the thought of him stopping what he was doing.

Eric kissed me behind my ear, where the almost-non-existent touch of his finger had made me shudder. His tongue flicked out and licked me there, hot and wet. It was over as soon as it started, but he blew a thin stream of breath over the wet spot.

I sucked in a breath at the shocking chill, the jolt of energy that poured through me.

"Okay?" he asked again. He pushed himself up on both arms, one hand on either side of me so he was leaning down over me, staring into my face with concern.

I nodded. "You don't have to keep asking. You'll know if I'm not."

"I know." He kissed my lips, but it was over too soon. "I just like to hear your voice."

"Okay."

Then he started kissing me all along the same path his fingers had taken moments before. Just tiny kisses. Dozens of them. One after the other after the other.

I couldn't catch my breath, and he didn't give me the chance to. He kissed me lower, dropping down toward the V of my dress and not stopping until he reached the cleft between my breasts.

He lifted his eyes without moving his head. "Okay?"

"Yes." My breathing was loose. Shaky. I couldn't take my eyes from him.

With the tip of his tongue, he traced a line along the tops of my breasts, following the line of my dress.

A completely unrecognizable sound came out of my mouth, and I fisted my hands in the comforter beside me. My hips shifted, rose up and twisted around almost of their own accord, needing to be closer.

I felt his hand between my breasts, his fingers undoing the top button of my dress.

"Okay?"

The button popped free, revealing the top of my bra.

"Mmm-hmm."

He licked me again, following the stretchy lace edging, and his fingers undid the next button, and the next, and then one more. When he lifted his head away, he eased the fabric of my dress to the side, until he could see all of my bra and my abdomen.

His mouth met mine, his tongue tangling with mine in a feverish battle while his hand moved down from my neck and settled just below my breast. The sensation of his skin against mine had heat flooding my body from head to toe and back again.

He moved his hand lower, down near the belt at my waist.

Panic hit me head-on, like running full speed into an oncoming race car.

"No!" I grabbed his hand in both of mine and pulled it up.

He tried to back away, to leave me, but I didn't want that. I held onto his hand with a death grip, keeping it between our bodies while I fought for air and to keep the shaking at bay.

"I'm sorry. Dayana, God, I'm so sorry." His voice was constant by my ear, soothing away the fear until it finally subsided.

When I looked at him, he was so filled with worry. I couldn't take it. I hated seeing him like that. I wasn't ready for this to end, not this time. Not yet. I wanted more, needed more.

I put one hand on the back of his head and pulled him down to kiss me again. "Don't stop," I whispered just before our lips met. "I need..." I didn't know what I needed. More.

He never stopped kissing me, just moved his kisses lower, dropping down my neck, to my chest, to my bra. His mouth came down over my breast, and he suckled my nipple through the lace fabric.

"Ah!" My back arched so much I nearly came up off the bed. When he did the same thing to my other breast, I felt a liquid pull in my center, like I was melting from the heat of his touch.

I rolled toward him, put both my arms around his shoulders and held on while he nuzzled my neck. He smelled so good, I wanted to be wrapped up in his scent. I couldn't get close enough and started undoing the buttons on his shirt like he'd done with my dress. I pulled it out of his waistband, attempting to tug it free.

He sat up on the bed. I tried to come with him, needed to touch him, didn't want to be separated from him. But he shook his head. "Slow down."

He took off his shirt first and then his undershirt, tossing them to the nightstand along with his jacket and tie. He was all muscle, with a smattering of dark hair over the middle of his chest and trailing down to his belly and below. A pink scar ran along his left shoulder from a surgery he'd had a few years ago. His right bicep had black tribal designs tattooed in a pattern that only emphasized his muscle.

Brenden had a matching tattoo. They'd gone to get them together the summer before their senior year at Yale.

I wanted him to come back to me, to come down over me so I could feel his skin against mine, so I could run my fingers over the lines of his muscles.

Instead, he went to the armoire and picked up that stupid vibrator.

My eyes bulged but I couldn't focus my vision, and my panic threatened to come back times ten.

I shook my head. "No—"

"Shh." He crossed back over to the bed, held his hands out to the side. "It's for you."

But I didn't understand. Couldn't think. I scrambled back on the bed, clutching at my chest like I could make my lungs work better that way.

He sat on the edge of the bed and reached across to me. "Here. Take it." He held the vibrator out in his hand. "I'm not going to touch you with it. It's for you to use. Only if you want."

I took it from him, clutched it with a white-knuckled grip while I tried to calm down.

"I should have told you what I was thinking," he said. He took my other hand, held it with our fingers linked. "Should have given you some warning. I just... You make it hard for me to think when you're squirming beneath me."

"It's okay." I had to be blushing. Besides, I might have panicked anyway just from the thought of using the vibrator with him even knowing about it, let alone with him in the same room.

With the worst of the attack easing, I inched closer to him again. He lifted our hands up to his mouth, kissed the back of mine. I stretched up on my knees until I could kiss his jaw.

He met my eyes. "Are you sure you're ready for more?"

Nowhere close to sure. "I'm sure."

Eric cupped the back of my head with one hand and kissed me, sucking my lower lip while he lowered me back to the bed. The hairs on his chest scratched and tickled against me. He kissed me until I felt frantic for his touch.

Then his hands and mouth were all over me, my neck, my breasts, the flat of my stomach, the ticklish spot under my arm, kissing and stroking and licking and kneading and nibbling—God, those tiny little nibbles—and I squirmed and ached and felt so good I could cry, but I still needed more.

I felt his hand coming over mine, the one still clutching the vibrator. He switched it on, and it buzzed to life in my hand.

"Only if you want," he said. His voice shook. His everything was shaking. The vibrator was barely shaking harder than he was as he leaned over me, looked down in my eyes. His were dark, so dark and intense as I saw so often when we were alone these days.

I felt like I was right on the edge of something, just on the cliff and ready to fall over to whatever was below.

I nodded. Couldn't speak. Slowly, tentatively, I lowered my hand down, down, past my waist and further. He watched the path of my hand at first but stopped when I went past my waist. Thank God he didn't watch the whole way. I didn't think I could touch myself with it if he was looking at me the whole time, looking at me down there. He bent over me again, suckled my nipple through the fabric of my bra. His tongue rasped over the nub, made the lace move against me in ways that pushed me closer and closer to insanity, and I arched up into him for more.

That made it hard to focus on trying to get the vibrator where it needed to be. I wasn't even sure I knew where that was. When I'd tried to use it the other night at his house, I'd fumbled around and found a few places that felt nice, but it had been nothing like what Laura and Sara had described.

I thought maybe I just couldn't have an orgasm. Maybe they were right—the people who say some women can't get there. After the rape, it wouldn't surprise me if I couldn't.

But I tried anyway because Eric seemed so intent upon making me feel good.

I slipped the vibrator under the edge of my panties, moved it around a bit to see how things felt. I was shocked to feel how wet I was. I found a spot that felt nice, the vibrations making my body thrum in new and slightly terrifying ways. But Eric suckled on my other nipple, and my hand slipped. The vibrator moved into a new spot, and I knew: this was it. My whole body tensed beneath him, taut as a bowstring.

"I can't," I panted. I'd never felt anything so intense before. Everything suddenly felt ten times as sensitive as usual. I couldn't take any more. I was desperate, needed something to ground me. My free hand fisted in the comforter beneath me, and my toes curled, trying to find a hold. "It's too much."

Eric spread both my hands over my rib cage, just under my breasts, and he leaned over me. "You can." Then he kissed me, long and deep and sweet, all the way through until I shuddered and felt everything contract to the point that I thought I would die and exploded in release.

Everything inside me was tensing and relaxing, over and over again, and I couldn't stop the shaking. But I didn't want to. I collapsed back against the bed, turned the vibrator off, and dropped it beside me.

Eric lay down next to me and pulled me close. He settled my head in a spot by his shoulder and wrapped his arms around me.

I felt so protected and warm. Loved.

With my fingertips, I traced the lines of his chest, breathing in the scent of him until I fell asleep.

ERIC

There was no chance in hell I was ever going to be able to let Dayana go. I couldn't let her leave me.

I watched her sleep, marveling at the feel of her body against me.

I was still hard enough to cut glass after helping her to climax, but my needs could wait. Mine didn't come close to comparing to hers. I knew at this moment I wanted to spend the rest of my life doing anything I could to meet her needs.

There was no way to delude myself into thinking I deserved that chance. But lying here, with her hair fanning over my shoulder and her breaths warming my chest, I couldn't stomach the thought of letting another man touch her. Of not being able to hold her as often as was feasible and for as long as possible.

I had to get through the rest of the season...and hopefully the playoffs. The Storm needed my focus right now, and besides, I didn't think Dayana was ready to start thinking about the future. Not like I was.

Once we got to the summer, though, I could start making plans. Buying rings. Making her fall as helplessly in love with me as I was with her.

But for now, I needed to get some sleep. We had a game to play tomorrow night. I needed to be sharp, refreshed. There was no chance I could get any decent sleep with her half naked and draped over me. Not without getting some relief, at least.

It would be better, probably for both of us, if I went into my room for the rest of the night. She hadn't ever spent the night with a man in her bed, other than maybe when she was a little girl and she got into bed with her parents. Definitely not since her rape. The risk of triggering a new panic attack if she woke up with me there was too high.

I tried to slip out of her bed without waking her up. As soon as I moved, though, her head lifted up.

She tensed and looked panicked, but then she recognized me. After a minute, she relaxed against me, her head dropping back onto my shoulder and her arm sliding across my stomach to pull herself closer to me.

She was asleep again in no time.

I slid out from beneath her, pulled the blankets over her, and made sure she had a pillow under her head. I picked up my discarded clothes, turned off the light, took the handle of my suitcase, and went out the main door from her room.

When I got into mine, I unlocked the connecting door. Just in case.

Even though it was close to midnight, I got in the shower. I doubted it would really clear my mind enough that I could sleep, but I had to try.

Chapter 16 - Breakaway

ERIC

We'd lost the game to Phoenix in overtime. When we got home and played Florida, we barely scraped out a win. Chicago beat us easily because we completely fell apart out on the ice. We'd come home for a game against Vancouver on St. Patrick's Day, where we managed to scrape out a shoot-out win, but we didn't deserve it. We'd played like shit through three of those four games.

Well, three and a half, actually. If Florida had managed to capitalize on the chances we'd allowed them, they could have beaten us handily. Lucky for us, they hadn't.

One of the biggest problems, at least according to Scotty (and for that matter, according to me) was that I wasn't scoring. I could complain about how he kept changing my linemates, but the truth was it had nothing to do with that. I've always been able to score no matter who I was playing with—my whole career. I'd been able to in peewee, in high school, in college, and in the pros. That was one of the main reasons I'd been given the big contract I was currently trying and failing to live up to.

I might have been letting all the stuff with Dayana get to me, but I didn't think that was the case. On the ice, at least, I'd been able to focus on the job at hand. More likely I was letting the pressure of trying to get the team back into the playoffs get to me.

Also, Hammer told me I was squeezing my stick. He was probably right. It was really hard to stop doing that once you start, though.

Everyone goes through scoring slumps in the league. It happens. If you somehow get to the end of your career without a slump like this happening at key times, you're considered to be a clutch performer, a real leader. When you hit a slump right when your team needs you to pull through the most? They say you choked.

I wasn't oblivious. I knew what they were saying about me, the national hockey media. The Storm had been on a downhill slide ever since I'd become captain, and they were pointing to my struggles right now as evidence I that couldn't cut it when it mattered. It was easy to put the blame on my shoulders instead of looking at any of the other mitigating factors involved—the poor management over the last few years before Jim Sutter came in, the multiple coaching changes, the constant roster turnover.

I needed to play better. Absolutely. I needed to lead better. But I wasn't the only problem. I couldn't believe that. If I let myself believe that, I might as well call it quits today, hang up my skates, and not look back.

No matter how I looked at it, though, this was not a good time for me to have a scoring slump. Not when every game could be the difference between the Portland Storm finally getting back into the playoffs or not. Not when we had so many guys injured and out of the lineup, when we were depending on so many rookies and AHL-level call-ups to fill those roles.

And it kept getting worse. We lost Pasha in the game against Chicago. He'd been racing for the puck and got tangled up with a Blackhawks defender, then went into the boards with his leg at a really awkward angle. He tore his ACL and was due to have season-ending surgery right after Casino Night.

That meant one of our best goal scorers was gone. That meant another call-up was on his way.

In last night's game, Razor twisted his ankle. Just a high ankle sprain and not a break, at least, but he was still going to miss at least a week.

There was only a little over a week left in the season.

Razor hadn't become the type of scoring defenseman everyone said he would become. Not yet, at least, but it was still just his first season in the league. The kid could move the puck well and get it out of our end and into the offensive zone pretty quickly. We needed him, and now we didn't have him.

And all of that meant I needed to be scoring, more so than ever before.

We were still right in the thick of the playoff race.

Somehow, Calgary was falling apart more than we were. They'd lost six straight and had pretty much been eliminated from the race. If Phoenix didn't pick up at least a point in every game from now until the end of the season, they'd be out, too. But we were still fighting tooth and nail for that eighth spot with Vancouver, Dallas, and Nashville.

All signs pointed to the final playoff spot not being decided until the very last day of the season. Maybe even the last game of the season. Which, coincidentally, we would be playing at home. By the time our game started, most of the others going on that night would have already been decided.

I couldn't let myself think too far ahead, though. I couldn't worry about that last game of the season when we still had four others between now and then. And we had Casino Night tomorrow.

"Don't forget, tomorrow night is not optional, and it is black tie. Brush up on how to deal blackjack, boys. And remember, it's about raising money. Let's make the fans happy." Scotty tossed a stack of pamphlets on a table near the front of the room—most likely containing blackjack rules. "Study up if you don't already know how."

It had been another rough practice. For a while, I'd thought Scotty was going to put us through a bag skate, kind of like that famous scene in the movie Miracle. I don't think bag skates ever have the sort of effect the movie tried to make you believe they could. At least none of the ones I'd ever been through had. Pretty much they just wear you out and piss you off. They're not really a way to bring a team together, but that doesn't stop coaches from thinking maybe this time it will.

It was too late in the season for that kind of thing, anyway. That's an early-to-mid-season trick coaches pull when teams aren't performing on the ice. With just a little over a week left in the season, it wouldn't make a ton of sense. But then again, it felt like Scotty was grasping at straws. It'd been a rough first year on the job for him, and it wasn't getting any easier.

Scotty cleared out of the dressing room, and the other coaches followed after him. They didn't seem to want to hear the groans coming from the guys. I couldn't blame the coaching staff for that. We'd been on a skid, lately, and the last thing some of the boys wanted to do was dress up and play nice for people. Yeah, it was for charity. It was for a good cause. But the timing was awful.

I made a mental note to talk to Jim Sutter about that sometime after we were done for the year. It would make a hell of a lot more sense to do the big charity events earlier in the season, when we weren't so beat up and broken down, sometime when we didn't need to conserve every spare bit of energy we could for a big push to the end.

Babs looked over at the stack of pamphlets Scotty had put on the table and sat down on the bench beside me. He started taking off his skates. "I've never played blackjack before. Don't have a fucking clue."

"You don't have to play blackjack," I said. "You just have to learn how to deal. It's easy. Besides, the people coming are there more to see and talk to us than they are to really play the games. Let 'em see your dimples, and you'll have the most popular table."

He looked at me like I'd lost my mind. One of these days, the kid would have a clue. For now, it wouldn't hurt anything for him to not understand his own appeal.

It was an annual event here with the Storm—our big fundraiser for the Storm Foundation. We all got dressed up and talked and schmoozed for the night, and in return people paid a lot of money for the opportunity to be there. There were other things going on during the course of the night, too: a silent auction with things like getting to go on a road trip with the team next year, a video game booth where they could compete against a few of the boys, that kind of thing. Babs was auctioning a day where a kid could take him to school instead of the prom date we'd tried to talk him into. And of course, there was plenty of food and drink for everyone.

I usually enjoyed myself at these things. They were a good way to interact with the fans and just be normal for a change, to have real conversations and not feel like we had to recite from a script of appropriate responses.

No pressure. At least not for me.

"Maybe we should practice tonight," Babs said. "Dealing."

"Yeah. Soupy can probably teach us both a thing or two." That'd be something we could do to all hang out together, me, Soupy, and Dayana. And Babs, too.

I'd been trying to find things to do where Dayana and I weren't always kicking Soupy out so we could be alone. It hadn't been easy.

"You mean maybe I can kick both your asses, right?" Soupy sat down across from us, getting out of his sweaty gear. "And the answer is yes, I can."

I'd let him have that one, for now. It felt more normal than things between us had been lately. "I need to make a stop before we go home, though."

We finished cleaning up, and the three of us headed out to my car. Laura Weber had told me about Dayana's dress for tomorrow night. I wanted to get her some jewelry to go with it. Nothing too elaborate or flashy. She'd never wear something like that.

Something simple. Classic.

For some reason, I kept thinking about a cheap vending machine locket I'd given her when we were kids. I had been hoping to get an egg with gum in it but instead I got the locket. I had no clue what I going to do with something like that, so I put a picture of a hockey goal in it and gave it to her.

But she'd worn it for years.

I figured it had finally fallen apart at some point. It was just cheap plastic. It wasn't designed for that kind of use.

I could get her one that was, though.

DAYANA

Once I'd put on a bit of lip gloss and mascara—Laura had insisted I had to at least wear that much since Casino Night is essentially a red-carpet event—I tugged down on the bottom of my skirt. That didn't really help it cover any more leg, though, and it made me feel like I was going to bust out of the top at any moment. I tugged the bodice up again, cursed Laura and Sara, and then made my way downstairs.

All three of the guys were waiting for me in the living room, dressed to perfection, when I got there. Seeing three good-looking men in tuxes isn't an everyday occurrence—not when you're surrounded by hockey players. Yeah, they wore suits to travel and all, but this was something else entirely. I did a double take.

Babs gave me a sheepish grin but quickly turned his head away.

I couldn't make myself look at Brenden. Not while I was dressed like this. I didn't want to see the dissatisfied, overprotective brother look I knew he'd have on his face. With the recent brief road trips the team had been on, he'd become more of a grouch than ever when it came to the time I was spending alone with Eric.

It couldn't be easy for him. He had always been my protector, the one who kept me safe except for that one time when he wasn't there. I knew he blamed himself, in much the same way Eric did, even though neither of them were to blame. Now the responsibility he'd taken on himself was passing to someone else, at least for the time being. And in some small way, he thought he needed to protect me from Eric.

None of that touched on how it must feel as though I was stealing his best friend away from him.

I wanted to tell him it was only for a little while longer, another week or so. Once I went back to Providence, he could have his best friend back. I'd be at home nursing my broken heart. Things could go back to normal for him, and he could pretend that this had never happened.

But he didn't want me to tell him those things. Brenden would rather sulk and glare and make sure everyone knew how unhappy he was about certain things. I couldn't very well deny him of the opportunity to do that.

Eric pulled me into his arms as soon as I was within his reach. I had already started feeling those anticipatory shivers I always got around him well before I came downstairs, and they only intensified once I was near him. They seemed to never stop these days. After that night in Phoenix, I was always anxious to be with him, to touch him and explore, to let him touch me. We hadn't had another night quite like that one since—the Storm had hit another rough skid, and I had been almost as busy as he was with helping to prepare for the players' wives' St. Patrick's Day event and a few other similar things for tonight.

At least that was all nearly complete. The raffle had been a resounding success at the game two nights ago, even though the Storm lost on the ice. And after tonight, we'd be able to put Casino Night behind us. Then our focus would be strictly on getting the guys through the final push toward the playoffs.

It felt good to have a moment to just be in his arms. I rested my hands on the outsides of his rib cage, delighting in the sensation of the smooth tuxedo jacket beneath my fingertips.

He held me for a minute, his strong arms making me feel warm and treasured, and he pressed a kiss to my temple. "You look beautiful."

I opened my mouth to deny what he'd said but stopped myself before I did. "Thank you." It shouldn't be so hard to hear those words. To believe them. I never used to have a hard time with it, if Dad or Brenden or Mom would tell me. It was just one of many things that had changed for me, like a switch that had been flipped.

He was helping me discover a means to flip it back the other way. It was getting easier, but I didn't know if it would ever feel normal again, if it would ever feel okay.

Eric released me but reached down for my hand. I thought we would be leaving, but instead of leading me toward the garage, he took me into the kitchen. A long, narrow black box was on the bar, with a thin blue ribbon tied around it.

I wanted to back away. He'd already given up so much for me, given me more than he should have. I couldn't accept jewelry from him. I was nearly panicking, almost couldn't breathe, and just because of a gift he was giving me.

It didn't make sense. He'd spent more than just a little bit of money on me in the five weeks I'd been here. He'd paid for all my expenses, bought me the dress and shoes I was wearing. He'd paid for everything, and I'd let him. If I could allow all that, what was so different about a piece of jewelry?

His hand squeezed mine, and he reached for the box with his other. He held it out to me. "Laura told me you'd be in blue."

The urge to shake my head, to tell him I couldn't take anything like that from him, was almost overwhelming. All I wanted to do was race back up the stairs, change into my yoga pants and T-shirt, and stay home with a book with my door locked.

"Just open it, Dayana," Brenden said.

I swallowed and took the box. After removing the ribbon, I flipped open the lid. It was just a simple chain, white gold with a few small sapphires and diamonds. It couldn't have been more uncomplicated, more delicate, more elegant.

"I thought it suited you," Eric said quietly. He took it out of the box and moved behind me. I felt his fingers brush my hair to the side. Then he draped the chain around my neck, and I stopped breathing. He fastened it behind me and kissed the top of my shoulder. "They didn't have a locket."

It was just hanging there around my neck, but I felt like it was clawing into me, strangling me. I reached up, grabbed it, tried to rip it free from my neck.

Strong arms came around me, trapping mine against my chest. "It's okay. I've got you."

"Take it off." I tried to pull my arms free, stretched my hands to reach it, but he shifted his grip and trapped my hands. "No," I said, frantic, crying. "Take it off me. Let go."

"Fucking let her go." Another voice.

More hands on me.

"It's the necklace. Get the necklace off her."

"I said to let her the fuck go."

I kicked. Clawed. Had to get away.

They had my arms. Hands at my neck, near my face.

I got a hand free. Made a fist, pulled my arm back. Punched like Jonny had taught me. Kept my wrist straight. Put as much force into it as I could.

"Shit, Dee."

I swung again. They caught my arm.

"It's off. Dayana, it's off."

This couldn't happen. Not again.

I squirmed, kicked. Fought until I didn't have any more fight. Couldn't stop crying. Couldn't breathe.

But then it was Eric's voice I heard in my ear. "I have you. I won't let go. No one's going to hurt you." Soft. Soothing. Over and over.

I collapsed against him, exhausted.

He carried me to the sofa, sat down with me in his arms, and he held me.

My breathing slowly leveled out, and my heartbeat became more normal, less erratic.

"I'm sorry," I said once I could speak again.

"Shh." Eric stroked my hair, kissed my temple. "No apologies."

Brenden cleared his throat behind us. "Dayana?" He sounded scared.

He hadn't seen me have an attack like that in years. No wonder he sounded scared.

I was scared, too. I hadn't felt quite like that—like I was back in that dirty janitor's closet, about to be raped—ever, other than that one time. Not until now.

I turned my head to him.

He held out a damp cloth. His hand was shaking.

In the kitchen, Babs was putting ice in a zipper bag. His eye was red and swollen.

"Oh, God." I'd never hurt anyone before. No one but myself.

"Take it. Your face—you have mascara running."

I took the cloth and wiped it over my face. When I pulled it away, Babs handed me a bag of ice and sat down in one of the recliners across from us holding another one to his eye.

"For your hand," he said. "You've got a mean right hook, Dee. Jonny'll be proud."

I wasn't proud. I felt sick to my stomach.

Eric kept running his hands over my arms, my hair, soothing me. "I usually know what brings them on," he said a minute later. "Your panic attacks. I can feel them coming. I didn't see this one until it was too late, and I still don't know what triggered it."

Brenden sat down too, his eyes on me.

I shook my head. "Don't we have to go? You'll be late."

"Then we'll be late," Babs said.

Even he was joining in this time, ganging up on me. There was no getting out of this one. No escaping it.

I swallowed, took a breath. "So, I guess you remember the locket you gave me..."

"You know I do, kid," Eric said, confirming it again even though I already knew it. He linked his fingers with mine and rubbed the pad of his thumb over the back of my hand. But he'd called me kid again, painfully reminding me of the rift that would always be between us.

I steeled myself against that pain and forced myself to plow through a different form of it. "I always took it off when I played. It got tangled in my hair and screwed with my focus. I would take it off and leave it inside the boards at the bench, with the water bottles and all. I forgot it that day. I didn't want to leave it behind. I'd never see it again if I did. So I went back for it before we got to the dressing room."

He didn't say anything, just kept rubbing my hand with his thumb. I looked away.

His lips came down, kissed me on the temple. I wanted to stay just like that, never move.

My hand hurt more than I'd realized earlier. I guess the adrenaline coursing through me after my panic attack had dulled it a lot, made it so I didn't realize just how bad it was. I flexed it while I watched the guys working their tables.

Eric was talking with the group sitting with him, smiling and laughing and doing all the things he was supposed to do, but I could tell he was distracted. His gaze kept flashing over to me at the little table Laura had snagged for the two of us and Sara. I tried to smile and reassure him, but there was only so much reassuring I could do from this distance.

A few tables over from him, buried in the middle of the crowd, Brenden was in his element. I knew he'd been pretty shaken up by what he'd witnessed, but dealing blackjack and talking up season ticket holders was right up his alley. He'd always been confident and comfortable at these types of events. They brought out the best of his personality. It was good to see him shaking off some of the negativity he'd been carrying around since his arrival in Portland—seeing him looking more like himself.

But it was Babs who kept drawing my attention tonight. His eye was red and swollen where I'd punched him, and that only seemed to draw the women in around him even more than his dimples normally would. His table was easily the most popular in the room, constantly full, pretty much entirely of young women who were flirting with him like crazy. He couldn't stop himself from smiling, but I knew it was embarrassment fueling the smile. He was too adorable for his own good, and the black eye he'd be sporting to finish off the regular season had only added to his appeal. It gave him a little bit of a bad boy vibe, even though that couldn't be further from the truth. Made him seem a little mysterious.

It was probably a good thing tonight was a school night and Katie Weber had been left at home with her younger siblings and a pile of homework.

A waiter was passing by us with a tray filled with wine glasses, and Laura waved him over. She handed him her empty and took a new glass. Sara did the same, but I shook my head.

"I've had all I can handle." With more than just alcohol. For the last half hour or so, the three of us had been hashing out the final plans for when I would leave. I didn't think I could face Eric, or really any of the guys, once they knew I was actually going to go. It would hurt too much despite the fact that I knew it was the right thing to do.

Eric still saw me as Brenden's kid sister. Earlier tonight had proven it.

"Spoilsport," Laura teased. She reached over and got another glass from him before he walked off. "Just in case."

I laughed. "Is that for me or for you?"

She shrugged.

Sara leaned over and set her glass down on the table. "Are you really sure about this?"

They both thought I was crazy. They were convinced that Eric loved me as much as I loved him, that he wasn't just playing the part and doing me a favor because I was Brenden's kid sister.

I knew better. "I'm sure." I couldn't deny that our relationship had changed, but the type of change I wanted was impossible. It was too much to expect of him.

"Surely they could extend your leave a little longer, though," Laura objected.

We all knew there was an expiration date for this arrangement. I'd changed my flight to a few days sooner than it was initially scheduled. It wasn't about my leave coming to an end. Not so much. There was only so much time I could afford to take off work, only so much time I could afford not to be earning my salary. Only so much time I could afford to fall deeper and deeper in love with Eric each day.

I had to cut the strings before I couldn't make myself do it.

"I've got to get back home. Back to my job, my apartment. Back to my life." I gave them a little smile, even though smiling was the last thing I felt like doing. "I'll stay in touch with you, though. Both of you."

The thought of getting through my heartache without at least being able to call them and talk was more than I could bear.

Laura finished off the first of her two glasses of wine. She frowned at me. "You're really not going to let us talk you out of this?"

I shook my head.

"Okay." Sara reached over, took my hand, and squeezed it. "I'll take you to the airport that day. But I'll be really pissed at you the whole time."

And I loved her for it.

Chapter 17 - Breakaway

- -

ERIC

We beat Nashville the night after Casino Night, but we'd let them push us into overtime to get there. They came out of it with a point, meaning we were tied with them in the standings. Again. We held the tiebreaker against them at this point, but the positioning and tiebreakers were changing daily.

Every night, back at the house, no matter what else was going on, we'd been turning on NHL Network and seeing what the scoreboards looked like. Soupy, Babs, Dayana, and I spent an awful lot of time watching that to see how things were shaking out.

It didn't ever make us feel any better about our position, any more comfortable. We couldn't seem to stop ourselves from doing it, though. Scoreboard watching gets to be an everyday part of life at this time of the season, especially if you're a fringe team like the Storm has been the last few years.

We had four games left in this last week of the season, two on the road, and then a back-to-back at home. Just this afternoon we'd flown into Los Angeles and got set up in our hotel. We'd be playing the Kings tomorrow and Anaheim two days after that. If there were any positives to take from playing against those two teams, it was that we didn't have to travel between those games. All of the games we had left would be in the same time zone, too. That should help with jet lag, if nothing else. Every bit of rest we could get was priceless right now. It could give us the advantage we needed to finish out the season strong and get into the playoffs.

After we got settled in our rooms, I'd gone out to dinner with the boys. Soupy and I both tried to get Dayana to come with us, but she said she wasn't up to a night out and she'd rather just stay in, order room service.

I hadn't pushed her. That last panic attack she'd had, when I'd given her the necklace, had taken a lot out of her.

Out of all of us, actually.

It hadn't just been panic. She'd felt like she was about to be raped again. Three big men surrounding her, me keeping her arms trapped, Babs and Soupy trying to get the necklace off—it didn't take a lot of imagination to understand how that must have been for her considering she was already in a panicked state. Not now, looking back at it.

We should have realized it at the time. All three of us had just been so focused on calming her down, getting the necklace off her, that it never crossed our minds.

This time, she seemed more than just exhausted afterward, though. She seemed really down. Depressed.

She'd talked to Laura and Sara quite a bit over the last few days. That had been helping, but we had to leave for this last road trip of the year.

I'd almost suggested she stay behind, spend some more time with the girls. Almost. We were only going to be gone a few days. I couldn't bring myself to do that, though. Maybe it was selfish, but I wanted her to be with me. Wanted to hold her as much as I could, try to soothe away her demons. Give her new memories to help wash away the old.

I didn't let myself think about how it would be next season, once she wasn't traveling with the team anymore. Jim and the coaching staff had been great about allowing her to come with us this year. That couldn't continue forever. Wives and girlfriends don't usually get to go with the team. Eventually, I'd have to start leaving her behind, but hopefully not until next season. She had plans to fly home in about a week, but I was determined to talk her out of it as soon as we finished the season.

The thought of leaving her at home when I was gone for road trips irked me more than it should. I'd never had a problem with leaving Kim behind. The other guys managed it with no problem.

I'd have to learn to deal with it.

After dinner, a bunch of the guys went out to a bar. Babs wasn't old enough to go, and with Razor back home with his injury, he didn't have anyone else to stay behind with him, so Soupy and I went back to the hotel with him. I wasn't really in the mood to drink tonight. There were way too many things on my mind for that.

Webs finished up a call on his cell and followed us out of the restaurant. He was scowling when he caught up to us. "Laura just gave Katie permission to go to prom with some dipshit I've never met. She didn't think it was necessary to talk to me about it first."

I didn't envy him, having a teenaged daughter who was a knockout like Katie was. It had to be hell on his nerves.

"How do you know he's a dipshit if you've never met him?" Babs seemed genuinely perplexed.

That only made Webs scowl even more than before, this time aiming a glare squarely in the kid's direction. "If he has the nerve to even fucking look at my little girl, he's a dipshit. Keep that in mind."

Babs shut up pretty quickly after that, staring down at his feet and trying to stay a few paces ahead of Webs.

I couldn't decide which one of them I pitied more. Probably Babs. I knew all too well what it was like to fall for a girl too soon, when you couldn't do anything about it yet.

For his sake, I hoped he wouldn't have to wait as long as I had.

After a minute, Webs caught up to him, grabbed him from behind, and gave him a noogie.

We stopped at the coffee shop in the hotel lobby and got beverages of the nonalcoholic variety. Then we went up to Webs's room for a while. As long as Webs wasn't thinking about Katie, he went a little easier on Babs, joked around with him. He really did like the kid. Everyone did. It would be pretty damn hard not to.

We talked a while and watched the season opener of Game of Thrones. But it was getting late. I was tired.

And I wanted to see Dayana.

I excused myself, leaving the other three to their own devices. I tried not to notice the look Soupy gave me when I left. I couldn't help it, though. He knew where I was going. What I was doing.

I knew he didn't like it any better than Webs liked having dipshits looking at his daughter and taking her to prom. It didn't help much that he liked me, just like it didn't help Webs much that he liked Babs.

When I got up to my room, Dayana had left the door connecting our rooms open. The lights in her room were low. I didn't hear anything coming from her side.

I knocked on the open door and poked my head in. She was already in her pj's. Her hair was pulled back in a messy ponytail, and she was lounging in bed with a single lamp on, reading a book on her e-reader.

She was smiling when she looked up at me. "Did you have a good time with the boys?" She set the e-reader aside on the nightstand and pulled her knees up to her chest.

I don't know if I'd ever seen anything so sexy. She'd looked amazing in that little blue dress the other night, and the shoes had made her already-stunning legs look so long and perfect that I'd had a hard time not thinking about having them wrapped around me.

But like this? She'd had that same T-shirt for probably a decade. It was an old castoff from Soupy, one he'd outgrown and was going to give to Goodwill until she'd snagged it for herself. It looked ridiculous on her, almost as ridiculous as her wild hair. Her yoga pants had seen better days...but not in a very long time.

"Yeah," I said when I was able to regroup. "Katie Weber apparently has a prom date."

She grinned, a mischievous glint in her eyes. "Babs?"

"Nah. Someone Webs doesn't know."

Dayana scooted over on the bed, making room for me. "How did Babs take it?"

"Better than Webs did."

She laughed. I loved the sound of her laugh.

"Come sit with me."

I took my jacket off and went to put it on the armoire in my room. I pulled my tie loose and toed my shoes off. When I came back and sat beside her, she let me put my arm around her and pull her into my side. She leaned her head back against my shoulder. A couple of the hairs sticking up from her haphazard ponytail tickled my chin, and I brushed them aside.

"What did you do tonight?"

"Not much." She snuggled closer, letting her hand rest on the top of my thigh. "I ordered a soup and salad and watched the news. I've been reading ever since."

"Good book?" I tried not to think about where she was touching me, how I wanted her to touch me. I'd made it a point to let her initiate any touching since her last attack. That was much easier said than done.

"Re-reading Harry Potter."

Now it was my turn to laugh. "You have to have read them all at least a dozen times."

"Probably closer to twenty."

That was so typical of Dayana. When she found something she loved—really, truly loved—she couldn't get enough of it. She grabbed on and wouldn't let go.

"Which one this time?"

"Prisoner of Azkaban. It was the best of all the books."

"And Goblet of Fire is the best of the movies," I said before she could. We'd had this conversation a few times. I didn't mind having it again.

"Exactly." She twisted her head around to look at me. She was smiling. I wanted to capture that smile and hold onto it forever.

I couldn't help myself. I stole a kiss.

Dayana melted into me even more than she already had been.

I could hold her forever and never get tired of the feel of her.

"Will you do something for me?" she asked. She sounded unsure, like she thought I might say no.

Didn't she know by now I'd do anything for her, give her anything I could?

"Of course," I said.

"I..." She looked so damn adorable with her bashfulness. "Will you sleep with me tonight?" Her blush was so intense it was going to drive me crazy. "I mean, stay with me. In my bed. Hold me, not—"

I put my finger on her lips, stopping her. "I know what you mean."

I knew very well what she wanted of me. I wanted it, too, but it would take a hell of a lot of restraint on my part. But that was my problem, not hers.

"Are you sure you're ready for that?" I asked.

"No. But how can I know until I try?"

I had to admire her courage. That had been her mindset through everything we'd done together these last weeks.

"Okay," I said. After all, I'd already admitted it to myself: I couldn't deny her anything.

DAYANA

I still didn't know where I'd gotten the guts to ask him to stay with me.

I'd been thinking about it for days. There weren't many more nights before I would be getting on a plane alone and flying back to Providence. I wanted to push myself, see if I could handle intimacy like that.

On a purely selfish level, I wanted to experience it with Eric, if I would ever be able to experience it with anyone.

After holding me for a while, kissing me here and there, but mainly just being together, Eric had gotten up and gone into his room to change. When he came back through the open doorway, my breath caught.

He didn't have anything on but a pair of boxer briefs. He was hard beneath them.

That scared me a little, but it was Eric. There was no reason to be afraid of him.

It was odd to see him so close to naked, though.

Eric wasn't one to go around partially undressed—at least not around me. I'd seen him plenty of times in workout clothes, T-shirts and shorts or athletic pants. Unless he was doing something active, he almost never went without at least jeans and a shirt of some kind or another. The other night, when he'd helped me to experience an orgasm, was the first time in a long time I could remember seeing his bare chest.

And it was a stunning chest.

But his legs were what had really caught my eye now. He had skater's legs, built with big, strong, powerful thighs. Back in my playing days, I'd had problems finding pants that fit me properly because of the size of my thighs and butt. I had no doubt that Eric had to have his pants custom-made. There was no way he could buy them off the shelf with thighs like that.

"You're still sure?" he asked. He'd been so patient with me. This whole time, he'd been far more patient than I'd ever imagined anyone could be.

I nodded. "If you are."

He let out a grunting sound that I couldn't have interpreted if I tried. But he came over to the bed and lifted the covers. He didn't get in. "Is this okay? Me sleeping like this? I can go put on something more if you—"

"It's fine." I didn't know how easily I'd be able to fall asleep with him next to me and so close to being nude. But then again, I didn't know how easily I'd be able to fall asleep with him next to me at all.

He still didn't get in the bed, so I scooted over a little further, giving him more space. The longer he just stood there, the more I studied him, and the more flutters I felt.

I shouldn't be this nervous just to have him in bed with me. Eric would never do anything I didn't want. He wouldn't touch me in ways I couldn't handle. He would always protect me, even from myself.

I knew that.

It wasn't fear that was causing the nerves. It was anticipation.

But he still hadn't gotten into bed. He hadn't even sat down on the edge.

I was asking too much of him again. Damn it.

"You don't have to do this, Eric." I rolled over so I wasn't facing him anymore. I didn't want him to see my disappointment, my hurt. I hadn't even left him yet, and the heartache was already starting, building, ready to overwhelm me. This was going to be hell.

"Please don't turn away from me."

"No, it's—" My voice cracked. If I wasn't careful, I would start crying. Crying could come later, once I was on the plane, or better yet, once I was back in Providence. Not now. I wanted to enjoy every moment I had left with him. I took a breath, steadied my nerves. "Really, you don't have to. I'm sorry. I shouldn't have asked."

The bed dipped behind me when he sat. He brushed the hair away from my face, kissed me on the cheek. "I didn't mean to upset you. And I want to sleep with you. More than I should." His hand stroked slowly down my arm. "The problem is I want too much. I have to hold myself back with you."

I knew all about wanting too much.

I stayed still while he settled himself beside me. He stretched out and filled the length of the bed, the heat of his body warming the entire back of mine.

"Can I hold you?"

I nodded. I didn't trust myself to speak without starting to cry. It was ridiculous, how emotional I was already feeling about all of this.

But he was going to give me this one last gift.

His arm, strong and sure, came around my waist and pulled me back against him. My knees bent around his and my hips curled back into him. I put my arm over his, and he laced his fingers with mine when they met.

I could feel his erection pressing against my butt.

"Is this all right?" I felt the words by my ear more than I heard them.

"Are you sure you want to do this?" I asked.

He shifted just a bit against me. "Positive."

I figured it was better not to question him anymore.

I lay still, listening to the sound of his breathing, feeling the beat of his heart against my back. His was as erratic as mine. The longer we lay like that, the more they slowed, calmed, came together like a single heartbeat.

He started snoring—very lightly, hardly more than deep breathing—and I let the rhythm of it lull me to sleep.

ERIC

It was still pitch black when I woke up. At first, I wasn't sure why I woke, but then I realized Dayana was jerking around in her sleep, making strange noises.

"Dayana?" I pulled her closer to me, hugging her body against mine.

She'd turned around in her sleep so she was facing me. Her breasts were pressed tight against my chest, her arms wrapped snugly around my waist, holding me as close as I was holding her.

But she stilled again, calmed down. I held her close until I was sure she was sleeping and still. I stroked my hands over her back, soothing her.

Soothing myself.

I kissed her forehead just before I fell asleep again.

DAYANA

The Storm managed to scrape out a win against Los Angeles. Things didn't go so well against Anaheim. The Ducks got a lead two minutes into the game, and their goaltender stood on his head the rest of the night. They beat the Storm one to nothing. Portland was the better team the whole night, apart than that goaltender.

He took home a shutout. The Storm took home nothing.

Still, those two points from beating Los Angeles were somehow enough to keep them in the playoff race. Three teams were still vying for that final playoff spot: Portland, Nashville, and Dallas. With each team only having a game or two left, they all had a legitimate shot.

Eric's stress only continued to mount with each game. He still hadn't pulled out of his scoring slump yet. Against Anaheim, he put up seven shots on goal against the Ducks' goaltender. Those were just the ones that got through the bodies in front of the net. He had another that hit the pipe and at least three more that got blocked by diving defensemen. At one point in the third period, he got so frustrated that he smashed his stick against the glass.

I wished there was something I could do to ease his stress. But he didn't want to talk about it. All he wanted to do was hold me, touch me. Be with me.

Both nights we were in the hotel in Los Angeles, Eric had slept in my bed with me. He'd held me close to him, his arms wrapped around me keeping me secure. Protected. Sometimes, I'd wake up in the night and feel his erection pressing into my belly or my butt. He never acted on it, though. He couldn't deny it was there, but it was like he'd been trying to ignore it.

I couldn't ignore it. I was fascinated by it. I'd been scared at first, when I saw that he was aroused that night. Ever since I'd been raped, I'd equated a man's arousal with all the awful and horrible things that had happened in my life.

That was starting to change for me, though. He'd helped me learn that my own arousal wasn't something to be feared but to be enjoyed. And this was Eric. Not a stranger. Not someone who intended to hurt me.

I couldn't delude myself into thinking that his arousal meant anything more than that he had been turned on. Not that he loved me. I supposed it was only natural for him to feel some arousal when he was sleeping in a bed with a woman pulled up against him. It wasn't because it was me.

A couple of times when I'd woken up, he'd been awake, too...looking at me. We would spend a few minutes kissing, almost lazily even though it was exciting. One time, while he was kissing me, he'd slid his hands up my torso, over my T-shirt, stopping just below my breasts. With his thumbs, he'd traced the lower curve of my breasts, teasing me like that until I arched up into him, nearly desperate for more.

That was as far as he took it that night. I wanted more, but I wasn't sure yet how much more.

When we got back to Portland, everything was different again. I had my room; he had his. Brenden was next door to me. Babs was downstairs.

It was about one in the morning when we got home, and everyone was tired. We all just went to bed—to our own beds.

And now, I only had two more days.

Chapter 18 - Breakaway

D AYANA

The Winnipeg Jets were up two to nothing, and it was only about halfway through the first period. There weren't many ways the beginning of the game could have been worse, at least from the Storm's perspective. They'd had defensive miscues right and left, hadn't been able to put out any kind of sustained offensive attack, and just generally looked like they were still warming up instead of playing the actual game.

At the moment, Eric was out on the ice with Brenden and David Weber as his wings. Babs would normally be playing with Eric and Brenden, at least lately, but he'd taken a high stick from Evander Kane a couple of minutes ago. He'd had to go back to the trainer's room to be stitched up. The refs completely missed it even with the blood coming from Babs's lip, so the Storm hadn't gotten a power play out of it like they should have.

Webs stole the puck from the Jets with a poke check at the blue line. Eric and Brenden started streaking up the ice immediately, and Webs got a pass through to Brenden's waiting stick. They'd caught the Jets defense pinching and had a three-on-one going. Brenden faked a shot and passed it to Eric, who was barreling straight down the center of the ice with his stick up for a one-timer. The one Jets defender flattened himself on the ice to block it, but he was in better position to prevent another pass than to block a shot.

Eric shanked the shot. The puck trickled in on net. The goaltender snatched it up easily in his glove and held on for the whistle.

The light over the penalty box came on, signaling a TV time-out. While Eric and the guys skated over to the bench, I leaned back in my seat.

"That was the best look he's had in a while," Laura said.

I shook my head. Not that I disagreed with her. "He's squeezing his stick. He's putting too much pressure on himself. It's all in his head." I just wished I could somehow help Eric ease his frustrations.

Even as I said it, Mattias Bergstrom was saying something over Eric's shoulder from behind him on the bench. Within seconds, Eric was on his feet and had spun around, getting right up in Bergy's face. They were yelling at each other, screaming. I was sure that the fans in the lowest ten rows or so of the arena had to be hearing every profanity-laced word from both their mouths.

Scotty just let them go at each other. He didn't do anything to intervene. After a minute, the other assistant coach tried to put himself between them, putting his hands on Bergy's chest and pushing him back away from Eric.

That didn't stop Eric. It didn't come close to calming him down. He just stepped over the bench and followed them. If someone didn't hold him back, he was going to hit Bergy. I could feel it all the way from the owner's box.

The ice crew was almost finished cleaning the surface during the TV time-out. They'd be back on the air any second, and then the whole world would see Eric losing it. Sure enough, the light over the penalty box went off, and Eric and Bergy were still going at each other with Hammer trying to separate them.

The puck dropped, and the game was underway again, but those three were oblivious to the action on the ice. I had no doubt that at least one of the TV cameras, and probably more, were focused on the fight behind the bench. It would be all over the hockey news tonight—maybe for a week or longer, depending on the outcome of the fight.

I wished I could be down there. To help calm him. To talk some sense into him. I had no idea what Bergy had said to him, but I had no doubt it was meant to help, not to hurt. Out of all the coaches on this team, Bergy really got Eric, understood what made him tick. Eric wouldn't necessarily agree with that, but it was more because Bergy tended to push all his buttons. I figured it came from all the years they'd played against each other.

A minute later, while Eric was still trying to get around Hammer so he could rip Bergy's throat out, Babs came back through the tunnel to the bench. Instead of sitting down, he grabbed a fistful of Eric's jersey from the back and pulled. Eric nearly lost his balance. He fell back onto the bench. For a second, I thought Eric might hit Babs. He didn't, though. He just turned around and faced the right direction, his glare visible all the way from in the owner's box.

A few minutes later, their line was back out on the ice for a face-off deep in their defensive zone to Nicklas Ericsson's left. Babs took his usual spot on the right wing instead of Webs.

Eric battled for the puck but only managed to tie up the Jets center's stick. Babs and Brenden both crashed into the face-off circle, and Babs somehow came out of the scrum with the puck. He sent it back to Burnzie, and in no time they were making their way up the ice as a five-man unit. Babs was streaking past the Jets defense. His speed forced the defender to hook him.

The referee raised his arm, signaling the delayed penalty.

Nicky Ericsson skated to the bench so the Storm could put an extra skater out. Jere Koskinen dove over the boards and joined the rush. He got the puck and slid it to Brenden, who was just outside the crease. Brenden shot it from in tight, but the Jets goaltender got over just in time with a kick save. The rebound bounced straight to the tape on Eric's stick.

He didn't shank it this time.

The goal horn sounded. Red lights flashed.

The team had gotten themselves back in the game.

Eric had finally gotten out of his slump.

"Maybe Bergy should have ripped Zee a new one a couple of weeks ago," Sara said beside me. "I'm sure that's what Daddy'll say."

Maybe he should have.

ERIC

Bergy tipped his chin up at me from across the locker room. I couldn't guess what that look was supposed to mean. I told you so? Nice job? No clue. I didn't respond.

I was still pissed at him for telling me I wasn't acting like a leader, even if it had resulted in me getting a hat trick. That maybe Jonny or Webs or Soupy or even Babs should have the captain's C on his chest, not me.

That was the second time in just a few short weeks he'd questioned my leadership. The first time, he might have had a point. But I'd been focusing on the team lately, doing all the things a leader should do.

I was still fuming when Soupy came over and sat down next to me. "Babs and I are going out with a few of the boys. You coming?"

This was the first time in a long time that he'd sought me out, invited me to do something with him. The first time he'd made the effort, initiated anything. It had been all me, lately, trying to salvage whatever friendship we still had. With the mood I was in, I didn't want to hang out with the guys, though. I didn't feel like having a good time. I just wanted to rest, to go home and get my head screwed back on straight for tomorrow.

We won the game tonight, but there was still one more to go. Tomorrow night, the St. Louis Blues were coming into our building. After all of the other games today, the Storm were sitting in a unique position. If we won tomorrow's game, we'd be in. Lose it and more than likely we would be out. Both Nashville and Dallas played tomorrow, too, and we held the tiebreakers over them, but it didn't seem too likely that they would both lose their games. Dallas was playing the worst team in the league at home, and Nashville had been on a serious roll the last couple of weeks of the season.

And us? The Blues had already cemented their place in the playoffs, but they were fighting with San Jose for the number-one seed. They wanted that for home-ice advantage, so there was no way they would roll over and let us have an easy win.

It would be a battle. I had to be ready for it.

"Nah," I said after a minute. I put my tie under my collar and knotted it. "I'm going home."

Soupy nodded. "I'll take Babs with me. Let him show off his new scar. The girls will go fucking crazy over him now."

Like they didn't already go crazy over him. I chuckled, but my heart wasn't in it. "Yeah. See ya."

It was only after they left that I realized Soupy was making it possible for me and Dayana to be alone for a while tonight.

I went up to the box to get her. She was sitting and talking with Laura and Sara, just like I'd come to expect. When she saw me, she smiled.

I reached for her hand, and she crossed over to me and took it.

"See you tomorrow," Sara called out as we left.

Dayana didn't say anything.

We didn't talk the whole way home. It wasn't an uncomfortable sort of silence. More like she was just giving me some time to cool off. I didn't want to take my anger out on her, so I was glad for the time to just sit. To just be with her.

When we got back to my house, she let me pull her into my arms and hold her close. We'd hardly gotten inside first. Only a few steps into the kitchen, I hadn't been able to hold out any longer. I needed to feel her against me, to smell the cucumber-melon scent of her soap and feel her curves hugging my body.

She wrapped her arms around my waist and tucked her head in against my chest. There was nothing better for soothing my anger, for calming my temper, than to have Dayana in my arms.

Even when the turbulence that had been blowing through my veins had stopped, she didn't let me go. After a minute, I realized she was holding tighter to me than I had been to her, clinging to me and not letting me go.

I tipped her chin up so I could see her. Her eyes, those big, brown eyes that had always been able to slay me with a single look, were filled with giant crocodile tears.

I brushed away one tear just as it fell over to her cheek. "What's wrong?" I hated that I'd been so caught up in myself, in being pissed off at Bergy that I hadn't recognized she was upset.

Dayana shook her head. "It's nothing. I'm just being silly."

There wasn't anything silly about her. I swept her hair back from her forehead and kissed her temple. "Please? Tell me." I wanted to know, wanted to do whatever I could to make it better.

Instead of answering me, she stretched up on her tiptoes and kissed me.

I couldn't stop myself from groaning. It felt so good, the sensation of her body tight against me, her lips soft and sweet over mine. Her tongue came out, slowly but confidently, and licked across the line of my lips.

I opened for her, reveling in her new boldness, in her unhurried exploration. She let her tongue tangle with mine, sucking here and easing off there. Just as she was pulling away, she took my lower lip between her teeth and nipped it.

That nearly undid me. I picked her up, moved her against the wall for support. Her head fell back when I kissed her neck, let my tongue run over the rapid pounding of her pulse. I put my hands on her ribs, wanting to touch her more intimately but not sure if I should.

Her hands landed on my chest, and she arched into me. With a feather-light touch, she moved her hands over me, tracing the lines of my pecs and running up to feel my biceps. In all our touching, in all the times we had spent in her hotel room alone together, she'd hardly touched me. It felt like heaven, having her hands on me. Like the most exquisite torture. I couldn't stop myself from exploring her further, seeing how far she would allow me to go before she retreated.

I let one hand slide down her side to her waist, then lower, to her hip, then her upper thigh. She pulled closer to me, instinctively lifting her thigh up to meet my questing hand. I let my hand slide down all the way to her knee, pulled her closer. Too late, I wished I hadn't.

She hooked her leg around me, grinding herself against me with a whimper.

My cock was hard. Too hard. With Dayana in this position, I couldn't stop myself from thinking about pulling her other leg up to my waist, driving into her, making love to her long and hard and slow until she came. But I couldn't. Not yet.

Sometime over the summer, maybe—when I went back to visit my parents in Providence, when I could convince her to be my girlfriend for real and not just pretend to be, when I could make her see that no one should ever touch her but me.

For now, though, if I didn't get hold of myself soon, I might push her too far. Too soon.

She still wasn't ready for what I wanted. What I needed.

I could wait. I'd already waited seven years. My needs had to come second to hers.

I forced myself to let go of her leg. To stop kissing her so I could take a moment, calm down, slow my pulse. I rested my head and my hand on the wall, one on either side of her.

Her breathing was shallow—as shallow as mine. Light fingertips trailed over my jaw. "I...I'm sorry. I shouldn't have..."

The thought that she was apologizing to me when I'd nearly lost control of myself was more than I could take with my already-frayed nerves.

"Stop, Dayana. Would you fucking stop apologizing to me?"

She flinched.

Damn it, I didn't mean to scare her, to sound so angry. It wasn't her fault I was more in love with her than I could handle, that I wanted her more than I wanted to breathe. "I'm sorry. I'm just frustrated. I can't do this."

Her hands dropped to her sides, and she lowered her leg to the floor. I instantly wished she was still touching me, wrapped around me. With a tiny nod, she ducked under my arm and moved away.

DAYANA

"Dayana?" He sounded pained, but he couldn't hurt as much as I did. Not right now.

I kept walking, needing to put some space between us before I shattered into a thousand tiny pieces. I didn't stop until I got to the other side of the kitchen island. I needed something solid between us so I wouldn't rush back to him, try to convince him to touch me in ways he didn't want.

But I couldn't look at him. I couldn't look in his eyes and let him see how much it hurt to know he could never love me the way I loved him. I didn't even know for sure what I wanted, other than that I wanted to touch him, him to touch me. I wanted to be with him. I wanted to feel all the things he made me feel all at once, like a giant explosion of sensation. I wanted to love him. I wanted so much more than what we'd had together so far, and that just couldn't happen.

Some things he would never be able to do with Brenden's kid sister. I was the biggest idiot in the world for thinking he'd be able to get past that huge detail.

"I know you can't," I finally said. My voice was so quiet I could barely hear it. "I asked you for too much when I came out here. I just..." I couldn't tell him what I hadn't even admitted to myself yet. I pressed my eyes closed and tried to calm myself again. "I should go to bed."

I swallowed hard and headed for the stairs.

His hand caught mine from behind. "Don't go. Not yet."

My chest squeezed, and I tugged to free myself. I had to get away from him, upstairs and into my room where I could lock the door and he couldn't see me fall apart.

But he didn't let me go. He moved in behind me, putting both arms around my waist without releasing my hand. I felt so protected like that.

I didn't want to feel protected. Not by him. It was like he was trying to keep me in this giant protective bubble, because I was safe in there. And I was, but I wanted to test my limits. I wanted to see the world outside my bubble. I wanted more.

"There's nothing you could ask me for that I won't give you if I can." He pulled me closer until I could feel how hard he was. "Nothing, Dayana."

"I know." I believed him. How could I not? But I didn't think I was brave enough to ask him for what I wanted.

I knew he couldn't give it to me. I was Brenden's kid sister. It didn't matter that he'd been able to put that aside to kiss me, to touch me some. This was different.

"Don't go up yet."

If I didn't go upstairs right now, I might cross all sorts of lines that shouldn't be crossed between us. The thought of that scared me, almost as much as the thought of how much it would hurt to leave him tomorrow.

I didn't go up.

I leaned back against him, letting him support my weight. The thumb of his free hand grazed the underside of my breast, teasing me with the faint touch.

It felt so good, but it wasn't enough. I wasn't sure there would ever be such a thing as enough. I arched back, took his hand in the one I had free and moved it higher. His touch was whisper soft, barely there, but it was perfect. I couldn't stop myself from moaning.

"Should I stop?"

I shook my head.

He let go of the hand he was still holding and moved both of his to the top button of my blouse. When he released it, I shivered.

"Okay?" It was just a breath next to my ear.

"Yes." It was so much more than okay.

He undid one button after another, all the way down the front of my blouse, and pulled it free from the waistband of my jeans. It slipped off my shoulder, and he kissed me where it had been while sliding the sleeve off my arm.

"Okay?"

"Yes." I turned to face him, reaching up to undo his tie while he took my shirt all the way off.

His hand came down over mine, stopping me from what I was doing. "Not yet."

I didn't want to wait, though. I wanted to touch him, to make him feel even half what he made me feel. I wanted to feel his body pressed against mine and discover the taste of his skin. "Eric, let me touch you." I didn't even care that it sounded like I was begging. I'd never felt anything like what he made me feel.

He looked pained, with that crease forming between his eyebrows like it always did when he was frustrated. "I want too much." The words were strained, cracking. "I don't trust myself right now to be able to stop when you need me to."

"I don't want you to stop."

I shocked myself when I said it, but it was true. I didn't want him to stop. I wanted him to make love to me, to touch me in ways that no one had ever touched me, to help me wash away the memories once and for all and replace them with something beautiful. I wanted to know, before I left, that with the right man, I could experience the kind of intimacy I'd never imagined I could have. I wanted to know, without even the tiniest semblance of a doubt, that I wasn't broken. That I could have a sexual experience without falling to pieces.

I wanted to learn all of that, to experience all of those things with him.

Eric shook his head, swallowed so hard his Adam's apple bobbed visibly in his throat. He took a small step back. "You're not ready." He still had my shirt in his hand, hanging limply at his side.

If I wasn't ready now, I never would be. If I couldn't have sex with Eric, how could I ever let any other man touch me in such an intimate way?

"I know I've asked a lot of you—"

He stopped me with a finger over my lips. "There aren't many things in this world I want more than to make love to you. Than being inside you, showing you how good being touched can feel. Taking you to bed wouldn't be any kind of hardship. Not for me." He handed me my shirt. "But it could damage you more than I can handle. I can't live with having something like that on my shoulders."

He still didn't understand. There was nothing he could do to mess me up worse than I already was, to damage me more than I had been for years. "I know you won't hurt me," I said. "But you can help me heal."

The shirt fell through my fingers to the floor. I left it there, kept my eyes on Eric while I reached both hands behind my back and undid the clasp of my bra. The straps fell down my arms when I brought them in front of me again. His eyes followed the cups, and they stopped on my bared breasts.

The urge to cover myself under the intensity of his stare had me lifting my hands, but he reached out and stopped me.

I let my hands drop, and my bra fell to join my shirt on the floor. My pulse was like a jackhammer in my veins, my breathing rapid.

With his fingertips, he skimmed over my newly exposed skin, the gentle contact nothing more than a flutter. My nipples pebbled immediately, and he hadn't even touched them yet. I trembled.

"You're sure?"

"Yes."

"Hell."

/

Chapter 19 - Breakaway

E RIC

The last thing I needed was Soupy coming home and seeing us like this. I doubted they'd stay out too late with a game tomorrow. Especially since it was the most important game of the year. Everything was riding on it, the whole season. He and Babs could be back any time.

I picked up Dayana's shirt and bra from the floor and took her hand. I'd only gone up two stairs when I froze.

"You have to tell me if you want me to stop. It'll be hell for me, but I will."

She was even more aroused than she had been that night in the hotel, when she'd used the vibrator and had the most beautiful orgasm I'd ever witnessed. Her eyes were almost solid black, and she could hardly catch her breath.

"I don't want you to stop."

She was killing me. I'd barely touched her, not like I wanted to, not like she wanted me to. But she was ready. Holy shit.

"But if you change your mind. You have to tell me."

Stopping would kill me.

Pushing Dayana too far if she wasn't really, truly ready for it would be worse. I'd never be able to forgive myself. I'd never deserve forgiveness.

"I won't change my mind." She climbed the rest of the stairs, pulling me behind her.

I overtook her by the time we got to the top. I lifted her into my arms, and she wrapped hers around my shoulders with a sharp intake of breath. Somehow, I had to keep myself under control enough—keep her from shredding the last vestiges of my restraint—that I could take things slow. I wanted her first time—her real first time—to be good.

Better than good. I wanted it to be perfect.

Almost as much as that, I wanted our first time to be colossal.

This wasn't something I'd planned to do at the spur of the moment like this. I'd wanted to take time to make things just right for her. Time to be sure she was ready. Time to be sure I was ready for whatever reaction she might have.

She didn't want to take that time.

I'd never been nervous about sex. Not even my first time. I was sixteen and stupid, and all that mattered to me had been finding a way to get off. I didn't know how to help my girl have an orgasm. I didn't even know that she could. Back then I hadn't known enough to be nervous, and the girl hadn't mattered to me like Dayana did.

Right now, I was nervous as hell. Nothing mattered to me like Dayana.

I carried her into my bedroom and shut the door before setting her on her feet. She lifted up on her toes and kissed me, wrapping her arms around my neck and tightening her fingers in my hair. The hard peaks of her nipples pressed against my chest, driving me crazy even with my clothes in the way.

I broke off the kiss and backed away enough that I could remove my jacket and tie. She stepped out of her shoes, her eyes never leaving me. I couldn't look away from her, either. Her hands were at the zipper of her jeans.

She lowered them over her hips, and I nearly lost it. I don't think I'd ever gotten my clothes off so fast before.

Dayana still had her panties on, those white cotton briefs that should have been anything but sexy but drove me insane with need. With needing her. I still had my shorts on, but I couldn't wait. I had to touch her again. Her thumbs were already hooked into the band of her panties like she was going to take them off, and she was so breathless and perfect and flushed and beautiful.

I kissed her and put my hands over hers, stopping her from removing her panties. "Let me."

She gave me a little nod. Her eyes never left mine, trusting and needy all at once.

I pulled her toward me even as I walked her backward, edging her toward my bed. She moved up on the mattress, sat in the center with her knees bent in front of her. I sat beside her, facing her. I shifted a bit, but nothing would help the built-up ache in my balls. Nothing but being inside her.

Her hands were on me before I could get mine on her. Velvet-soft tickles, everywhere. All over my abs and chest and arms and thighs. I had to bite down on my tongue to keep from rushing her, to stop myself from tossing her onto her back and forgetting everything I'd ever promised myself about how it should be.

Dayana pulled my hand toward her, kissed the inside of my palm. A strangled sound came from me, nearly choking me, and her eyes shot up to mine.

"Okay?" she asked, and I almost laughed that she'd turned it around on me.

"Always," I somehow got out.

She inched closer to me on the bed, angled herself so she had better access. Then she stretched up further, and her lips hit me where my neck and collarbone meet. I nearly came unglued. I had to lay back and support myself on my elbows. She followed, letting her fingertips explore every line she could find, letting her lips and tongue follow.

She moved in a straight path down the center of my chest and abdomen, moving lower. "Okay?" she asked me again just before her tongue flicked in my belly button.

I hissed in a breath and nearly came right then and there.

She was going to make me lose control. I reached for her, took her hand, and pulled her toward me. Her hair fell down near my face, tickling my chest and the hollow of my neck where it brushed against me. I put my other hand on her waist, guided her to straddle me. I wished I hadn't. I needed to let her take the lead, determine how this would go. The memory of how she'd panicked the last time she was straddling me wouldn't go away, but Dayana didn't panic this time.

She let herself drop down over me, the heat of her sex melding with the heat of my cock like an inferno. She was wet, so wet. I could feel it through her panties and my shorts. She ground her hips, rolled them instinctively, and her head dropped down onto my shoulder.

"Okay?" she asked me again.

I could hardly breathe. Couldn't focus on anything but how good she felt over me. "If you do that again, I'm going to lose control."

"I want you to lose control." Dayana nipped the curve of my neck where she'd kissed me earlier.

I tried to brace myself. Knew it was coming. I grabbed her hips with both hands like I could stop her. But when she rolled them against me, I pushed her down onto me, lifted my hips up, intensified the contact.

She arched her back and sat upright, gasping for air.

And I was lost.

I rolled up with her, flipping our positions until she was on her back against the pillows and I was over her, grinding against her, supporting my weight on my elbows.

Her legs came around my waist, her ankles hooking behind my back, and she put both hands behind my neck. She pulled me down to her, so low I could kiss her, so close her breaths were fanning over my face.

I'd been dreaming of having her just like this for so long. Now it was happening.

"Okay?" she asked again. She sounded as winded as I felt.

I didn't answer her. Not with words.

I kissed her under her chin and let my tongue lead me where I wanted to be.

DAYANA

Eric's tongue was taking the same path down my body as I had taken down his earlier, scorching me with heat and leaving wet shivers in its wake. I had to release my grip on his waist with my legs as he moved lower.

He didn't stop when he got to my panties, though. He kissed me through them, over them, lower and lower.

I squirmed, embarrassed as hell but wanting more. Wanting to be closer.

His fingers dipped beneath the elastic band at the top of my panties and he lowered them, inch by inch, so slowly. I didn't want him to be slow. I wanted him, all of him, now.

I tried to help him get them off, but he wouldn't let me rush him, wouldn't move any faster. He licked me through my panties, and I shuddered, so close to finding the same type of release I'd had with the vibrator.

"Please, Eric." My words came out as a whimper.

He pulled his head away just a bit and blew a cool stream of air on me. I arched up again, nearly frantic with need, my hips moving in ways I wasn't telling them to move.

Finally, he pulled my panties down to my knees, then further, to my ankles and off.

I was sure that he'd take his boxer briefs off now, that he'd stop torturing me and making me wait, but he didn't. He put one hand on each of my knees and pushed them to the side a bit at a time. He brought his head down to me again, kissed the inside of one thigh, then the other.

I was mortified to have him so close to me there, with nothing hiding me from him when I knew how wet I was. I wanted to close my legs, to go back to my own room and shut the door. But I couldn't. This was my one chance, the one opportunity I would have to prove to myself I could experience a normal sexual relationship with a man.

My last chance to be with Eric.

I fought off the panic, fought down the urge to run.

I'd barely gotten myself back under control when I felt his tongue on my clitoris, right where I'd held the vibrator the other night. He swirled his tongue around it a few times and sucked it between his lips. His stubble scratched against my sensitive skin, driving me insane.

I let out a tortured sound, and my hips bucked up into him. I needed something to hold onto. Something to ground me. Something to keep me from flying off the bed completely. My hands grasped for something, anything. One fisted in a pillow, and I brought it over my mouth. The other fisted in his hair.

He growled low in his throat but kept licking me, sucking and swirling and kissing me until I thought I would die.

When I felt his finger slide into me, so easily, so perfectly, so carefully, so unthreateningly, I started crying from relief. Sobbing. Great, heaving, reassured sobs behind my pillow.

He slid his finger in and out of me, then added another, his tongue never leaving my clitoris, until I shuddered and cried out with my orgasm. He kept licking me, caressing me, all the way until the quaking subsided, until I felt like I had melted into a puddle of contentment.

I still had the pillow over my face when he moved up to lie beside me.

"Okay?" he asked.

I nodded. Even just the tiny movement that required seemed too much. I felt limp and liquid and as good as I'd ever felt in my life. I sucked in a breath of air, but it went back out of me on a sob.

"Dayana? Look at me." He put one arm around my waist, pulled me closer to him. He took the pillow away. "Damn it. You should have stopped me." There was so much anguish in his voice, so much concern in his expression when he looked down at me. He brushed my tears away, his big, strong hand caressing my cheek gently, tenderly, lovingly. "Why didn't you stop me?"

"I— No." I shook my head and kissed him, tasting my release on his lips. The thought of speaking, of explaining my tears to him right now, was overwhelming. But he had to know, to understand. "I'm not hurt or scared or panicking. I was just—" I broke off, distracted by his hands stroking my back, soothing me. "I was so scared before, scared that I couldn't handle having something—you—inside me. That it might trigger me. Take me back to that night."

"Hell, Dayana." He still looked tormented, as tormented as I'd been for years. He brought his hand back to cup my cheek, kissed my forehead. "I knew I shouldn't have— I knew it was too soon."

"You still don't understand. It didn't trigger me. I'd never felt relief like that."

Eric searched my eyes, my face, his gaze traveling over every inch of me. He brushed more tears away with his thumb. "You're crying because you're relieved?"

I nodded.

"You swear? Dayana, I can't—"

I shushed him with a finger over his lips. "I promise."

He sucked my finger into his mouth and slowly released it. I shivered, and he did it again. "You have to talk to me about these things. You have to tell me what you're scared of, what you want. What feels good."

"Everything you do feels good."

He kissed me, slow and deep. I could still feel the heat of his erection, how hard it was pressing against my belly, but he didn't seem in any big hurry to do anything about it. I slid my hand down his stomach, reaching for him.

He stopped me before I got there, his fingers circling my wrist. "Not now. Another day. Let's just take it one step at a time."

There wouldn't be another time, though. I was flying home tomorrow, back to Providence, back to my own life. He was staying here to go on with his.

I didn't have any more time for one step at a time.

"Please? I want..." I got my wrist free, reached further. I stroked him over his boxer briefs, and he sucked in a breath. "I want you. I want this."

Eric put his forehead against mine. His staggered breaths flitted over my lips. "You're sure? Absolutely sure?" he ground out.

"Yes."

He kissed me hard but pulled away all too soon. I reached for him instinctively, wanting to pull him back to me. He got off the bed, slipped off his boxer briefs, and took a condom from the drawer of his nightstand. I watched, a little more fascinated than I would have liked to admit, as he ripped open the wrapper and slid it into place. At least it was fascination I was feeling, though, and not fear.

When he climbed back onto the bed, my mouth felt dry with anticipation. He lifted himself over me, one of his thighs slipping between mine, and he ran his hands from my waist up my ribs to tease my breasts.

"Promise me you'll stop me if—"

I cut him off with a kiss. Even if I got scared, even if panic hit me, I didn't want him to stop. I put my arms around his waist, drew him down to me. The feel of his bare skin on mine was overwhelming, almost too much to bear.

He didn't stop kissing me when he moved one hand down between us and stroked my vulva, my clit. I was still so sensitive from earlier. Every little touch was magnified. He guided himself inside me, just a little bit at a time before retreating.

He rocked over me, gentle movements that drove me wild. My hips rolled up to meet him, and I lifted my free leg, stretched it up to curl around his thigh. When I did that, he slid deeper into me. I felt stretched and hot and wonderful.

Eric kissed me everywhere—the underside of my chin, the hollow of my neck, the lobe of my ear, the hard peak of my nipple—always rocking. Always tender. Perfect.

I slid my hands down his back, caressed his butt, and pressed him closer to me. And then it got to be too much. My muscles contracted, tensed. I knew I was about to have another orgasm just before the tremors started.

It felt like he got bigger inside me, and he rocked harder, a little faster. He let out a shout and stilled above me, our bodies quaking together for a few moments.

I wrapped both my legs around him, wanting to hold onto him as long as I could, wanting to remember the sensation of having him inside me. After a minute, he lowered himself down onto me, kissing my cheeks and lips and eyelids while I reveled in the moment.

Eventually he rolled off me, pulled me to rest my head on his shoulder. I lay my hand on his stomach.

"Okay?" he asked me again. He sounded so unsure it broke my heart.

"Wonderful," I whispered. I was afraid if I spoke louder, I'd fall apart already.

After a minute of holding me like that, he got out of the bed and disposed of the condom. When he came back, he had a warm, wet cloth in his hands. He reached out with it like he was going to clean me. I tried to close my legs and stop him. It felt so insanely intimate to me, so embarrassing.

"I just had my tongue there, Dayana. My cock."

"I know. I just..." I'd started building a new wall of protection around myself the minute he'd gotten out of bed. It was already going to hurt more than I could stand to leave tomorrow. I couldn't let myself fall any more in love with him than I already had.

He sat down by my legs and carefully cleaned me with the cloth. He set it on the nightstand and got back into bed, pulling me into his arms and situating the blankets over us both. He tucked my head into his shoulder and trailed his hand over my arm.

It was too perfect.

I knew I should get myself up from the bed, put my clothes on, and go back to my room. Staying with him tonight after he'd made love to me so sweetly—it would only make things harder.

I didn't get up, though. I lay there in his arms, listening to the beat of his heart and the depth of his breaths until they leveled out and he was asleep.

I tried to memorize every detail of this moment. The warm feel of his skin contrasting with the coolness of the sheets. The musky scent of sex in the air. The tingles still coursing through me from his touch. The rise and fall of his chest beneath my head.

I was still cataloging memories when I fell asleep.

Chapter 20 - Breakaway

DAYANA

Eric spent longer kissing me before the guys left for morning skate than he normally would. I held on tight, wishing I could make the moment last forever. There were only so many more kisses I would get from him. Even when he broke off the kiss, he held me close to him for a minute.

It felt good to be in his arms. Too good.

"I love you," I whispered in his ear before he let me go. It wasn't fair of me to say that to him, to tell him the truth. I knew it. Love had never been part of the deal. I'd known before I ever flew all the way across the country that I might get hurt in the end.

Telling him I loved him wouldn't change how he felt about me. It wouldn't change how things had to be. It would only make things awkward between us when it didn't have to be that way. I should have kept it to myself.

He pulled me closer, held me tighter. "I love you, too."

But he didn't. Not like I wanted. He loved me like he would love his best friend's kid sister, nothing more. I had to keep reminding myself of that so I wouldn't hope for the impossible.

I couldn't miss the angry glares Brenden was giving him when they left. I guess they were inevitable. Things had been tense between them ever since Brenden found out I was here. He'd probably realized I hadn't been in my room last night when he and Babs got home. For all I knew, he might have heard what was going on in Eric's bedroom.

I hated that this had driven a wedge between them, but I didn't know how to make it better. Maybe once I left, once Eric wasn't touching me anymore—maybe then Brenden could see all the good Eric had done for me and ignore the parts that upset him.

"See you in a couple hours," Eric said. I nodded, and he closed the garage door.

After they were gone, I packed my suitcases and set them by the door in my bedroom. Then I waited.

I had to sit and wait far too long. I'd been traveling with the team so much that I'd become an expert at packing. It only took me about fifteen minutes to get everything I had with me situated. Even with walking through the whole house twice, looking to see if I'd forgotten anything, I had too much time on my hands before they would be back for lunch and their pregame naps. Too much time to think. Thinking was dangerous right now, because it could only lead to my getting upset.

I checked in for my flight. I texted Sara to make sure she could still pick me up and take me to the airport this afternoon. I wrote Eric a letter, then tore it to shreds and started over again. On my fourth attempt, I had something I didn't completely hate. I put it in my bedroom and came back downstairs to start making lunch.

The guys would be hungry when they got back. On game days, they usually liked to eat a big lunch and mainly just snack for dinner. I took out some chicken breasts and salad fixings and put a pot of water on to boil for pasta.

I'd almost finished cooking, and I looked up when the garage door opened. They were pretty quiet when they came in. Eric was last. He had a black eye like Babs had had on Casino Night, after I'd punched him.

"What—"

He just shook his head.

I didn't have to wonder much what had caused it. Not with the way Brenden kept flexing his fingers.

Babs came into the kitchen and helped me finish up the salad. "Smells good, Dee. You're going to spoil us."

I'd completely lost my appetite, though.

ERIC

I pulled Dayana into my bedroom with me when I went to lay down for my pregame nap. I usually slept during that time, but there was no chance I would actually sleep today. There was too much adrenaline coursing through my body, between everything that was riding on tonight's game and the fact that Dayana had told me she loved me. Then there was the small matter of Soupy wanting to go a round during the skate this morning.

I couldn't fight him. I wouldn't.

I would have done the same thing to him if our roles had been reversed.

Since I knew there was no possibility I'd be able to sleep, I figured it would be a good opportunity to at least hold her. Just hold her.

So I brought her into my bedroom and tugged her down on the bed with me. I pulled her into my arms, wrapped her up, and held her close. She put her hands on my waist and tucked her head in by my shoulder.

We didn't talk. We didn't need to.

It felt right to hold her like that. I let myself imagine how it would be to hold her like this every day, to keep her close to me and never let her go.

When I had to get up to dress and head out for tonight's game, she lifted up and kissed my swollen eye just like she'd done that night when she was drunk.

"I'm sorry," she said.

"You didn't hit me."

"I know. But I'm still sorry."

I was starting to wonder if I'd ever convince her to stop apologizing to me. I kissed her on the cheek. I put my suit on. She was giving me the strangest look when I finished. Like she wanted to say something but wouldn't. I reached for her, holding out my hand. She came to me and let me wrap her up in my arms.

"Have a good game tonight," she said after a minute.

I figured she was feeling awkward about last night. Or maybe it was because Soupy had hit me because of last night. It should pass soon, whatever she was feeling.

"I plan to," I said. I kissed her, long and slow. "I'll see you after."

She came with me down the stairs, letting me hold her hand the whole way. Babs and Soupy were waiting in the kitchen when we got there.

Babs tossed me an apple. "Later, Dee."

"Yeah," she said. But she sounded distant. "Good-bye."

I couldn't take any more time to wonder what was going on with her or we'd be late. We'd have to talk about it tonight after the game.

I kissed her on the forehead, and then I headed out to the garage with the boys.

DAYANA

I kept it together until I heard the garage door close behind them. Only then did I let myself cry—but only for a minute. Not a good, solid cry like I wanted. Like I needed.

Sara would be here to get me anytime now. I didn't have too long to wallow in my self-pity. I dried my tears and went back upstairs. I put the letter I'd written Eric on his bed before lugging my two suitcases down the stairs.

I'd only been on the lower level for about five minutes when Sara rang the doorbell. Laura was with her when I opened it. Sara had chocolate; Laura had a bottle of red wine and a teddy bear.

"The bear's from Katie. The wine's from me."

I laughed. "I don't think that'll fit in my quart-sized zipper bag."

"All the more reason for us to drink it at the airport before you go through security."

With that, they helped me wheel my bags out to Sara's car, and we were off to the airport. We finished off the bottle, drinking from red plastic cups Sara had stashed in her car. We got through about half the box of chocolates, too, before I had to leave them.

I hugged them both and took the teddy bear, but Laura stopped me before I could go.

"There's a code," she said. I turned to her and shook my head, confused. She tucked her dark hair behind her ear. "The guys have their code, and we have ours—the wives and girlfriends. Once you're one of us, you're always one of us. It's a sisterhood, and you can't just walk away. So no matter what happens, wherever you are, you call me if you need me. Okay?"

I nodded, trying to fight back another round of tears.

"Even if it's just to talk about what new vibrator you're thinking about buying next. Lord knows I've tried them all and can give you plenty of opinions."

At least she made me laugh at the end.

"Deal," I said. I walked around the corner and allowed this phase of my life to stay behind.

"I'm coming to visit you this summer whether you like it or not!" Sara shouted as I left.

I might not be closing a door completely, but it was still time to open a new one.

ERIC

There was only one minute left in our season.

The Blues had been taking it to us all night, using their size and skill to punish physically as much as they were punishing us on the scoreboard.

Now we had two minutes to tie the game and take it to overtime or else we could just pack up our skates and work on our golf swings all summer. No matter how much the boys liked playing golf, we'd all rather keep playing hockey.

Scotty called for time-out and brought us all in. "One shot," he shouted. "That's all it's gonna take is one shot. Don't you fucking give up now."

Hammer pulled out his marker and whiteboard, drew up a play for the face-off. I followed him, but I was focusing more on getting enough air in my lungs to stay upright. Soupy, Babs, and I had already been out for an extended shift, and Scotty was leaving us out there for the next one. He'd pulled Nicky to the bench and told Sarge to head out with us as the extra skater.

"Zee, don't you fucking dare lose that draw," Hammer said to finish up. "But if he does, you boys know what to do."

David Backes was waiting to take the face-off against me at the dot. He looked ready to rip my head off, but that was just how he always looked, at least on the ice. It didn't intimidate me.

I got down low, positioned my stick over the ice, and waited for the puck to drop.

Backes expected me to pull it back on my strong side and get it to the D, but I surprised him. I shot it forward, straight at the net. Babs and Soupy were both streaking in toward the goal, and Sarge skated into position at the half-wall. I won the draw a little too cleanly. The puck went in hard on the Blues goaltender, and he made a kick save. The rebound shot out clear past both Babs and Soupy, heading toward the blue line.

Burnzie and his partner had both already gotten into position at the points, and it streaked right between them even though they both dove back toward the middle to stop it.

They were both flat out on the ice. Backes was flying after the puck. I was the only one with a chance to catch him.

I gave chase. Tried to hook him.

Missed.

He scored an empty-net goal and put an end to our playoff hopes.

Back in the dressing room after the game, Scotty gave a big speech about all the progress we'd made over the course of the season, how we were a better team than last year, how next year we'd be better yet. Jim Sutter came in and said a few things about being proud of us and how we'd pulled together even through all the adversity of injuries and personnel changes and a new coaching staff. None of it made me feel any better. None of it could change the fact that for four years in a row, we would be calling it a summer much earlier than we would have liked. And I was the captain. It was on me.

When Jim finished, he and the coaching staff left. It was just me and the boys. Everyone was quiet, sulking or reflecting, pissed off. I was pissed. Pissed at myself.

It was the quietest I'd ever heard a locker room after a game in all the years I'd been playing.

I took off my jersey and tossed it in the laundry, then my pads, hanging them up behind me in my stall. "I'm sorry, boys. I blew it." I blew it in so many ways. What happened in those dying moments of the game, the final moments of our season, they were barely scratching the surface.

That was all I could say.

I finished changing out of my gear, did a few interviews with the press, made my way to the showers, and got dressed.

Babs was waiting by my stall when I finished, but pretty much everyone else was gone. "You didn't blow it, Zee. There were twenty of us out there every night. Not just you."

I nodded and clapped him on the back, but I couldn't really talk.

"Soupy headed out with Burnzie," he said a minute later. "Said not to wait up for him."

"Yeah." It didn't really surprise me, but it hurt more than I wanted to admit. "You ready?"

He gave me a sheepish grin. I admired that about him. Even after losing, after just missing out on our shot to get to the playoffs, he could smile.

"Come on. Let's go get Dayana and head home." I wanted nothing more than to console myself with a beer or three and another night with her in my arms.

Dayana wasn't in the owner's box when we got up there—no one but Webs, Laura, and Katie had stuck around.

My gut clenched, but I ignored it. "Did she leave with Soupy?" It was ridiculous to be jealous of her brother, but I was. I would have thought that she would have at least let me know if she wasn't going to be here when I got done, called me or sent a text or something.

Laura shook her head. "She's not with Soupy. She's on her way back to Providence."

"No." I'd been holding her only a few hours ago. Dayana hadn't said anything about leaving. She'd just told me she loved me, for fuck's sake. She couldn't have left me. "No, that can't be."

"Sara and I took her to the airport this afternoon. She's gone, Zee."

I felt like ice was clutching my lungs and squeezing. I had to get out of there or I was going to hit something, someone.

I spun and headed toward the parking garage, pulling my cell phone out of my pocket as I walked. No missed calls. No texts.

She wasn't gone. She couldn't be gone.

I called her phone. It went straight to voice mail. I hung up without leaving a message.

I texted her.

Call me as soon as you get this. Anytime. I love you.

Babs got into the car beside me. Shit, I hadn't even thought about him. I'd just left without anything in my head other than for Dayana.

I was probably lucky I didn't get pulled over for speeding. The post-game traffic had all cleared out well before I left. Got home in record time.

I leaped out of the car and ran into the house. The lights were all out.

"Dayana?"

No answer.

I flipped on lights as I went. Raced up the stairs and down the hall. Opened the door to her room.

She wasn't there.

I went to the closet. Empty. Same with the bathroom. All her stuff, all her clothes and luggage and that cucumber-melon soap she always used—it was all gone.

I went to my room, holding my breath.

Nothing.

She was gone. She'd left me.

I sat down on the edge of my bed and dropped my head into my hands. How could I fuck everything up so badly, all at once? I'd let my team down. I'd let myself down. Jim Sutter was probably going to trade me this summer. Dayana had left me.

She'd given me the chance to love her, to really love her the way I'd wanted to for so long I couldn't remember ever not loving her, and I'd blown it.

Now she was going back to Providence, back to her old life. She might date someone else, let some asshole touch her.

I didn't want anyone to touch her but me. Ever.

Just thinking about it made me sick to my stomach.

I reached behind me and grabbed for a pillow to throw across the room, but my hand landed on an envelope first.

It had my name on it. Dayana's writing.

I slid my finger under the seal and pulled the letter out. The necklace I'd given her fell out on my lap as I unfolded the paper.

Eric,

I'm sorry I left without saying good-bye. I didn't trust myself not to fall apart, and you've seen enough of that for this lifetime.

You warned me, when I first asked you to help me, that for women physical intimacy and emotional intimacy go hand in hand, that if you have one, you start to feel the other. You were right. I knew going in that I might start to have feelings I wasn't prepared to have for you, but it was a risk I had to take if I was ever going to be able to live a normal life.

Now I have to leave before I can't make myself go. You did all that I asked you to do, even when you didn't want to. You told me you'd do anything you could to help me, and you did so much more than that.

I asked too much of you. You've always seen me as Brenden's kid sister, not as a woman you could love the way I love you. I didn't realize I would fall as hard as I did. I didn't think it would happen so fast. I didn't realize it would hurt to leave as much as it does.

You've done so much more for me than I could ever deserve, more than I could ever thank you for. You've been my rock. You gave me more than you could ever know. You gave me my life back.

You gave me myself back.

You put me back together again. I'll always love you for that. But now I have to go find out who this version of me is.

Dayana

I read her letter three times, berating myself the whole time, hoping I'd find a gotcha hidden in there somewhere on another read-through, and it would all have just been a joke. Why hadn't I told her I loved her sooner? Why hadn't I told her over and over and over again until she started to believe it?

I'd been so careful with her, trying not to push her too far, too soon. The whole time, she'd been pushing me for more. I was an idiot for not seeing that what she was really asking me for, the whole time, was to love her. She may not have realized that's what she wanted from me, but it was.

And now she was gone.

Chapter 21 - Breakaway

D AYANA
Dad was waiting for me at baggage claim. He was a slightly more wrinkled, salt-and-pepper version of Brenden, towering over most of the people milling around and waiting for their bags or their loved ones.

I ran straight into his arms as soon as I saw him.

He nearly jumped, I startled him so much, but then he hugged me back like he had when I was a little girl, practically lifting me off my feet in his exuberance.

"I missed you," I said when I could catch my breath.

"I missed you, too," he said, but I knew there was so much more behind that simple statement than just missing me over the last six weeks.

We went to the baggage carousel to wait for my suitcase. Dad handed me a mug of coffee, which I immediately started guzzling. The sun wasn't up yet after my red-eye. I hadn't been able to sleep on the plane. Every time I'd shut my eyes, I'd thought about Eric—how he would hold me when we flew together, how it felt to sleep in his arms, how safe I felt when he held my hand. It made me want to cry.

I couldn't keep crying, though. I'd made my choice. I'd done this with a full understanding of what might happen, even if I didn't understand how a broken heart would feel. Now I had to deal with the consequences.

"Your brother already called this morning," Dad said. "Wanted to know if you're here. He was worried when you weren't home last night."

I hadn't told any of the guys I was leaving. They'd become a sort of family to me since I'd been traveling with the team.

Brenden would come back to Providence for the summer, though. He had to stick around Portland for a few days, go through exit interviews with the coaches and Jim Sutter, that type of thing. But then he'd come back. He always did.

Eric would probably be back at some point, too.

His first couple of years in the league, he'd spent most of his off-season in Providence. But how long he stayed had gotten shorter each year. He'd bought his house in Portland and stayed there a little longer. He had commitments with charities in the area that he'd stuck around to help out.

He'd started training with a big-shot personal trainer in Minnesota. That usually took at least a month or two out of his summer—a month or two less that he'd potentially be around Providence.

I half hoped he wouldn't come home at all this year. It would be easier for me to get over him if I didn't have to see him so soon. But at least I could console myself with the knowledge that he shouldn't be around much if he even came at all. After everything I'd put him through, he might just stay away the whole summer—especially since all of that had soured his friendship with Brenden.

I eyed my dad over my mug. He didn't look upset with me. Just concerned.

"I didn't tell him I was coming home. I didn't want to distract any of them from finishing the season out strong."

That lie sounded hollow even to my own ears, but Dad just nodded. "Your mom's got your room all ready for you."

My subletter wasn't supposed to be out of my apartment for two more weeks, so I was going back home, at least for a little while. "Thanks, Dad."

He saw my suitcase come onto the conveyer before I did and grabbed it. We walked out to his car and drove into the rising sun.

"Jim Sutter told me you got back on the ice," he said, trying too hard to sound casual.

"I did. It felt good." I didn't miss the little smile on his face. "He said something to me I've been wondering about. He said he owed you. Made it sound like a really big deal."

Dad fell silent, his fingers drumming on the steering wheel. That was as sure a sign as any that he didn't want to talk about something. It was probably where I'd picked up the nervous habit, the need to be doing something with my hands all the time.

I didn't press him. Not now. That could come some other time.

"The peewee league asked me to referee a tournament this week," he said a minute later. "I agreed, but I could use some help. Someone who knows the game as well as I do."

I stared out the front windshield, watching the sky change from purple to pink to orange in front of my eyes.

My trip to Portland hadn't just been about letting men back into my life. It had been about letting my life back into my life. If I didn't start doing that, it was all a waste.

I couldn't waste the gift Eric had given me.

"Okay," I said. "I'm in."

ERIC

Martha Alvarez looked up over her bifocals, squinting at me. "Jim's waiting on you, Zee. Go on in." She immediately went back to whatever she was doing on her computer and ignored me.

I knocked on Jim's open door, and he waved me in.

I'd never dreaded an exit interview at the end of a season quite like I was dreading this one. The Storm hadn't had a good year, and I felt like it was a direct reflection of me and my personal performance. There was no reason to expect Jim Sutter wouldn't agree with that assessment.

"Have a seat, Zee." He came around his desk and took the chair next to me instead of sitting across from me. "How's the eye?"

"Healing." Better than my heart.

He nodded sympathetically. "I already met with Brenden—Soupy." He chuckled. "His dad is still Soupy to me. I don't know if I can get used to calling Brenden Soupy like everyone else does. He's assured me he can keep personal matters off the ice next season if we bring him back."

I grunted. I hadn't just lost Dayana. I'd lost her whole family. She hadn't answered any of my calls since she'd left. It went straight to her voice mail every time I called. The only response I'd gotten was a single text message.

Home. I'm fine. Thanks for everything.

Since then, nothing.

Soupy had come back to my house to get his clothes, but he hadn't really said much of anything. I asked him about Dayana, and he gave me a go-to-hell look as his answer. I'd only seen him in passing ever since. He wouldn't talk to me, would hardly look at me.

"Do you think I should bring him back next season?" Jim asked. "He played really well for us in a difficult position, I thought. But you know him better than any of us."

I shot my eyes up to meet his. "Am I still going to be here?"

"Do you want to be?" He leaned back in his chair, crossed his ankles and kicked them out in front of him. "I'm going to be totally honest with you, Zee. There are going to be changes this summer. There have to be. I don't think you're part of the problem, though, and I do think you can be part of the solution. If you want to be. But it won't be easy. There are going to be some growing pains."

"Pain doesn't hurt," I said without thinking. That was bullshit. Pain hurt like hell. It was all I'd felt since Dayana left, and it didn't feel like it would ever end.

"Spoken like a true hockey player."

I ground my teeth together, wishing I could cause myself enough physical pain to erase the rest. "I want to be here," I finally said. "This is my team."

"Good. So tell me what you think about Soupy. Should I bring him back? Can he contribute like he did the last month for a full season? Can he stay healthy?"

It didn't matter that Soupy wasn't talking to me right now. He'd busted his ass for years for this shot. "There's no one I'd rather have beside me, no one better to have in the room. He just needs a chance to prove it."

Jim smiled. "I already knew that. You just proved to me why this is your team, why you and only you are the captain."

I nodded. It felt weird to get complimented like that after the shit job I felt I'd done lately.

"Got plans for the summer?" he asked. "Going home to visit your family?"

"Heading to St. Paul for a couple of months to train with Larry Daniels."

"Good, good. Be sure you take some time to just enjoy yourself, too. Play a few rounds of golf." Jim had a sly look in his eye that had me curious. "I was talking to Mark Campbell this morning—Soupy and Dayana's dad. He was telling me about a peewee tournament going on in Providence later this week. Said he and Dayana were going to be refereeing it. It'll be good to see her back on the ice again, don't you think?"

Better than he could ever know.

DAYANA

It felt weird being in zebra stripes. It felt even weirder to see Dad in them. I'd always been a player on the ice, not a referee, and he had always been either a player or a coach.

At least these kids were all young enough that I was still taller than them. Peewee hockey is made up of eleven- and twelve-year-old kids. This league was coed, so both girls and boys could play if they were good enough to make the team. The teams were out on the ice for their warm-up, skating through the passing and shooting drills their coaches had taught them all season long.

I took a final look at my cell phone before the game. Brenden might be flying home today, and I thought maybe he would have texted me his flight information. There wasn't anything from him. I had two more missed calls from Eric, though, and two more voice mails to go with the dozen others I hadn't listened to yet.

He was being persistent, which didn't surprise me. Not really. He'd always been stubbornly persistent. He wouldn't have made it into the NHL otherwise. In some ways, it was a really good trait for him to have.

But I wished that with this, he'd back off a little.

I couldn't talk to him. Not yet. Just thinking about him made me want to curl up in a ball in my room and cry for hours. Maybe getting over a broken heart would have been easier if I'd had one before. I didn't know. All I knew was I would break down if I heard his voice on the other end of the phone, no matter what it was that he wanted to say to me. I couldn't imagine anything he could say that wouldn't hurt.

The only thing he could say that would ease the constant ache in my gut was that he loved me, not like a kid sister, but like a woman.

That wasn't going to happen. There was no point wasting time wishing for something that would never happen.

Now was not the time to start wallowing in my self-pity again. There was a game to officiate and kids who were counting on me. I put my phone in my gym bag and set it next to Dad's in the scorer's box. I stretched my legs one more time. The officials in a game had to do just as much skating as the players. I didn't want to get a cramp or not be able to keep up. Some of these kids could really fly out there. There was one girl, a little redhead who was about half the size of most of the others, who looked like she was just floating over the ice out there. She made it look easy.

Skating like that is anything but easy.

Dad skated over to me and tossed me a whistle. "Ready?" he asked.

I smiled. "Yeah. Ready as I'll ever be."

We skated out to center ice and met up with the two linesmen who were working the game. Dad took charge. "All right, let's make sure these kids have fun out there. Keep it a nice, clean game."

The four of us put our fists together in the middle and gave each other a little bump. We skated out and took up our positions. The coaches got their teams organized and sent out the players who were going to start the game. I got a nod from both coaches that they were all set, and I caught Mom's eye from the stands behind the home team's bench. She winked at me.

Game time.

I raised the whistle to my lips and blew into it. The linesman at center dropped the puck, and the game was on.

By the time the horn blew to signal the end of the first period, I was exhausted, but a good kind of exhausted. The kind that meant I'd been working hard, skating fast. The two teams were tied at two heading into the locker rooms, and Dad and I had only had to call a single penalty—a trip. We knew the kid didn't mean to do it, that he was reaching for the puck and not her skates, but he'd sent the little redhead sprawling to the ice when she was about to get free on a breakaway.

The coaches ushered their kids off the ice and down the tunnels for intermission. Dad skated over to me to help with the net I was closest to, and the linesmen went to move the other net out of the way. We had to clear the ice for the Zamboni to come on and resurface it.

I'd barely lifted my goalpost free of its moorings when Dad cleared his throat. I brought my head up and he gave me a funny look. "Seems like someone wants to talk to you."

I followed the path of his eyes. Eric had climbed over the glass into the team benches, gone over the boards, and was walking across the ice toward me in his shoes. None of the arena crew had stopped him. He's a local celebrity here, a home-grown kid who made it big. Everyone involved in the Providence hockey community knew him.

They all loved him. If he wanted to come out on the ice, they would let him.

Damn it.

I almost started crying just seeing him. Even more humiliating, I almost skated across to him and threw myself into his arms.

Dad pushed the goal out the door the ice crew had opened, leaving me alone to figure out what to do.

I didn't do anything. I just froze, watching him walk across to me. He'd finally gotten a haircut. It was still a little longer than he used to wear it, but it looked neat and tidy. And he'd shaved, too, eliminating the five-o'clock shadow he almost always had. He was in jeans and a T-shirt, not a suit and tie like I'd gotten so used to seeing him in.

My breath hitched, and not just because he was here when I hadn't been expecting him. It was more the look in his eyes, as though he couldn't decide whether he wanted to yell at me or kiss me. Maybe I was just hoping that he wanted to kiss me. That meant he probably wanted to yell. Not that he would. He'd never lost his temper with me, not even when he should have.

He stopped about a foot away from me and shoved both hands in his pockets. He was close enough to touch. Close enough that I could close the distance between us in half a second and fall into his arms.

I wanted to touch him. I wanted him to touch me.

What I wanted hadn't really changed.

My mouth felt dry. I swallowed and licked my lips. "What are you doing here?"

"Seemed like the only way I could talk to you. You won't answer your phone, and you left me without giving me a chance to convince you to stay."

I shook my head. "You'd keep helping me until I'd taken everything you have to give if I let you. I can't let you do that. I can't be a leech like that."

The Zamboni came out of the tunnel and started its path around the outside of the ice. We needed to get out of the way so the driver could do his job. I skated toward the tunnel, but Eric stopped me by taking my hand. It felt electric, full of heat and so much more than simple hand-holding.

"That's what you do when you love someone."

My chest ached, felt tight with all the tears I'd been holding inside me for days in trying to convince Mom and Dad I was fine.

"You give all you have to give," he said, "and they do the same. You fill each other up." He twined his fingers with mine, rubbing the pad of his thumb over the back of my hand. Our hands were between us, and he kept pulling me closer to him, inch by inch.

"It doesn't work if it isn't even, though," I said. "If one does all the giving and the other does all the taking."

The Zamboni driver passed us and waved as he went. I tried to pull Eric toward the tunnel with me so we could get out of the man's way. He didn't let me tug him. He just dug in and pulled me closer, until I could feel his warmth only a hair's breadth away from me.

"You give me so much more than I deserve. You give me your trust. I know how hard it is for you to trust anyone, and you trust me completely. You give me pieces of yourself, pieces you don't share with anyone else. And you're standing on your own again. Maybe I've been giving more lately, but you needed it. It won't always be that way. You're back to being the Dayana I've loved since you were too young for me to do anything about it. Someday, I'll be the one who needs more. I know you'll give it to me."

I couldn't take it all in. Even though I'd been fighting against letting myself hope, I was losing that battle. Fast.

"You love me like a kid sister," I argued, but it felt feeble.

"I did once," he said. "Years ago. That changed so long ago I hardly remember loving you any way other than how I do now. I think I realized it that first semester Soupy and I were off in college and you were here. But you were just a kid still. It was like Babs and Katie. I thought I could just wait until you grew up." He brought my hand up to his lips, kissed the backs of my knuckles, and left me shivering. "I waited too long. I don't want to wait anymore."

I wanted to believe him. Everything in me was desperate to believe that he could love me like I loved him. It felt too good to be true, though.

He brought his other hand up to my face and brushed away a tear from my cheek. "I couldn't have touched you like I did if you were still like a kid sister to me, Dayana. I couldn't have made love to you."

The Zamboni circled past us again. We had to move. On his next pass, he needed to go right where we were standing. I couldn't make myself move, though.

"You love me?" I asked. I hated that I could doubt it, that I ever had. He was right. I couldn't have even let Brenden hold my hand, and it had nothing to do with trust and everything to do with the type of love I felt for each of them.

"I love you so much it felt like you ripped my heart out of my chest when you left. I love you more than I know what to do with."

"I love you, too."

He smiled at me, the half-smile that could melt me and turn my bones to mush. "I know." Then he took off my helmet and kissed me, and I fell against him, wrapping my arms around his neck and holding on with everything I had.

He broke off the kiss too soon and backed away from me. I wanted to move with him, to keep holding him and never let go. It felt so good to have his arms around me again, I didn't want it to end so soon.

But he pulled a box out of his pocket, another black jewelry box with a blue ribbon around it, like the one the necklace had been in. Only it was small. Square.

My pulse was roaring in my ears when he held it out to me.

"It's not a locket," he said. "It's not a necklace of any type."

My hand was shaking when I took it from him. I took off the ribbon and tentatively lifted the lid. I laughed and cried at the same time.

It had a ring in it—a cheap, vending machine prize ring that could have matched the locket he'd given me years ago.

"I'll give you a real one when you're ready. Until then, will you come back to me? Be my girlfriend for real?"

"Are you sure about this?" I asked him, teasing him with the question he'd asked me more times than I could count. "Really sure?"

"I've never been more sure of anything in my life than I am of the fact that I love you and I can't stop loving you. I tried. God knows I tried, because I didn't think you'd ever be able to let me love you like I wanted to. But I failed, and now I love you even more than I did before." He kissed my forehead in that way that made my blood sing and my breath stutter. "Let me love you."

I couldn't answer him with words. There were none to explain how my heart felt like it would explode with love, how protected and cherished I felt when he touched me. I could only answer him with a kiss. Even that couldn't possibly convey half of what I was feeling, but I tried.

I stretched up as far as my skates would allow and pressed my lips to his.

The crowd around us roared with applause and cheers and whistles, jolting me back to reality, to the fact that a whole arena full of people were watching everything we were doing. I tried to pull away, but Eric put his arms around me and held on tight.

When he broke off the kiss, the Zamboni driver was grinning down at us. He'd had to stop his work because we were in his way. "Nice one, Zee. How's Soupy supposed to top a proposal like that?"

Oh, God. "They think you just proposed to me." I felt like my cheeks must have just traveled through ten thousand shades of red in half a second or so. I buried my face in his chest, wishing the ice beneath me would melt and I could just fall away, as long as Eric was still holding me.

"I will," Eric said, laughing. "When you're ready."

Epilogue

ERIC

It felt good, sitting on the sofa in the Campbells' TV room with my arm around Dayana. She had her feet up beside her and her head resting on my shoulder. Comfortable. Casual. She didn't care that her dad was sitting across from us. She didn't care that her mom could come in at any minute with a tray of freshly baked cookies or a big bowl of popcorn.

She just sat there like that, letting me hold her and occasionally playing with that stupid ring I'd given her.

I was pretty sure she was almost ready for me to give her a real one. To pop the question for real, not just accidentally lead a lot of people to think I'd already popped it. I hadn't meant to give her that ring while so many people were looking on like that. It had just happened.

She didn't seem to mind, though. Not once her initial embarrassment wore off, at least.

Mr. Campbell picked up his remote control and flipped it over to the Stanley Cup Finals. I didn't really like watching the playoffs. Watching them on TV just reminded me that I wasn't there, that I wasn't getting my chance to raise the cup. But that was good, in a way. It helped fuel my fire for next season, made me hungrier to get the Storm back there.

They were just playing the national anthem when Soupy came through the front door.

He stopped short when he saw me on the couch with Dayana. For a second, I thought he was going to turn around and leave. He'd been doing a lot of that lately, ever since we'd both been back in Providence. Hell, he'd been doing it since the morning of our final game of the season, when he gave me a black eye because I'd slept with his sister.

But he didn't leave. He flopped down on the other end of the sofa, leaving Dayana between us.

Mrs. Campbell came in from the kitchen with a plate of cookies as I'd been expecting. "Brenden! I didn't know you were coming tonight. I would have made oatmeal raisin."

He took a cookie off the plate before she set it on the coffee table. "Just got off a conference call with my agent and Jim Sutter."

Everyone stopped paying attention to the pregame chatter and turned to him.

"Jim wants to re-sign me. One-year contract at a million bucks. One-way."

A one-way contract would mean they'd have to pay him just as much to play on the minor-league team as they would when he was playing with Portland. And a million dollars was almost double the league minimum. It wasn't big money compared to a lot of contracts out there, but it was more than a lot of guys made. That meant he'd be much more likely to stay in Portland instead of being sent back to Seattle. It also meant it was a prove-it sort of contract. Jim wanted Soupy to prove he could hack it at this level consistently, that he belonged in the NHL, before they gave him more years and more money.

Dayana and their parents chattered and congratulated him, all the kinds of things families do. I kept quiet, even though I felt a swell of pride for him. He'd worked so hard to get this shot. Now he was really getting it.

It got quiet when the puck dropped. We all focused on the game and on eating our cookies.

But Soupy turned to me. "Jim said you told him there's no one you'd rather have on the ice with you."

I nodded. I'd said that, and I meant it.

"So you think I should take the deal?"

There wasn't a team in the league that would offer him anything better if he went into free agency. He knew that. But that wasn't what he was asking me.

I pulled the throw pillow out from behind my back and tossed it at his head. "Take the fucking deal."

He threw it back, but it hit Dayana.

"Now you've done it," I said.

"You've just started a war," Dayana said.

Before I could grab another pillow, she leaped straight at her brother and wrestled him to the ground.

I had to protect my girl, so I got in on it, too.

When we came up for air, laughing like lunatics, Mrs. Campbell gave us her best Mom look. "You three are acting just like you did when you were kids. If you break my sofa, you're going to buy me a new one."

It was just like when we were kids. Only better.

Lightning Source UK Ltd.
Milton Keynes UK
UKHW051500211122
412554UK00024B/759